And then I kissed him, just like that—

a shy little girl kind of kiss, a geeky peck on the cheek. I slapped a hand over my mouth.

He froze, his golden-brown skin darkening slightly. This would be the moment where he would tell me he had a girlfriend in L.A. or wherever he was from. A girlfriend way prettier than I, who didn't try to drop barbells on him or trip over her shoelaces. He stared at me for the longest two seconds of my life.

"Hey, come on," I joked. "It wasn't that bad."

He gave a peculiar little smirk and turned away, planting his hands on his hips as if he were angry or thinking hard about something. I was fourteen the last time I'd tried to kiss a guy first, and it had gone as well as this seemed to be going. I looked down at the grimy concrete floor and opened my mouth to apologize.

Evan spun around with a fluidity that startled me. He caught me by the elbow and pulled me close. He pressed his other hand against my neck so his fingers were tangled in my hair and his thumb teased the corner of my lips. Then he ducked his head down and kissed me, long and hard. My hands slipped around his back as if they were used to going there. I staggered a bit as his tongue slipped into my mouth. When we stopped for breath, he pressed his forehead against mine and sighed.

"That was incredibly unprofessional of me," he murmured.

Praise and Kudos

THIRTY-NINE AGAIN finaled in the 2007 Marlene Contest sponsored by the Washington, DC Romance Writers Chapter of RWA.

Thirty-Nine Again

by

Lynn Reynolds

Thirty-Nine Again

Cover Art by *Rae Monet*

The Wild Rose Press
PO Box 708
Adams Basin, NY 14410-0706
Visit us at www.thewildrosepress.com

Publishing History
First Last Rose of Summer Edition, 2009
Print ISBN 1-60154-517-7

Published in the United States of America

Dedication

In memory of my mother, Catherine Whalen,
who always believed I could do it.

.

One

The day of my second thirty-ninth birthday began beautifully. The unseasonably mild autumn blossomed overnight into full-fledged spring, with sunshine and temperatures expected to reach the seventies. All day, childish glee bubbled in me at the realization I'd lived to see another birthday. It bubbled even bigger as the workday drew to a close—I had planned to knock off work early to run with Evan down at Harborplace.

I blew off the gang at the office, even though they wanted to take me to some hot, hip, new nightclub to celebrate. Because I'd had no energy for celebrating my first thirty-ninth birthday—chemotherapy and radiation treatments will do that to a person—they wanted to make it up to me this year. I felt a little bad when I broke the news, but they weren't too put out. In fact, a round of cheering went up. Everyone knew Scott and I had been drifting apart, so they were pleased to hear someone else had inched into the picture. I denied that was the case, of course, even to myself.

"Evan's just helping me get back into shape after surgery. He's my new personal trainer, and he figured I'd stick with running more regularly if I had a partner."

"I'll bet he can think of a few other things you'll do better with a partner, too!" Andy, the good-looking blond from Information Services, laughed.

"Not true!" My friend Jess winked at him. "Sabrina says he's gay."

"Really?" Andy's interest wasn't all that

altruistic. He *is* gay, and he'd seen Evan once when we ran into him during our lunch break. "Are you sure?"

As a matter of fact, I wasn't. I had never said I was sure. I'd only mentioned it in passing, a point of curiosity because of the whole earring thing. He wore earrings in both ears, and I was old enough to remember a time when only gay guys did that. But Jess and Andy reminded me that wasn't the case anymore.

How do men know when a shift like that takes place? How, as a straight guy, would someone know it's now safe to wear earrings in both ears? Does someone send out an official memo about these things?

"No, I'm not sure he's gay," I admitted.

"Mmm-hmm," from both of them.

"Cut it out. If he is straight or bi or whatever, it doesn't matter. I'm sure I'm too frumpy for the likes of him."

"Oh, girl, have you looked in a mirror lately?" Jess sighed.

Of course I hadn't, not closely anyway. I avoided mirrors as much as possible. First, I'd been a chubby, freckle-faced teen, then last year I'd been bald. Now I was missing a sizable part of one breast—euphemistically called a lumpectomy. Bottom line, mirrors had never been my friends.

"I have to go." I snatched up my gym bag. "I'll try to come to the restaurant later tonight."

"You'll try?!" Andy shook with laughter. "You'll try? You mean, if you aren't too worn out from all that *running*?"

"We won't hold our breath," Jess added.

I exited to the sound of clapping and ribald whistling.

****

Evan and I were supposed to meet at the

amphitheatre in front of the harbor, but when I arrived, I saw no sign of him, so I paced around nervously. Then I decided I shouldn't look too interested, so I strolled over to the angled steps near the water taxi's passenger loading area. I sat down and further decided my left shoelace was too tight and my right shoelace was too loose. So I untied them both and began to retie them.

Evan jogged around a corner and stopped beside me. "Hey, I thought maybe you decided not to come!"

I looked up, disappointed to discover his dark eyes were hidden by a pair of wraparound sunglasses.

"Ready to go?"

"Yeah, sure!" I felt my face heating up and heard the perky little exclamation point in my voice. It made me ill. To cover my own embarrassment, I charged up the steps, but I had never finished with the whole shoelace-tying thing, so I got tangled in my own feet and stumbled. Badly.

I stumbled in a way only I could stumble. I started to fall face forward right into Evan's arms. That threw me into such a huge panic that I windmilled my arms wildly and tried to arch away from him. I flailed backwards, somersaulting down the steps and coming within a millimeter of rolling into the dirty, oily water of the Patapsco River. The only thing that saved me was Evan, who dove down the steps with incredible speed and grabbed me by the arms. I wound up with my legs in the water but my clothes unscathed. He pulled me onto the steps, and I buried my face in my hands.

"Oh, that went way better than the gym," I muttered.

Evan snorted, blatantly failing to hide his amusement. "Are you okay?"

"No," I replied. "I am not. I have a bloody knee that's probably been exposed to all sorts of mutant flesh-eating bacteria. And my pride is utterly in tatters."

"Not to worry." He left me there and jogged over to the Light Street Pavilion, the one with all the food places. When he returned, he was carrying two cups and a little plastic shopping bag.

"Water, bandages, and lemonade." He knelt beside me.

"What good will all that do?"

He hooked his sunglasses over the neck of his t-shirt. Then he lifted the lid on the cup of water, put his hand under my knee, and poured the water over the wound. The water was warm, but it stung nonetheless. Still, I was impressed at the effort he'd made to get the water temperature right.

I peered at him surreptitiously. His head was down, and the sun's rays glinted off shoulder-length hair so black it almost seemed blue. He wore it tied back in a ponytail, which looked natural, not phony and pretentious. At my firm a couple of investment bankers with receding hairlines had adopted that mini-ponytail look in some lame effort to compensate. On them, the effect was comical. Not on Evan though.

The hard lines of muscle in his shoulders and back flexed as he leaned forward and blotted at my knee. To my surprise, he used the hem of his olive green t-shirt to clean the wound.

"Oh, Evan, don't," I protested.

"It needs cleaning." He glanced up with a reassuring grin. His almond eyes were so black I couldn't even see the pupils. But his smile was so open and honest, like none of this was the least bit of trouble, and there was no place he'd rather be.

"This is an old shirt," he added. "From my Army days. It's seen worse than this. Anyway, time to let it go."

We both laughed, because when he laughed, I

4

couldn't help but join him. His eyes gleamed, and little crinkly lines formed at their corners. How could a woman not want to laugh with him? No wonder Scott had blown a gasket when I'd said I was going running with Evan.

Scott and I considered ourselves engaged, even though no ring had ever been proffered. He was an immigration lawyer at Homeland Security, and he came from an uptight, politically well-connected Southern family. They didn't blow gaskets in Scott's family, so his display of temper had come across to me as almost flattering. Making Scott a little jealous last night had been one thing, and not necessarily a very classy thing. So enough was enough. He wasn't even here to watch, yet I continued to sit, immensely enjoying the feel of Evan's hands all over my leg. Guilt fluttered at the base of my skull, like a moth trapped in a light.

Evan pulled a box of large bandages out of the little bag he'd brought with him.

"Where did you find those?" I peered over at the pavilion he'd just left. Baltimore's big tourist Mecca was full of overpriced chain restaurants and gift shops. Drugstores didn't exist in a place like that.

"They have a security and first aid station in there. Any big mall does. People are always getting lost or injured or sick in malls, Sabrina. I went in, told them what happened, and asked if they had some first aid supplies. No big deal."

He shrugged in that mellow way he had. Everything about Evan as my personal trainer was like that—laid-back, low-key. He ripped open a packet of antibiotic cream and dabbed the antiseptic all over my knee as I winced.

"That's what this is for." He handed me the lemonade. "To take your mind off the pain."

"I'm sorry I'm being such a girl," I said.

"I'm not." His voice sounded uncharacteristically

husky. When his eyes tried to meet mine again, I looked away.

"I should go." I half-rose from the step, his hands still wrapped around my leg.

"Come on. First let me bandage this," he insisted.

I sat back down. He laid a piece of non-stick gauze against my knee before fixing the big square bandage on top. His hands were broad with long, thick fingers, and they moved with swift confidence, like he'd done this a million times.

"Were you ever a medical student or something?"

"Army medic."

That jarred me. How pathetic I must look complaining about my poor knee. But then I told myself he'd probably been in and out before the world went all to hell, so maybe he hadn't seen anything gruesome at all.

"Can you walk okay?" He rose with a lithe, animal grace and offered me his hand

As I took it, I realized I'd never remotely believed he was gay or bi. Except in a couple of really weird fantasies involving him and me and Andy. I shook my head hard, trying to knock those embarrassing images out of my head.

"Does your head hurt?" Evan threw his arm around my shoulders, not in a romantic way, but like he was trying to steady me.

My head did hurt now, mostly because I'd shaken it so hard. I'd almost been able to hear marbles rattling around.

"It's fine." I squirmed out of his unexpected embrace.

"Where's your car?"

I'd left my car in the office parking garage after visiting a client that morning. When I told Evan where I'd parked, he said that was a long walk with a sore leg, which it wasn't. Then he offered to come with me. I don't know why I said yes. Okay, I do know why I said yes. But at least I had the dignity to hesitate a bit.

We lumbered down the street side by side. By this time of the year, people usually needed to bundle up in heavy jackets, but the weathermen were calling it the warmest November on record. People in their business suits and designer dresses brushed past us, wrapped up in their cell phone conversations and oblivious to the warmth of the evening or the beauty of the Inner Harbor. Yeah, the water was disgusting, but the place was picturesque in the extreme, something I'd only noticed around the time my hair started falling out.

I used to joke that with less weight on top of my head, I could think more clearly. During chemo I'd dug out my old sketchbooks and pastels, and on my good days, I'd come down and sketch the boats in the harbor or sketch the people strolling hand-in-hand around the promenade. At the time, I'd promised to spend more time on my art and less on adding up columns of numbers, but it had been months since I'd taken time to do any sketching.

Evan interrupted my musings, laying a hand on the middle of my back as he guided me into the garage. We came to a halt in front of a bank of elevators.

I turned to face him. "I'm on the top level. Thanks for walking with me."

And then I kissed him, just like that—a shy little girl kind of kiss, a geeky peck on the cheek. I slapped a hand over my mouth.

He froze, his golden-brown skin darkening slightly. This would be the moment where he would tell me he had a girlfriend in L.A. or wherever he was from. A girlfriend way prettier than I, who didn't try to drop barbells on him or trip over her shoelaces. He stared at me for the longest two seconds of my life.

"Hey, come on," I joked. "It wasn't that bad."

He gave a peculiar little smirk and turned away, planting his hands on his hips as if he were angry or thinking hard about something. I was fourteen the last time I'd tried to kiss a guy first, and it had gone as well as this seemed to be going. I looked down at the grimy concrete floor and opened my mouth to apologize.

Evan spun around with a fluidity that startled me. He caught me by the elbow and pulled me close. He pressed his other hand against my neck so his fingers were tangled in my hair and his thumb teased the corner of my lips. Then he ducked his head down and kissed me, long and hard. My hands slipped around his back as if they were used to going there. I staggered a bit as his tongue slipped into my mouth. When we stopped for breath, he pressed his forehead against mine and sighed.

"That was incredibly unprofessional of me," he murmured.

He surprised me. I had suspected personal trainers were like tennis pros—that a fair percentage of them were in the job for the extracurricular benefits. Last night Scott had implied I was trying to bait Evan. I'd denied it heatedly, but now here I was proving him right. I've always hated women who try to make their boyfriends jealous. If a girl is that insecure about a guy, why not dump him? Why, indeed? Years of accumulated stuff, inertia, the cowardly fear of an ugly scene, and lack of confidence in my own attractiveness—that would be four answers off the top of my head.

"I should really go. Now." The elevator doors opened and for some insane reason, I started crying.

"Hey," he protested softly.

He raised a hand again, as if he wanted to touch me. But then he drew it away, balled it into a tight fist, and clamped his other hand on top.

"I'm sorry," I babbled. "Scott and I had a fight yesterday, and he left for his business trip in a really bad mood. He was so flustered he even took the wrong damned laptop, which is not like him. He never lets me touch his computer. Barely lets it out of his sight. He's going to be in such a mess at his meeting in Mexico, and then he'll be in an even crankier mood when he calls later."

Behind me, the elevator doors whooshed closed again. Evan's face twisted, a deep line creasing his brow.

"Do you have the laptop with you?"

Talk about a non sequitur.

"What, when I go jogging I should bring someone else's computer? Not even my own?"

I laughed but he didn't. His whole demeanor had changed somehow, like a panther sighting a wounded rabbit.

"It's not in your car either?" He said it with a weird, disconcerting urgency.

"What do you care?" I was baffled and even a little alarmed. The kiss had rattled us more than it should have. "I need to leave." I thrust out a hand to keep him at bay and backed up a little.

What did I know about him, except he looked hot in a muscle shirt and could probably wrestle me into submission with frighteningly little effort? As I stepped away from him, two silver-haired businessmen approached the elevator and pressed the call button. The doors slid open again.

"Sabrina," Evan said. "Wait. I need to tell you something."

"Please don't."

I positioned myself close to the two, fatherly businessmen, who eyed the earring-wearing longhair

9

with condescending smirks. One of them moved to block the center of the elevator doors. He pushed the "close" button before Evan could follow me.

****

I called Jess at the restaurant and told her I wouldn't be coming. I was tired and embarrassed, disgusted with my lame attempt at flirtation, and in a significant amount of pain. My knee had grown to the size of a grapefruit, and I worried something important might have been torn or damaged. I went home and put an icepack on it, reminding myself where I'd been one year ago and remembering how much worse a birthday could be.

Scott fancied himself a bit of a gourmet cook and wine connoisseur. To cap off my festive birthday, I broke out a bottle of one of his most expensive red wines and consoled myself with a glass. And another. And another. Soon I was feeling pleasantly drowsy.

I found myself in my mother's condo in Arizona. My father was there, which was strange since he'd never been near the place in real life. Weirder still, the two of them weren't trying to kill each other.

"Honestly, what kind of man misses his girlfriend's first post-cancer birthday?" My mother snapped as she set the table for dinner.

I muttered some half-hearted defense about how busy Scott was at work.

My father lifted a cup of coffee to his lips and slurped loudly.

Mom winced and frowned at him. "All I know is, Hugh would never do that to me."

Hugh was my stepfather, and the reason my parents' marriage had broken up.

"Honey, you need a new man." Mom waved a fork in my direction. "One that can make a commitment."

My father smirked at her. "You should talk about

10

commitment."

God, even in my dreams they couldn't hold a civil conversation with one another.

"Oh, stop it," I said.

Just as things looked like they might escalate, my sister Angie walked into the room. As always, she was heavily pregnant.

"What about that guy from the gym?" she said.

My mother's eyes went wide with horror. "She can't go out with him! He's gorgeous, so what would he want with her? Plus, he's a lot younger than her, and he's incredibly dangerous."

"Dangerous?" I repeated.

"You just have to look at him to know," my father piped up. "Looks like he probably deals drugs on the side, if you ask me."

"Well, you would know." My mother shot him her trademarked, condescending eye roll.

She put down a plate and turned her attention to me. "In any case, dear, that's not a recipe for a quiet life, is it? And you know that's what you need after the last couple of years—quiet."

"Hey." I started to splutter a protest, but she was right. I abandoned the effort and went back to her earlier remark. "Do you both really think he's dangerous?"

My father took a last gulp of coffee and stood to go. "All I'm saying is, remember what your old dad taught you about using a gun."

"Excuse me?"

My sister's cell phone had begun to ring. She dug it out of a diaper bag slung over her shoulder. "Look, sis," she said to me. "I'm outta here. Dad just means, don't forget that thing about the trigger."

She wiggled her fingers at me and hurried out the front door.

"Trigger thing? What trigger thing?"

"Look, Kid, I'm sorry, but I have to go, too." My

11

dad leaned across the table and gave me a quick peck on the cheek. Then he got up and headed out the door, too.

My mother went into the kitchen and turned a knob on the oven. Suddenly, she looked back at me and said, "For God's sake, Sabrina, don't step on the broken glass in your bare feet."

"Don't what?" I looked down at my favorite old brown loafers and then up at my mother again. "Bare feet? What broken glass?"

The oven door gave a weird muffled thump as she threw it open.

I shook myself from my confusion and discovered I was on the sofa in my own living room. I'd managed to down most of the bottle of wine during my little pity party and had no idea what time it was. For a second, I thought Scott had come home. Maybe that thump had been him putting down his suitcase.

But no, he would be in Mexico for the rest of the week. I sat straight up on the couch and strained to hear any other sounds. There were none.

I told myself I was being crazy. Also, I needed to pee really, really badly. So I struggled to my feet and limped down the long corridor toward the bathroom. I saw a light where there should be none and stumbled into what I thought was my den. Unfortunately, I had stumbled into a whole new universe, one where a man wearing a stocking over his face spun toward me, pointing a dark, shiny metal thing, and bellowed, "Get on the floor, bitch!"

Two

"Um," I replied. "I need to pee."

He waved the dark, shiny thing wildly. "Just do it!"

I noticed he held Scott's laptop under his other arm. I'm not brave, but I do have a bit of a temper. Plus my knee hurt, I needed to go to the toilet, and I was muzzy-headed from all the wine.

"What are you doing with that?" I came at the guy like he was some rude shopper who'd picked up the pair of shoes I wanted at an after-Christmas sale.

He fired the dark, shiny thing. At me. A bullet sailed right past my ear. I wet myself the teensiest bit. Right about then, the word *gun* finally formed itself in my head.

I backed up and ran down the corridor toward my bedroom, thinking to barricade myself in there and call 911. But the guy in the stocking mask sprinted after me.

I ducked around the corner of the bedroom door, and at the last second, I stuck out my leg. Believe it or not, it worked. The guy went sprawling past me, and Scott's computer flew across the room, hitting my vanity table mirror, which shattered into dozens of pieces.

I spun away, but the thief was already up on his knees. He lunged and grabbed me by the ankle, bringing me down on my sore knee. I screamed like a banshee and kicked him in the face harder than I knew I could, hard enough to make him let go. After scrambling to my feet, I ran back into the corridor and flattened myself against the wall. When the guy followed me, I dove back into my bedroom and tried to close the door. But he was too quick, thrusting an arm and a leg inside. I kept slamming the door on his body parts, but he had the resilience of a freaking robot.

"Give me that computer, you bitch!" he shouted.

His hand scrabbled around grabbing for me and connected with my wrist. I let out a throat-tearing shriek, and then I heard two pops, like the sound of a car backfiring. The arm and leg wedged in my bedroom door suddenly spasmed, then relaxed and sagged toward the floor. I waited what felt like forever before I threw open the door. The man in the stocking mask slumped face down into my bedroom doorway.

I looked up and away from him. I could make out a tall silhouette at the opposite end of the dark corridor. He lowered a gun, tucking it into his waistband or a holster as he strode toward me.

"Officer?" Maybe some neighbor had complained about all the tumbling around in the bedroom. But even as I spoke, I stepped back. Faint light spilled in through the open door of the den as this stranger approached, and I saw the shine of leather gloves on his hands.

"Who—?"

I never finished that question. It wasn't necessary.

"Okay." Evan spoke brusquely as he closed the distance between us. "We need to hurry. Where's the laptop?"

"Not you, too!" I dashed into the bedroom, but shutting the door against him wasn't an option, what with a dead guy lying in the threshold.

"Where is it?" he asked again.

I began shaking all over. My hand trembled as I pointed to the far side of the room.

"He dropped it—well, threw it. I don't know if it's working anymore."

Evan sidled past me as though we were strangers—which, I realized in amazement, we apparently were. Using a gloved hand, he brushed aside some glass and flipped open the laptop.

"You should get dressed," he murmured without looking at me.

"Do what?"

"Get dressed," he repeated. "Now."

"No." He wanted to take me somewhere. And do what? Rape me? Torture me? Kill me? All of the above? I was not moving one inch.

"Do as I say, Sabrina." His tone was much firmer than I'd ever heard. I'd always liked that he wasn't one of those drill sergeant-type instructors, but now his voice made the hairs on the back of my neck prickle.

He sighed and tore his gaze from Scott's computer screen, which was looking very blue.

"More of them are coming." He jabbed a thumb in the direction of the dead guy. "And they *will* kill you. Among other things." He spoke with elaborate care, as if he were talking to someone who didn't speak English.

I stayed where I was.

"Right. This is going to take you a while to process, and even longer for me to explain. I'll make it simple." He crossed the room in a few smooth steps and threw me over his shoulder like a sack of garden mulch.

I snarled and pounded on his back as he carried me over to my walk-in closet.

With his free hand, he threw open the door. "Last chance, or we leave with you in those pink kitty-cat jammies."

I had no doubt he could drag me pretty much anywhere he chose. My good girl modesty kicked in.

I had no desire to be paraded all over my condo building in the kitty-cat jammies. And I wanted shoes, too. Mom had been right about that broken glass. Even when she wasn't around, she knew more about my life than I did.

Whoa. Maybe now wasn't a good time to consider the significance of having my future foretold by a character in a dream.

"Fine. Put me down and turn around."

He gave a faint snort of laughter.

"I'm sorry, I suppose it's a quaint notion that not everyone gets to see my naked body." I threw back my shoulders, displaying a confidence I didn't feel. "I'm sure it's not all that interesting to men anyway, since the—the—"

"Cancer," he finished for me.

I blinked. Scott had never said the word out loud. My parents referred to it as *my illness.* Even I usually called it *the C word.*

"Turn around."

This time, he did.

I removed my shirt and grabbed a pair of jeans and a pink blouse from a drawer to my left. Then I realized I needed underwear, which was on the opposite side of the closet where Evan stood.

"I need a bra." I choked back tears. It was worse because I'd thought I'd known him. Good God, I'd even kissed him. For a fleeting second, I imagined that was why he was here—I'd ignited the psycho fantasies of a latent stalker without meaning to do so. Then I remembered the other guy, the one whose corpse was cooling in my bedroom doorway. What was his excuse? Even though the bedroom was warm, my skin prickled with goose bumps and my teeth chattered.

"Which drawer?" Evan glanced at me. I clasped my pajama top over my chest and pointed. He yanked the drawer open, flinging one of my bras at me. I didn't have the nerve to ask for one of those horrible enhancer shells—the silicone cushion that fills the empty space where about half of my right breast used to be.

"Here, you'll want these too, I suppose." Evan's low voice sounded strained and almost angry. He reached a hand over his opposite shoulder and held out one of my nicer pairs of panties, the creamy lace ones with a little red bow at the front of the waistband. They were special-occasion panties, not the comfy cotton undies I wear every day. In fact, I had worn this fancy pair only once. When I realized Scott was never again going to look at my naked body with the lights on, I'd come to hate their pointless extravagance and stuck them in a corner of the drawer to gather dust. I considered explaining these were the wrong panties for wearing with jeans, but it seemed like a bad idea to be too picky about my wardrobe with an armed man doing the choosing.

"Thank you," I whispered. I slipped on the panties and then my jeans, buttoned up my blouse, and turned back around as I slipped into a pair of canvas sneakers.

Evan had moved out of the closet doorway and was now crouched down on one knee fiddling with the computer.

"Is it all right?" I asked.

"Blue screen of death." He made a low noise of disgust. "But we have to get it and you out of here. The information's still in there. We'll get it to Philly and let the guys up there wrestle with it."

He closed the laptop and strode away from me with it tucked under his arm. When he got to the other man's body, he stepped over it like it was a mere ruck in the carpeting, like he stepped over bodies everyday—no biggie.

"Ben, any newcomers?"

17

I looked down in confusion, thinking he was speaking to the body. Then I noticed he was wearing something that looked like one of those Bluetooth headsets.

After a moment of listening, he cursed under his breath.

"Tweedledee woke her up. She's right in the middle of this now."

"What am I in the middle of?" I demanded, but he held up one gloved hand to silence me as he stepped into the den.

He found the carrier bag for Scott's laptop and zipped the computer into it as he listened to his invisible friend. "Yeah, that'll be Tweedledum. We should assume he called for more help. Have your engine running. Oh, and get a clean-up crew in here pronto. Out."

I found time to snicker a bit.

"Ooh, have your engine running," I mocked in a cavernous voice.

He glared at me and shook his head. Then he grabbed me by the elbow, ushering me out of my own apartment.

"I need to pee," I remembered suddenly.

"Not now you don't. We'll stop at a fast food place along the way."

"Along the way to where?" I demanded as he propelled me toward the elevators.

"Can't say." His eyes were everywhere as he spoke, moving so swiftly he seemed to be looking in both directions at once. As the elevator indicator dinged, he shoved me behind him and reached around to the back of his waistband. If anyone were in that car when the doors opened, he'd fire first and ask questions later. But the car was unoccupied, and he nudged me into it. As he did, the door to the fire escape opened, and a burly man with a scar barged into the hallway. Another gun, for crying out loud! I thought Baltimore had all these gun control laws. What the hell?

Scarface glanced in the direction of the elevator and instantly a little dark spot appeared on his forehead. He flew backwards against the wall opposite the elevators. When he slid down the wall, he left a long, wet trail of redness. I hadn't seen Evan get the gun out or take aim, he was that fast. When I understood what had happened and looked his way, he was already tucking it under the back flap of his jacket.

I lurched into a corner of the elevator car and sank to my knees, struggling against a powerful wave of nausea. I turned and sat down, trying to back even further away from him.

"There are cameras in this elevator," I said. "Security is going to stop you when we get to the lobby."

"No they won't," he replied with a chilly smile. "We replaced your security people last month, around the same time we replaced your personal trainer."

****

When I first met Evan, he stuck out his hand and grasped mine in a fierce shake. I remember getting a stupid, plastered-on grin on my face because my hand hurt and I didn't want to act like a total girl and complain about it.

"Hi." He had beamed at me that day. "I'm Evan Garcia. Mitzi had an accident, and she'll be out of commission for a few months. I'm your new trainer."

He was the tallest guy I'd ever seen off a basketball court, with lots of muscles rippling all over his chest and back. Big, powerful shoulders and biceps—but not ridiculously so. Not one of those muscle-bound apes who can't even hold their arms down at their sides. More like a statue of a Greek god. Even through the snug tees he wore at the gym,

I'd seen the fantastic definition of his abs. Sometimes I wanted to reach out and put my hand there, which of course I would never do in a million years. Of course, there are girls who would have done that upon being introduced to him—Jess, for example. I could imagine her patting his flat belly and saying something like "Ooh, can I have a taste of your six-pack, honey?" But me, I wanted to get as far away from him as possible when I first met him, he made me that tense. I was used to pin-striped, button-downed men, and Evan most definitely wasn't one of those.

When he spoke, he sounded like the classic California slacker—his voice low and easy-going. Come to think of it, he even looked Californian—like he'd just surfed out of the Pacific and landed on the wrong beach. He had a perfect, golden-brown tan and almond eyes so black I couldn't even see the pupils. I'd figured him for at least partly Native American, because of the black hair. The strands in front were shorter and curled under to frame his face.

And his lips—oh, boy. His lips just knocked me out, right from the get-go. His bottom lip jutted out a little, looking almost pouty. It gave him an insolent male-model look, like something out of a gay porn magazine. Those lips looked silky—like they would *be* silky-smooth and delicious. And they had been that afternoon. Now all I could do was feel hot with shame at having been so thoroughly played by this—this—I didn't even know what to call him. Charlatan? Con man? Gangster? Psychopath?

"Augh!" I moaned in frustration, putting my head down between my knees.

Then I quickly looked up again, afraid to take my eyes off him. He regarded me with an almost apologetic expression, which only made me angrier.

"What did you do to Mitzi, whoever you are?"

He furrowed his brow but then his face lit up as he finally dredged up her memory. "Oh, her! The trainer. She's fine. We gave her a paid vacation in the Bahamas. Guess she'll be bummed to hear it's over so soon. I wasn't expecting us to get a break like this thing with the laptop."

He smiled, flashing the same open, boyish grin he'd used when he handed me the lemonade.

"Who is *we*?" I demanded. "You said *we* replaced the security personnel, too."

Evan didn't answer me. The elevator stopped moving right then, and he reached a hand down to me. I batted it away like some pesky fly, unintimidated by his firepower. I suppose on some unconscious level I'd already realized he would have killed me by now if he meant to do so. He took a step back and put his hands up, then watched as I struggled to my feet. I was really feeling the after-affects of all those glasses of wine, the tussle with my first assailant, and my sore knee—but it was too late to ask him to help me up without losing all remaining dignity.

As the doors opened, Evan did his owl-like scan of our environment again and hustled me out to the parking garage. A blue coupe sports car idled a few yards away in the central aisle of the parking garage. The tinted driver's side window rolled down, and an unassuming guy in his twenties with kinky-curly hair peered out at us.

"I don't think we should bring the girl with us, Ev," he said. "Didn't Tyrese tell you the other day—"

"Ben," Evan retorted, "if we leave the girl, I might as well shoot her in the head right here and now."

My eyes popped open so wide, I half-expected them to fall out of my head and roll around a bit on the garage floor.

"Anyway, I've known Tyrese longer than you

have. Trust me when I say he has extraneous issues on this one."

The man behind the wheel shrugged. I couldn't help thinking that with his rosy, round face and wiry hair, this new guy looked an awful lot like Frodo Baggins.

"Shouldn't we be more worried about protecting that laptop?" Frodo asked. "She'll slow everything down."

"I don't know what to think anymore." Evan gave me a cursory glance that wasn't entirely friendly. "I was looking at the security monitors before I went up there. She ran right at Mendoza's man when he picked up the laptop. Jesus, I can't think why she'd take a risk like that unless she was trying to protect Scott Bennett. Which would mean she knows way more than I thought she did."

"Hah!" Frodo said. "Even the great Evan Desmond has to have a few wrong hunches. Otherwise you'd have to wear a blue leotard with a big S on the front."

Evan Desmond? I repeated it out loud, twice for good measure.

"Oh, come on," I sneered. "That's even phonier than Evan Garcia."

"What makes you say that?" Evan asked in a particularly brittle tone. He shifted Scott's laptop off his shoulder and passed it through the car window to Frodo. Then he pulled me around the vehicle to the passenger's side. He wasn't gentle either.

"News flash," I hissed. "People named Desmond look like me, not you."

He threw open the car door with a violent yank. I saw Frodo's eyebrow go up, and I could have sworn he was shaking his head at me in some attempt at a warning.

"Evan Ignacio Garcia y Delgado Desmond," Evan announced, with a sarcastic little bow. "I'd shake your hand, but we did that already. And you probably had to wash it off after touching someone as brown as me."

I may have still been a bit drunk, but I'd sobered up enough to blush at the suggestion of prejudice on my part, even from a gun-toting kidnapper.

He reached into the passenger seat behind me and picked up something off the floor. I twisted around in my seat and leaned over the back so I could watch him. Frodo stuck one hand out to hold me back, and the other went under his windbreaker, the implied threat all too clear.

"Get your hand away from me." I tried to shrug him off, but he was stronger than he looked. I shifted my gaze to Evan. "I don't know what you all want with Scott's computer, but I'll remind you he's a lawyer for Homeland Security, and his uncle is a Senator. You boys are in over your head. And that's not a real name. Do I look like a fool? That's like two completely different names sandwiched together. Evan Desmond sounds like someone I'd meet at my stepfather's country club. As for Ignacio Garcia Delgado—you're probably a hit man for some Latin American drug cartel."

I can be pretty vicious when I go past one glass of wine. Evan's head jerked upwards and his nostrils flared. I felt certain I'd hit the mark, and I grinned triumphantly. He muttered a string of Spanish words at me, including *puta*, which I had learned from Scott many years ago before we started dating. He was fluent in Spanish and several other languages, and he took a frat boy's delight in being able to cuss in all of them. *Puta* was not a compliment.

The abrupt shriek of skidding tires prevented any further culture clashes for the moment.

Evan backed out of the car with a canvas bag slung over one shoulder. He was holding a rifle, and not the kind my dad uses when he goes deer hunting either. More like the kind the SWAT team uses when they bust down somebody's door. I scrunched down in the front seat and shut my mouth. He dashed over to the low wall dividing the entrance and exit ramps of the garage, and he peered down at the lower levels.

"Ben, get her out of here!" he called back to us. He stepped away from the wall and threw open the driver's door on a truck parked nearby. "And don't let Ty question her without me."

"But Ev, what do I do with her then?" Frodo said.

"Do I arrest her? What do I charge her with?"

"Arrest? Hah!" I spat at him and twisted in my seat, flailing at the locked door. "My dad's a cop! Cops don't act like this, mister!"

"Go!" Evan barked at the younger guy. "Now!"

"Go?" I repeated, squirming around as Ben reached over and fastened my seatbelt. I could see an ivory pallor to his face where before he'd had that nice Hobbity glow.

The screaming drone of an engine grew louder, and I heard tires cornering sharply.

"What's happening? Where are we going? Why is he staying?"

"He's going to try and stop them. Or draw their fire. You can never tell with him." Ben threw the sports car into gear. "Geez, I hope you're worth all this."

I had no answer.

We sped down the sloped ramp of my parking level as a battered white sedan zipped up the ramp on the opposite side of the dividing barricade. The men inside looked like they were wearing suits. Now, my dad is a retired police detective. Nothing says cops to me like guys in cheap suits in a plain vanilla sedan. I was sure they were the cavalry coming to rescue me, but I knew they wouldn't get to me in time. I grasped the sides of the passenger seat and peered into the side mirror as the sedan whipped around a support column at the rear of the garage.

Then I heard the cavernous echo of a rifle blast. I craned my neck to peer into Ben's rearview mirror. The white car fishtailed; its windshield spiderwebbed into a million little fragments. I watched in horror as it veered toward my next-door neighbor's expensive new foreign car. She'd only bought that car two weeks ago. Although I squeezed my eyes shut at the moment of impact, I could still hear the crunch of metal against metal.

Ben rumbled out of the parking garage and merged into traffic on Key Highway.

"What will Evan do?" I said when I could breathe again.

"He'll catch up to us in the truck." Ben spoke without taking his eyes off the road. "He'll phone me and tell me where he wants to meet, once we're sure no one else is following. Then I guess we take the laptop up to Philly. I don't know what we do with you. Tyrese is going to want to question you. But he's in DC, so it'll take him a while to find out we've got you. And I'm sure Evan will keep that information to himself for as long as he can. I don't know what the heck I'm going to do, I am way too low on the totem pole to survive if I get stuck in the middle of a turf war between those two."

I nodded in mute agreement. Most of what he'd said was incoherent, but I recognized the universal grousing about territorial battles between bosses.

"So Evan—or whatever his name is—he's not some Colombian drug lord's hit man?"

"Geez, don't ever, ever say anything like that to him again, lady." Ben whistled. "You are so lucky he didn't throw you out of the car and leave you to those guys after a remark like that."

I grunted. It seemed to be a safe, all-purpose answer.

"He must like you an awful lot." Ben shook his head as he turned onto Light Street.

I could feel my face coloring again. I still needed to pee, and I had my legs squeezed together tight. I told myself the effort of holding it in was making me turn red.

"Can you at least tell me who you people are?" I pressed my clammy hands to my burning cheeks, trying to cool them down and distract myself.

"No, I can't," Ben answered, licking his lips.

"Why the heck not?" I lowered my hands again.

"Because, first, Evan and Tyrese are in charge, so they should be the ones to talk to you," he answered. "And second, there's a black Ford Explorer following us. It's coming on fast, too. I need to focus on that right now."

"Oh, brother," I groaned.

It was going to be a long night. And that was only if I got lucky and didn't die with wet panties sometime in the next few minutes.

Three

I reached down and dug my fingernails into the sides of the passenger seat again. Just in time too, because I needed that extra leverage to stay upright when Ben whipped across two lanes of traffic and sped down Key Highway, past the big train mural on the retaining wall. The tires shrieked as he turned onto McComas, where it runs past the loading docks of the city's commercial port. The road there is bleak even in broad daylight. An overpass blots out both sun and streetlamp glow, and there's always a puddle to splash through coming around the corner, even in a drought. Suddenly the interior of our car glowed blue-gray from the Explorer's headlights. A brighter glare bounced off the side mirror and blinded me. I squinted and turned my face away.

"They turned on their high beams," Ben explained as he drove a little faster.

We were hurtling toward the Fort McHenry Tunnel and the toll plaza that led out onto I-95.

I gulped. "Shouldn't we slow down?"

"No," he replied. "If I can get a few cops between me and that Explorer, I'll be happy as a pig in mud."

"Charming metaphor."

"Lady," Ben spared me a hasty glance. "I'm from Iowa, give me a break,"

We zoomed into the tunnel at a hair-raising speed. Fortunately at that time of night it was empty. I never liked the tunnel in the best of times—the weird dappled light, the white tiled walls curved to hold out the deadly weight of the water surrounding them. When we emerged, we blew right through one of the toll lanes without even a pause. The Explorer was closing on us, and the sound of sirens loomed in the distance.

Ben fixed his gaze on the road. "Open that glove compartment."

I did as I was told and found the usual pile of papers, yet another gun—boy, were these guys loaded for bear—and what looked like an antique cell phone.

"That's a satellite phone. Now call Evan. Push the one."

I fumbled with the big clunky satellite phone while Ben talked me through how to operate it. Evan answered on the second ring.

"I thought you'd be dead." What an idiotic thing for me to say. He'd think I was still pining for him.

"Well, I'm fine," he snapped. "I'm behind the Explorer."

"Can't you shoot their tires or something, like they do in the movies?"

He said something in Spanish again.

"Tell Ben to get off the highway," he added. "Tell him to take the next exit. I radioed the state troopers, so they know not to shoot at us. But I'd like to get us off the main road anyway, away from other drivers, in case things get ugly."

"In *case*?! In *case* they get ugly? What, they aren't ugly now?"

He ignored my tirade and hung up. I conveyed his message to Ben, who threw the wheel hard to the right and screeched over to the Boston Street exit in the nick of time. For a second, it looked like Ben was in the clear, that the Explorer would miss the turn, but then it loomed up behind us closer than ever. I couldn't see behind the hulking SUV, but I could hear the sirens getting louder. We wove in and out of sparse traffic and turned onto a dark, deserted two-lane road. I peered out the window and saw a low stone wall and sagging arched gates, mounds of earth and stone statues—a cemetery. Oh, what a grand omen.

As if to confirm my worst fears, the Explorer picked that moment to catch up and ram us from behind. I jolted forward and then sideways and hit my head against the passenger window. Ben pressed hard on the gas but only a few inches separated us from them. Abruptly the Explorer slowed and veered over the yellow line. Ben cursed under his breath as the vehicle crowded back in toward us, pushing us off the road and into the cemetery wall.

"Get the laptop," he told me.

"What, now I can have it?" I spluttered.

"It's on the backseat, reach around and grab it, and be ready to run."

"Run?! Run where?"

"Anywhere. Evan will find you. I'm going to hold them off while you go, okay?"

His bleak tone gave me a shiver. I still didn't know who Ben and Evan were, but the guys in the Explorer sure didn't act like cops either. What if two different gangs were after Scott and me—for whatever reason? I liked Ben's team better than the one in the black Explorer, that much was certain. I felt an almost maternal desire to hug him and pat his woolly head.

"I'm so sorry," I told him.

He nodded to me right before the little coupe plowed into the stone wall. A big, grey rock bounced off the hood and hit the windshield, chipping it. We were engulfed in a hail of stones, and the clatter on the car was horrendous. I expected something to come through the roof and kill us both at any second. We coasted through the cemetery, heading straight for an above ground crypt. The car smashed into it, and things truly seemed to happen in slow motion. The whole time I thought I was going to be thrown from the vehicle because the airbag hadn't opened. I kept praying and praying for it to open, but I never saw or felt a thing. After the impact, I smelled something like gunpowder. I choked and my eyes stung, but as the smoke cleared, I saw a big white blob of parachute material in front of me and another in front of Ben. The airbags had deployed after all, even though I hadn't noticed them at the time.

Ben slumped back, rubbing his temples.

"Are you hurt?" I asked.

He pulled the gun from beneath his windbreaker. "Get out, *now*."

As he wrenched open his door, I did the same with mine. I remembered the laptop at the last second and almost wanted to leave it behind. But I was feeling some weird attachment to Ben at this point. I envisioned some cartoon-like ogre named Tyrese kicking the crap out of him if he came back without the computer. I turned back, threw open the passenger door, grabbed the machine, and stumbled into the pitch darkness of the graveyard.

I ran without looking back, my sneakers getting wet and suctioning into the soft earth. Voices drifted toward me from far away, but no one was coming after me, yet. An open grave brought me up short, and I nearly fell into it. I crawled around its perimeter and settled behind a big mound of dirt piled up on its far side, taking a second to breathe.

When I'd recovered a bit, I chanced a look around the corner. Flames shot out from under the hood of the smashed vehicle and illuminated my surroundings. A few yards in front of me I could make out the shape of Ben as he headed in my direction. A lanky silhouette loomed up behind him. Right about the time I'd made up my mind to call out a warning, Ben must have heard the guy. He spun around, pointing his gun and firing. The thin stranger fired, too, and Ben ducked. His assailant stalked closer, firing again, and Ben went down. I let out a strangled whimper, then clapped my hand over my mouth. My fingers had dug into the pile of dirt, and my hand carried the pungent aroma of clay and decay and wet, rotting leaves. I gagged on the smell.

Ben's attacker stepped closer, raising his gun to fire again, when he was thrown off balance. Someone had come flying out of the darkness and broadsided him, taking him down to the ground. His gun fell away as the newcomer pinned him down. I stood to get a better view and recognized Evan's tall form and big shoulders. He sat astride Ben's attacker, pounding his fist into the guy's face over and over again. Occasionally, he would aim a blow at the guy's stomach or ribs, but mostly he focused on the face. I'd never seen someone waling on another human being like that. The sound was what got me, the soft grunting noises from Evan as he landed each punch and the gasps and moans from the other man. His ferocity was impressive and repellent all at once.

Sudden light flooded the cemetery. A police helicopter hovered above us, and a whole cavalcade of squad cars squealed to a stop in front of the cemetery gates. Cops poured into the space, but none made any move to stop Evan. They all carefully pretended not to see him trying to beat this other man to death. Paramedics came in and worked on Ben, loading him onto a gurney, even as Evan stood up and kicked the gunman in the head a couple of times. I couldn't look anymore. I turned my back and sat down behind the pile of dirt. I understood that skinny guy had been a bad man. But there's more than one way of dealing out justice. Evan's way made me so sick, I had to choke down the sour taste of vomit.

The laptop lay in the grass beneath me.

Someone would be looking for it soon—Evan, the police, one of those mysterious guys who'd been chasing us all night. I didn't know what any of them wanted with it, but at this point, I decided no one was going to touch it again until I had a lawyer present. I crawled past the mound of dirt, scooted my legs around, and jumped down into the open grave, taking the laptop with me. I stood it upright against one of the short sides of the grave, hoping that position would keep it out of the way if someone did get buried before I could return. They must have to allow an inch or two of wiggle room on each side, mustn't they? Otherwise it would be way too hard to get the coffin into the ground.

"Sabrina!"

Evan's voice chilled me. I didn't ever want to see him again.

But fear is a terrible thing for many reasons, not the least of which is that it can make a girl forget some very important details. Details like—I'm allergic to mold and standing in a big wet hole in the ground is like standing in the middle of Ground Zero for mold. I sneezed.

"Hey!" Evan leaned his head over the edge of the grave. "Clever. Good thing you didn't sneeze while Mendoza's man was on the loose. Here."

He stretched out on the ground and reached his arms down to me. He caught me under my shoulders and lifted me clear like I was no more trouble than a child, and then he sat me down at the edge of the grave. In the glare from the hovering chopper, I could see red spatters on his shirt and even his face as he knelt down beside me. My expression must have betrayed my disgust because he rubbed self-consciously at his jaw.

"Your forehead." I looked down and away. "There's blood there and—and everywhere."

"I thought you might have been in the car." He

made no move to wipe away the blood. "It was burning, and I didn't see you. And then there's Ben. He's a kid. The bastard didn't need to shoot him. Mendoza's goon could see he didn't have the computer. He should have gone after the car or looked for you. He just shot Ben because he could, for his own amusement."

"I'm sorry."

"He's as good as dead." Evan's voice sounded weary and old. "That bastard shot him in the head. They aim for the head now, because everyone's wearing vests."

"Well." No other words would come. He'd had such a fuzzy puppy quality to him, Ben had.

"And now the laptop's gone, too" Evan stood and looked across the field to Ben's car, which was being doused with foam by a crew of firefighters. Then he clenched and unclenched his right hand a few times. I was still sitting, so his hands were right about my eye level. His knuckles were scraped raw and bleeding. Until then, I'd never contemplated how much damage hitting someone else could do to a person. Seeing the aftereffects up close creeped me out big time. That must have been one hell of a burst of adrenaline.

I'd almost spoken up about the computer, but seeing his bloodied hands made me bite my tongue. What had happened to Ben was tragic but didn't change the facts as I could see them. Someone had broken into my apartment to steal my boyfriend's computer. Evan had killed that guy, but I still didn't know who or what Evan represented or why everyone wanted Scott's laptop so badly. I kept my own counsel.

A female state trooper approached us, directing her words to Evan. "Excuse me."

"Yes?"

"They're taking your partner to UM, to the

Shock-Trauma Center. I think the suspect's going to Bayview."

"I could kick him a few more times, then they can take him straight to the morgue." Evan smirked.

"That won't be necessary." To my horror, the corners of the trooper's mouth turned up a bit as she spoke. She was smaller than I am, with blond hair in a ponytail. I couldn't imagine her being much of a threat to the bad guys of the world.

And I couldn't believe the familiar, almost condescending tone Evan used in speaking to her. Maybe they knew each other? Maybe he was a police informer?

The blond trooper jotted something down in her handy notebook and passed it to Evan. "Can you come back to our barracks to fill out some paperwork on the suspect, sir?"

"Yeah." Evan agreed as he looked at the paper she'd handed him. "I need to clear up some loose ends here first. I'll meet you back there. Golden Ring station?"

She nodded. She had green eyes and obscenely long lashes with no hint of mascara on them. I glanced up at Evan, but he didn't seem to be noticing her Bambi eyes right now. The fact I cared one way or the other must be an indicator of my own mental incompetence.

"This is Sabrina O'Hara," Evan said to Blondie. "She's not a suspect, but she is a material witness in the case."

Blondie nodded at me, but I was too busy trying to keep my eyes from bugging out of my head to nod back.

"What case?" I demanded. Loudly. "How can I be a freaking material witness when I don't even know what's going on?!"

"We'll talk back at the barracks." Evan sounded eerily like Scott trying to shut down a discussion of wedding plans. Do they give guys a handbook full of phrases like that? *We'll talk later. This isn't the appropriate time, honey. I can't think about that now.*

"You woke me up, damn it!" I shouted. Disconcertingly, I noticed Trooper Blondie covering her mouth with her notebook.

Evan glared down at me. "No, I didn't wake you up. That would be the man who tried to kill you, Sabrina. I'm the one that saved you."

He looked away from me to the blonde.

"Can you take her back to your barracks and keep an eye on her until I get over there? I shouldn't be long."

I suspected he was hanging around to look for the laptop, but I didn't feel like offering any assistance. Now I was a material witness? What the hell did he mean? Visions of my being tossed into one of those witness protection programs danced in my head. And I'd seen enough TV movies to know that was as good as a death sentence.

****

The state and county police decided I would have to ride in the back of Trooper Blondie's car, which was horrifying. I had to fight down an urge to put my shirt over my face so no one would see me and think I was being arrested. Not that anyone I knew was likely to be around the area. But television reporters were starting to show up outside the gates of the cemetery, and I could imagine Jess and Andy and everyone else seeing me on the morning news. *Boy, that must have been some birthday celebration, Sabrina! Now we know why you didn't invite us.* I would never hear the end of it.

"No cameras." A huge, bear-like trooper made a shooing gesture as we approached the gates.

The reporters shifted uneasily but continued to set up their equipment.

"I said, no cameras," the trooper growled. "This is a Homeland Security matter. Under the terms of the Patriot Act, I'm ordering you to put your cameras away. Unless you want to disappear into Gitmo and never come back."

"Can you guys do that?" I whispered to Trooper Blondie.

"Not sure," she whispered back. "I'm kind of a rookie. But the threat alone usually does the trick."

Sure enough, the reporters stowed their cameras back in their vans and muttered unhappily to themselves. So much for freedom of the press. At least my face wouldn't be splashed all over every television and newspaper in Baltimore come the dawn, so I couldn't be too outraged by the situation.

I watched two ambulances speed away from the scene as Blondie helped me into her squad car.

"What exactly is Evan?" I asked. "Is he an informer? An undercover cop?"

"Oh no, ma'am," she answered as she started the car. "He's a Federal agent. This really is a Homeland Security matter."

Four

No one wanted to say much to me at the barracks. The building was the typical squat, utilitarian government building, dull reddish-brown.

Trooper Blondie, whose real name was Gloria Petty, led me to a room she called a conference room, but it looked like an interrogation room. Before my parents' divorce, my dad would sometimes take us kids for visits to his station house. The room with the big mirror was the interrogation room there, so I was sure it did the same duty here. Still, no one seemed inclined to do any interrogating of me, so I chilled out. Gloria showed me where the bathrooms were and waited for me outside the door. No questioning, no Mirandizing—but no leaving me unattended either.

"Am I under arrest?" I asked as we walked down the corridor and returned to the *conference room.*

"No, ma'am!" She spoke in the emphatic tones of a high school kid.

"Please stop calling me ma'am." She looked younger than I but not young enough to be assaulting me with the dreaded use of that word.

"Sorry." She grinned and sat next to me at the long table. The door to the room remained open, which reassured me.

"I honestly don't know what's going on," I said. "I fell asleep on my sofa and woke up to find a guy in a stocking mask and the man I thought was my personal trainer engaged in a life-or-death battle for my fiancé's laptop."

"Who's your fiancé?"

"Scott Bennett. A lawyer at CIS—used to be INS. Actually, fiancé is an overstatement," I admitted. "He's never given me a ring. And the date for any possible wedding keeps getting pushed further and further into the future."

Gloria instantly won my affection with her disapproving harrumph and a shake of the head.

"Yeah, I had one of those, too," she sighed. "Then I found him with my best friend and all that ambivalence became painfully clear. So I quit being a paralegal at his firm and joined the state police. That was about a year and a half ago."

"Wow. All I did was cut my hair the last time I broke up with a guy."

"Why don't I get us some coffee?" she offered.

"Sounds good." I nodded, thinking Gloria and I could be good friends in real life.

At the door to the room, she turned back to me and said, "You will stay right here, won't you?"

"I promise." Honestly, I was too tired and too curious to contemplate making a break right then.

Besides the mirrored wall, the room had a big window on the opposite side, looking into the central bullpen office. The blinds were down on the window, but I rose from the table and peered between the slats, watching Gloria making her way to the far side of the room, where a water cooler and a couple of coffee pots were ranged against the wall next to a door. She stopped to chat with the brawny trooper, the one who'd threatened the reporters with internment at Guantanamo. The two of them glanced over at me in the non-interrogation room, and I gave them a cheery little wave. Gloria looked away quickly, embarrassed. That wasn't encouraging. That had to mean whatever they'd been saying about me was not good.

Evan appeared in the main doorway of the outer room. He'd cleaned the blood off his face and stripped down to the plain white tee he'd been wearing under his button-down shirt. He also had on a dark blue windbreaker with "POLICE ICE" emblazoned on the back. He wore a small wooden cross on a leather cord around his neck; I'd seen it sometimes before in the gym. While I spied on him, he tucked the cross under his shirt. I guessed he probably wore it all the time, even when I couldn't see it. Did he wear it because of some devout belief or out of sentiment or superstition? Cravenly, I wondered whether I could use this information to my benefit. Maybe he'd go easy on me if he found me praying in the interrogation room?

He spotted Gloria and her partner and strode toward them. Heads turned and even though I couldn't hear much noise from within my sequestered area, I could sense the outer room got a lot quieter. When my dad was a cop, I couldn't tell who irritated him more—the criminals or the Feds.

Evan spoke to Gloria and the Bear and then looked over at me. I didn't wave this time. In fact, I dropped the shade and found myself backing away from the window as he approached.

"Hey." He walked into the conference room like he owned the place. Then he closed the door.

"Hey," I returned, trying to stay cool. "So you're a Fed. I guess it's no surprise you got upset when I said you must be a drug dealer. But I guess someone like you has to pretend to be one a lot, huh?"

He gave me a look that wasn't quite angry but might be a stop on the road in that direction.

"What does that mean?"

"I mean, you know, since so many drug dealers are Latino, you know—"

"Met a lot of them, have you?"

"No!" I exclaimed. "None! Not ever! I've never even smoked pot! Not even when I had cancer and my doctor suggested it for the nausea. I was afraid

I'd survive cancer only to become some spaced-out junkie!"

The stony set of his face wavered. He'd taken a turn off of Angry Road and was now heading down the more familiar Have-a-Laugh-at-Sabrina's-Expense Avenue.

"So what's ICE?" I said, nudging him along. "Is that anything like SMERSH?"

Evan smiled broadly then, revealing deep dimples in his cheeks.

"ICE is Immigration and Customs Enforcement. I'm a contract agent for the Feds. I used to work for DEA, now I mostly work for Homeland Security. And if you're that conversant in James Bond lore, you'll know SMERSH were bad guys."

"And you're not? Despite this habit you have of beating people to a bloody unconscious pulp. Oh, and shooting first and not even bothering to ask questions later."

"What question would you have liked me to ask the guy in your apartment, Sabrina?" Evan said. "Wait, here's one. Why did you miss that shot you took at Sabrina? You were only about two yards away. No one misses a shot that close, especially not someone who's good enough to work for the Mendozas. So why did you miss that shot?"

All night I had been pushing that question aside.

"There are only two answers I can think of, Sabrina." Evan counted them on his fingers. "One—his employer told him not to kill you, which would mean you work for the Mendozas too, or at least know about them. Or two—the guy wanted to scare you then have his sick bit of fun with you before absconding with the computer."

I winced.

"Of course, the two possibilities aren't mutually exclusive," he went on. "You could be under the

Mendozas' protection, so he wouldn't dare kill you. But maybe he thought he'd be allowed to play with you a bit."

"Stop it!" I sat down at the conference table and laid my head on the cool wood veneer for a moment.

"The other question is why so many people were after you tonight," Evan mused.

I'd wondered that, too. Initially, I'd believed those other people in the SUV were the good guys—cops—until they'd run us off the road and shot Ben in the face. Between seeing that and then watching Evan beat the crap out of that other guy, I questioned whether there *were* any good guys in this situation.

"I came to your place to tell you who I was and get you to give me the laptop," Evan went on. "And right about the time I got there, our guard saw the intruder jimmy your door open on his monitor. That's why I came in unannounced—I knew you were in danger."

"My hero."

He laughed a little and shook his head. Then his smile faded, and he stroked a finger over his jaw, contemplative.

"I can't figure out who the guy at the elevator was, or the ones chasing Ben. Unless the Mendoza brothers are at war with each other now. We've been considering that possibility since their father died, but we didn't think Hector was that ambitious. Guess we were wrong."

"Look, whatever you think I've done, I haven't," I snapped, straightening up. I truly was not interested in his off-the-cuff musings about a bunch of crooks I'd never heard of.

"I don't even have any speeding tickets! And Scott—Scott can be an insensitive jerk, but honestly Evan, he's a nice guy. He's a nice, solid Methodist, goes to church every Sunday, which is more than I do. He found the lump, for God's sake!"

Evan tilted his head at me in a questioning way.

"My lump," I explained. "He found the lump, and he pestered me for a week to call my doctor. I was too young for regular mammograms. He saved my life."

I didn't add that was probably the reason I'd been so willing to overlook his lack of support during the actual treatment. It had been unspoken between us that he'd somehow already done his part by finding the damned disease in the first place.

"Look, this is obviously some misunderstanding. Tell me what you think he's done, and I'm sure I can help you figure out what's really going on."

"Your fiancé makes a lot of trips to Mexico," Evan said.

"Because he works for CIS," I cried in utter exasperation. "Customs and Immigration Service."

"I know what it stands for. It's another branch of Homeland Security."

"Then why are you after us?" I pleaded. "We're all on the same side."

"Not Scott Bennett. He's not playing on my side." Evan managed to look so tired and so angry all at once. A hard light gleamed in his eyes as he continued. "We have photos of Scott meeting several times with associates of the Mendoza Cartel. The Mendozas used to focus exclusively on drugs, but over the years they've diversified. Think of them as a supermarket of organized crime."

I smiled in spite of myself. "So my Scott is dealing drugs for the local grocery store?"

Evan ignored me. "They're branching out. Now they sell people. Young girls mostly, but sometimes even boys. Some get pressed to work in brothels or child pornography rings. The really unlucky ones get sold to private collectors."

"Oh." I fumbled with my hair and looked away.

"Oh, my. Those poor girls."

"This is where your fiancé comes in."

"It's not official," I hastened to say. "There's no ring and no date."

As soon as the words were out of my mouth, I despised myself for being a coward. Of course I didn't believe Scott was involved in this thing. But Evan clearly did—and in the absence of my lawyer, a little calculated distancing seemed like my best protection from a similar charge.

Evan peered at me with those smoldering brown eyes, and I regretted saying anything. He probably thought I was trying to tell him I was available and interested. And I really wasn't anymore. The guy who had kind of interested me—my sweet-faced, laid-back personal trainer—that guy didn't exist. This guy he'd morphed into was still good-looking in a rough-edged way, but I'd always been a man-in-a-suit girl. I guess that was the influence of my mom, who always referred to her marriage to my scruffy, rough-and-tumble dad as her "period of slumming." My stepfather was a nice, respectable university administrator, and all the men I dated were like that. Men in good clothes who sat behind desks, maybe played a little basketball or touch football on the weekends. No guy I'd ever dated would know how to load a gun without blowing his own hand off—something my dad had taught me when I was a teenager—and they sure wouldn't be able to beat a man into submission with their bare hands. I shuddered again at the memory of that beating, but Evan's voice brought me back into the present.

"I'm part of a joint task force investigating what happened to those girls. We believe Scott's using his access to resources at the Department of Homeland Security—and maybe even higher up—to manipulate data and falsify records. He and whomever he's working with fake up the necessary documents, enter false data into the system, and pay off people to look the other way. That's how they get these girls into the country and keep them here. I want that laptop because I'm betting it'll show dates and times of meetings with some pretty important businessmen and politicians here. Our task force thinks Scott makes contact with some of the Mendozas' private American clients—wealthy men who think it would be cool to have their very own teen or even preteen plaything."

"So he's like a pimp? He's selling girls to rich men, is that what you think? Why him? Surely other people are involved in this scam. Why would you think Scott's the one contacting these wealthy clients?"

"Personally, I think he's being introduced to them by his uncle." Evan answered without meeting my gaze.

"Uncle Carlton?"

Scott's Uncle Carlton was also Senator Bennett, the senior senator from Virginia. A courtly, good-humored Southern gentleman, who'd always been kind to me.

"I'm sure Carlton has nothing to do with this," I sniffed. "Anyway, how do I know you're telling the truth? First, you were my personal trainer, then you were all hot for me in that garage. Now you're some top-secret federal agent? Why should I believe a word you say?"

"You have no reason to believe me," he replied calmly.

I got up from the table and peered through the blinds again. Gloria and the Bear were peering back at me, pacing uncomfortably. I turned back to face Evan.

"About the garage," he said. "I mean what happened earlier today. Or yesterday. When you hurt your knee."

"You don't need to say anything." I softened, trying to shrug indifferently. I was the one who had pecked him on the cheek after all. "You had a job to do. I set myself up for what happened. You don't need to explain. I'm sure you get information out of people any way you can."

"But I do have to explain." He turned his liquid brown gaze on me. "Because I want you to know I didn't do that in an attempt to seduce you. Or I guess I did mean to seduce you. But I meant it sincerely, I meant to kiss you because you're pretty and funny and smart. And very capable despite that shoelace problem."

I fought a smile, squeezing it down hard, until it felt like I'd swallowed a rock.

"I like you a lot, despite your smart mouth," he continued. "Or maybe even because of it. I swear that kiss wasn't part of some nefarious plot to coax secrets out of you."

"Uh-huh."

"That was completely unprofessional of me in any case. I want you to know I try not to work that way." He scratched his head like a kid having trouble with the answers to his geography quiz. "Anymore," he added, losing an awful lot of points on the quiz. "I try not to work that way *anymore*. If I can possibly avoid it. Which I usually can."

I crossed my arms over my chest and glared at him with a level of disapproval that would have pleased my Nanny O'Hara.

"Okay, look," he snapped. "This isn't about me."

"Obviously not."

"Sabrina," he went on. "I promise I wasn't using you. I'm sure you think I'm lying again, and I don't blame you. But I'm not."

Flattering, but a little too convenient for me to believe.

"Am I under arrest?" I asked.

"What?"

"You heard me."

"No."

"Then I can leave here now? Go stay with a friend, get a shower, call a lawyer?"

"Why do you want a lawyer?" Evan asked, all sweetness and innocence now. "I told you you're not under arrest."

"I want a lawyer." I reminded myself that at least half of everything he'd ever said to me was a lie. "And the woman trooper, I want the woman trooper back in here."

Evan sighed and rolled his eyes.

"Will you sit down and relax? You're not under arrest. Not yet."

"What does that mean?" I remained standing, wrapping my arms around my chest so tightly I could barely breathe.

"It means I don't think we should arrest you. It means I believe you can give us any information you have without being arrested, and frankly, I don't think you know that much about what's going on with Scott Bennett. But my boss thinks differently."

"This is that Tyrese guy you two mentioned?"

Evan sat down and gestured to a chair next to him at the conference table, but I stayed right where I was.

"He's on his way up from DC," Evan said. "And boy, is he pissed."

"Why? Because of what happened to Ben? But that wasn't your fault."

"Yes, it was, Sabrina. Because I was in charge of this investigation and repeatedly ignored Tyrese's warnings."

"Warnings about what?"

"About you, about how I was treating you," Evan said. "I've been letting my personal feelings interfere with the conduct of this investigation, and now Ben is probably in critical condition because of it."

Oh, here we go again. The only thing more preposterous than Evan as a federal agent was Evan too dazzled by me to successfully complete his assignment.

"You were so overcome by your passion for me, you nearly let the Maltese Falcon slip through your fingers, is that it?" I sneered down at him.

"I should have arrested you or turned you weeks ago." Evan covered his face with his hands and then ran them upwards, as if he could bring order to his thinking by using brute force.

"Arrested me? Turned me? What the hell do you mean?"

"Sabrina," Evan said. "I'm trying to protect you. I've been trying to protect you almost from the minute I met you. And that was a mistake. As soon as I believed you were innocent, I should have told you who I am. But that would have put you in more danger. If I'd taken you into my confidence, Tyrese would have wanted to turn you—enlist you to spy on Scott for us—and I didn't want to put you in that position. Now you're in danger anyway."

He pounded a fist on the table, then rose, and walked toward me. He had a smooth rolling gait, like a big jungle cat. I usually liked to watch him walk, but now as he loomed nearer, I felt trapped.

"You have to be wrong." The closer he came to me, the more panicky I felt. "No one I know could do the kinds of things you're talking about, Evan."

He'd moved closer as he spoke, and now he stood only inches from me, peering down at me like a disapproving big brother. "I would think cancer would have made you reassess your life and become more honest with yourself."

That was below the belt. Everybody thinks when you have a brush with death you automatically wind up like that guy in that country music song, the one where the singer boasts about going skydiving and bull riding and being wiser and nicer to everyone when he finds out he's dying. Me, I just went bald and threw up an awful lot.

"What cancer should have done for me is not for you to say," I told Evan.

His face, I was gratified to see, turned a little red.

"I figured a lot out when I thought I might die," I said. "And I'm still working it all out. One thing I figured was I don't want to be alone my whole life. So I stayed with Scott even though I don't exactly hear angels singing when he kisses me, okay? He's unexciting but decent. He stuck around when I had my surgery, even though he doesn't cope well with sick people. He doesn't abuse me, he doesn't cheat. He's not this man you say he is, he's not."

Evan rubbed a hand over his jaw, then massaged his neck. His disagreement couldn't have been clearer if he'd said it out loud.

I continued despite the expression on his face. "I've figured out a lot of other things. You spend a lot of time making lists of the stuff you're going to do if you get to live. But hey, guess what? You get better, and you don't get to give up your job in accounting and take a cruise or learn to fly or retire to Spain to paint. You know why? Because those things cost money, Evan. They don't give you a free ticket for a cruise with your last chemotherapy treatment; they don't give you a certificate for free flying lessons when they shave off the last scraggly bits of your hair. And best of all, Evan, when it's all over, you have a gazillion bills, and you're pretty much uninsurable. So, you go back to work and try to pay off all the bills the insurance didn't cover. Fortunately for me, I have Scott, and he's paid a lot of my bills. I don't know what the heck other people who aren't so lucky do."

Oh, the chill that went down my neck in that instant.

"How long has Scott being doing this?" I asked.

Evan hesitated, and that should have been answer enough, but I asked again.

"We've only found out about his involvement in the last six months, thanks to an informer at CIS."

I'd lived with a lawyer long enough to know an evasive answer when I heard one.

"I didn't ask you how long you've known about him," I said. "I asked how long you believe he's been involved with these people?"

"For at least the last year."

My silent dread must have shown on my face.

"You didn't make him do this!" Evan insisted. "There are other ways to pay bills. You're an accountant, you know this."

I don't think I even nodded; I felt so cold and sick and angry with God again.

"Scott Bennett is not some hero who sacrificed his principles for the good of the woman he loves."

"How do you know?"

"Because heroes don't sacrifice their principles," he replied. "That's what makes them heroic in the first place. Damn it, he's a fucking weasel with no moral compass whatever, a man who does what's convenient."

Poor Scott. He did do it. He did this awful, terrible thing, and he did it because of me. It almost sounded noble.

"Sabrina, he might have used your financial situation to justify this to himself. But some of those girls smuggled into this country are dead now. That's evil, pure evil."

"You can pass judgment," I retorted. "You aren't the one who was in our position."

"No, I'm the one who's seen some of those girls, seen their bodies when the men who bought them were through with them. That's who I am."

"But he didn't know that would happen, I'm sure. If he did this thing, he must have believed those girls were going to decent homes, to some place safer than the place they came from!"

"Scott is into this way too deep to not know what happened to those girls!" Evan retorted ferociously, his voice growing hoarse as he tried not to shout. He shook his finger at me. "And if he did it for you, I don't think he'd be cheating on you now with one of Mendoza's whores down in Mexico!"

Well, that certainly had the desired dramatic affect. I thrust my open hand against his rock-hard chest, as if I were strong enough to shove him out of the way. His own eyes went huge, almost round with amazement at his own indiscretion. He caught my arm and held me in place.

"Sabrina." He gathered me into an embrace. "I am so sorry. I didn't mean to tell you like this, I didn't mean to tell you at all."

"I don't believe you," I said, squirming free.

But it would explain so much. It would explain how Scott could be okay with having sex once every two months or so. It would explain him pushing me away that night when I tried to spice things up by trying the whole oral sex thing for the first time since college. Probably she was way better at that than I was. I could feel myself going red with shame, and I couldn't stand it. He had to be wrong about Scott, had to be.

I looked Evan up and down. The long hair, the earrings, even the glimpse of a tattoo I'd seen peeking out from the sleeve of his t-shirts at the gym—this had never been my kind of man.

Why should I believe a word he said? I'd known Scott for about six years before we became lovers. I'd known Evan for one month and most of it had been a big lie. What was I doing taking his word for anything?

"No!" I cried. "No, no, no!"

"Sabrina," he said. "I'm sorry, but it's the truth."

So I slapped him. Hard.

Five

My hand stung from the impact, and his head jerked backwards and to the side. Instantly, his cheek began to turn scarlet. I swallowed hard and raised my hands toward him in some helpless placating gesture. He rubbed his jaw and turned away from me.

"I liked the Sabrina in the gym better," Evan muttered. "She wouldn't have blamed the messenger for the bad news."

"She wasn't sleep deprived and in pain and covered in dirt from someone else's grave!"

"It could be worse." Evan cast a glance over his shoulder at me. "It could be dirt from your grave. And believe me, the Mendozas would have you dig your grave before they throw you into it."

Gloria came into the room, holding a cardboard drink carrier in one hand and a notepad and pen in the other. She sat it all down on the table.

"Hi, I brought lots of strong, hot coffee. It's not particularly good, but it is strong, and it is hot."

She glanced from Evan to me and back again. "Should I come back?"

"No." Evan took a cup from the holder. "We're done here. But I need to see your lieutenant before I go to the hospital."

Neither of them paid any attention to me now.

Gloria tossed her head in the direction of the squad room, which had the unfortunate effect of showing us the extreme bounciness of her blonde ponytail. "Trooper Shaunessy is going off duty. He'll take you to the hospital in the squad car if you're in a big hurry to see your partner."

"Oh, Frodo!" I stepped out of the corner and approached them. "How is he?"

Evan turned toward me, his brows knit together in a look of confusion.

"Ben." My face felt red again, which happened entirely too often around Evan. "I meant Ben. He seemed like a nice guy."

"He is. I don't know anything about his condition yet." Evan looked away from me and took Gloria's elbow. He gestured toward the corridor, and they left me alone in the room.

"I think I'll take Shaunessy up on his offer," Evan murmured, his voice barely audible. At least he wasn't asking her for a date. But damn it, why did I care?

"Let him know I won't be long with your lieutenant. I need to update him on what's going on and warn him my boss is coming up from DC. He's in a big hurry to take over from me on this one, so he might get here before I'm back from the hospital. "

"Oh, geez, two feds! The lieutenant will love that," Gloria said. "What about—?"

I glanced into the hall and watched the female trooper toss her head in my direction. Her ponytail gave a cute little bounce. I couldn't see Evan from where he stood, and I wondered if he'd noticed how young and pretty and healthy she was.

"Are we locking her up until you get back?"

Oh, hell. I had really done it. I had slapped the guy who decided whether or not I got put in a holding cell. I sat down at the table with my back to them, snatched one of the cups of coffee, and took a gulp. Then I gasped at the burning sensation in my mouth. I pushed it away and shifted the little notepad closer to me, hoping to gain some insight into their plans for me. But the last page with any writing on it didn't give me any insights. All she'd managed to jot down so far was the date and my name.

I picked up the pen and ripped out a blank page. I didn't want Gloria to find me going through some confidential notes about folks she'd arrested. She'd been irresponsible to leave the book out on the table in the first place, but she was young, after all. Maybe she was thinking more about the hot guy talking to her right now and not so much about proper police procedures.

"She's not a criminal," Evan murmured. He sounded torn, and I'm ashamed to say that pleased me. *Take that, Trooper Blondie.*

After a moment of hesitation, he spoke again. "She's been through a lot tonight. Can you stay with her until I get back from the hospital?"

Gloria spoke inaudibly.

"No, no, I'm not charging her with anything yet," Evan replied insistently. "Tyrese might, but I can't see it. I don't believe she knew what her boyfriend was up to. And when my boss questions her personally, he'll come to the same conclusion. At least I hope he will."

A weird sensation of vertigo washed over me. I laid my head down on the desk. After another minute, Gloria came back into the room.

"This is the second-worst birthday I've ever had." I turned my head to the side so I could look at her.

"Only the second-worst?"

"I had cancer for my last birthday."

As it usually did, that put a halt to conversation. I snuffled and raised my head an inch or two. "Is Evan gone? I mean Agent Desmond?"

"Yeah. Looks like you've got man troubles, among all your other problems." Gloria sat down across from me. She flashed an amazing smile that lit up her whole face, adding dimples to the blonde hair and perky breasts. She looked like a cheerleader in the wrong uniform.

I dashed off a few lines on the sheet of notebook paper, capturing her prominent cheekbones and little pointed chin pretty accurately, considering the tools I had to work with. I held it up to show her.

"Cool!" Gloria held her hand out for the picture and I passed it over to her. "That really looks like me! Are you an artist?"

Ah, that was the question.

I slid my coffee cup closer and braved another sip. Art—drawing and painting—had been my refuge when I was a freckled, fat teenager. Then it had become important again while I was battling the cancer. I'd sworn this time I would stick with it if I recovered, but in truth, I hadn't sketched or painted anything in months. And I'd never quite gotten around to signing up for those evening art classes I'd talked about taking when I was sick.

"I used to paint a lot," I told Gloria. "My degree's in art."

"Agent Desmond said you were an accountant."

"I am. All a degree in art gets you after graduation is a choice of jobs in retail. A classmate of mine took some accounting courses and sat for the exam. I figured if he could do it, I could do it, too."

Back then, I believed I'd be able to keep painting in my free time. But it hadn't worked out that way. The real job takes more and more time and mental energy, and then there are networking lunches and professional organization meetings. One day I woke up, and I wasn't a painter, not even a museum curator. I was a tax accountant—and one who was wanted by Homeland Security. So much for making the safe career choice.

"No." I handed her the scribbled drawing. "I'm not an artist. It's just a hobby."

"You're pretty good." She looked pleased by the

portrait. "So—what the heck did Agent Desmond say before I came in? I could still see the mark from your hand on his face. He does look like the cocky type."

"I've never slapped a guy in my life," I confessed. "Not even Jeremy Tollmayer when he put his hand up my skirt in his office a few years ago. Tollmayer's our managing partner. The day he groped me, I picked up my files, walked out of the room, and went home sick for the rest of the day. He called later to apologize. It was February, and you don't want to lose a tax specialist in the middle of tax season. I cannot believe I slapped an agent from Homeland Security."

Gloria laughed appreciatively. "You're not having a good night, are you?"

"First, I made fun of his real name." I sighed and rested my chin on my fist. "Then I made a rude remark about his ethnicity. And next, I slapped him. And of course, I got his friend shot."

"You didn't do that," she reassured me.

"But Ben was trying to protect me."

"That was his job. It's what we do. We know the risks."

"He was awfully young. Honestly, I might even be old enough to be his mother. Just barely, of course. But I didn't understand what was happening. They didn't explain; they just came in and rushed me out of my home, and people were getting shot and—. They didn't explain."

"Yeah, Feds are like that." She shrugged. We sat together in companionable silence for a moment.

"Evan—Agent Desmond—says my boyfriend is an international criminal who helps sell little girls into prostitution or slavery or something worse." I was a drowning woman, throwing up my arms and begging to be saved, but she only nodded and made a faint "mmm-hmm" noise with her lips.

"The last guy I fell for," she said, "was a bounty

hunter. I don't know what I was thinking. He'd had more scrapes with the law than he had piercings. I think I dated him to make my ex-fiancé crazy."

I gave a weak laugh. "I have trouble believing my Scott Bennett is the man Agent Desmond wants. Scott is—well, he's cute, and he's sophisticated with great taste in music, art, and wine. That's why we got together. We met at a single professional's night at the Walters Art Gallery. He never does dangerous or impulsive things. He's not a deeply emotional guy."

That could be because he's living his real life somewhere else, a voice like my mother's whispered in my head. Her opinion of Scott had gone downhill during my cancer ordeal, when he'd found so many ways to be out of town during my chemo sessions.

"Of course my mother doesn't like him anymore," I said. "And my dad never did like him. You know, my father and mother might have trouble agreeing on the time of day with an atomic clock in the room, but they agreed to dislike Scott. Should that have told me something?"

"Hard to say." Gloria shook her head. "My parents never like anyone I date."

"Yeah. Neither of my parents likes my sister Angie's husband either, and she's been blissfully happy with him for about ten years now. Even my brother Tim's spouse they can barely tolerate."

"Oh, yeah, who's he married to?"

"God," I answered. "He's a Jesuit."

Gloria sputtered out a mouthful of coffee and swiped at her mouth with the back of her hand.

"Agent Desmond also says Scott has been cheating on me." I picked at an imaginary spot on the conference table, unable to look at her. "How could he? He never even uses a condom. That would be putting me at risk. He wouldn't do that to me, would he?"

"I assume you're supposed to be a monogamous couple?" Her tone was blunt and matter-of-fact. "If he whipped out a condom, you'd pretty much know he was being unfaithful."

"How can men be like that?" I demanded.

"I don't know! I'm thirty and I'm still single, so I doubt I understand them any better than you do. Maybe he wears a condom with the other woman, so he figures you're both safe."

"Or maybe Agent Desmond's information is wrong," I pressed her.

She gave a slow shrug that made it painfully clear she wouldn't buy my explanation for a dollar. I opened my mouth to make a case for Scott, but at that moment, the glass window vibrated, and we heard a loud thud in the main room. Gloria dashed across the room and pulled up the blinds.

"Oh, geez. Those Pagan guys again."

Two big mountains lumbered through the squad room. Both mountains had wiry, long, graying hair and beards, both sported scuffed leather jackets emblazoned with the image of an ugly troll-like creature wielding a sword, and one of them carried a state trooper on his back. As I watched, one mountain backed up and slammed the trooper against the window of the interrogation room. Gloria's partner lunged at the biker, and Gloria scrambled out the room to assist him.

When I was a little girl, I had a parakeet. It got so used to being in a cage; if my mother left the door open, that bird would sit there and look at her funny. Didn't even try to escape. I didn't want to be that parakeet. I felt bad for Gloria, knowing she'd get into huge trouble for not guarding me properly. But after all, I reasoned, she was a rookie—how else was she going to learn this stuff?

I waited until Gloria and her partner had waltzed the mountain man to the far side of the squad room. The two of them were sitting on the guy while someone else clamped him in leg irons. I sidled past a couple of empty desks—everyone in the sparsely populated room had thrown their attention to controlling the two crazed bikers. I came to the sergeant at the front desk, who was staring raptly over his shoulder at the commotion.

"Excuse me?" I used my mildest good Catholic girl voice. "Can you tell me where the ladies' room is?"

He jabbed a thumb down the corridor, barely noticing me. I didn't look particularly criminal; people were distracted by the spitting, cussing biker dudes, and if someone acts like she belongs in a place, she can slip by pretty much unnoticed. I learned that from my mother the newspaper reporter, who got many exclusive stories by being able to fake her way into forbidden locations. She told me once the two most essential skills in her profession were the ability to fake sincerity and the ability to read upside-down. I think she was serious.

****

Once I was out on the street, I had a new dilemma—where to go and how to get there. I was in a slightly shabby part of east Baltimore County, something that had probably been industrial once and now looked to be undergoing a bit of a renaissance. The roadside landscape alternated between old truck dealerships and new big-box stores under construction. I was forced to walk on the narrow shoulder of the road, and traffic whizzed past me at an unnerving pace. I knew I was on or near Route 40, an area notorious for its high quotient of hookers. Somebody would probably pull over and try to pick me up soon. The best I could hope for was that it would be the local cops handcuffing and arresting me this time around. After all, officers of the law could only stand to overlook so much, and escaping from their custody had not demonstrated good faith on my part.

I needed a better plan than trying to walk back to the city on Route 40, so I chose the Catholic Girl Strategy. I said a "Hail Mary."

My mother hardly ever goes to Mass. I mean, she's a member of the liberal media, and her husband is a college professor. They're both practically atheists, except that would require too much of a commitment on either of their parts. But my father and my paternal grandmother are as Catholic as they come, and they'd both been part of my daily life until I was fourteen. Nanny O'Hara especially had trained me early in all the important Catholic traditions—make three wishes in a new church, pray to St. Anthony when something's lost, and always say a "Hail Mary" when in trouble. If it's really big trouble, call in St. Jude.

Jude is to the apostles as Bashful is to the seven dwarves. He's the one people always skip when they're going down the list of names. But he's important, because he's the patron saint of lost causes—Jude, I mean, not Bashful. When I found I was still walking without direction ten minutes after leaving the station, I abandoned the Blessed Mother and appealed to Jude. A chill had crept into the air, so I wiggled my hands into my jeans pockets to warm them. And there I found a twenty.

And then a car pulled over. I flinched and hopped up on the tiny piece of curb, thinking some guy was about to proposition me. But it was a big yellow taxi. I hadn't even needed to whistle for it. That Jude, he knows about customer service.

"Excuse me, miss." A turbaned driver leaned his head out the window. "It is not safe to walk on this road. Will you be needing a ride somewhere?"

I was going to reach through the window and kiss him as I shouted, "Yes, yes, yes!" But I didn't want to frighten him. Instead, I thanked him as calmly as I could and climbed into the backseat.

"Where is it you would like to go, Miss?"

I thought about going after the laptop. I'd go get it and maybe get Andy to help me boot it up. I'd show that cocky Latino bastard. I'd show him the most incriminating thing on that computer was probably a copy of USCIS Form M-685 (Revised), "Pathway to Citizenship." Sure, Scott's laptop was probably password-protected, but how hard could that be to figure out? If he behaved like most of our clients at the accounting firm, he probably even had the password written on a sticky note stuck right on the screen.

"I'd like to go—" I began, and at that moment two things happened simultaneously. The driver pushed the button on his meter which started racking up dollars, and I remembered I had no clear idea where I was now or where the cemetery was in relation to this place. It could take us hours to find the cemetery. At any rate, it would take way more than my measly twenty.

I cursed softly to myself. I needed money and a cell phone. At the very least, I needed a map. If I had that, I could retrace the route we'd taken after getting off at Boston Street and find the name of the road where the graveyard was located. One of those supersize books would be fantastic because they even have things like cemeteries marked right on the maps. I asked the driver if he had one.

"Oh, no, ma'am!" His reflection beamed at me in the rearview mirror. "I have the GPS now, so I do not need maps!"

"Fine," I sighed. I slumped back against the seat, in defeat and despair. All I wanted anymore was a shower and a nap, not even in that order. I told him to take me home.

Six

The sheets beneath me were satin, the color of champagne. My gown, of the same material, was cool against my hot flesh as it slid up over my legs. Strong, golden brown hands pushed the fabric above my knees and stroked my skin. I knew his hands right away, even though at first I could see nothing else of him. Then his long black hair ranged into view, falling loosely around his shoulders, tickling the insides of my thighs. He said my name and his cool, moist lips brushed against my knees, my thighs, higher. I arched my back and sighed as he began to caress the warm darkness between my legs. He traced a line of kisses up to my bellybutton, and then he raised his head. His big dark eyes were shining and wet.

"I thought I'd never see you again in this life," he said. His graceful hands caught the hem of my nightgown and pulled at it. Obediently, I sat up and let him lift the gown over my head, leaving me naked.

He froze, dropping the nightgown to the floor beside the bed. His hands fell to his sides, and he sat back on his heels, turning his face away in revulsion. I had forgotten. How could I have forgotten, even for a moment? He rose from the bed and walked away as I crossed my arms over my hideous scars...

****

"We are here, Miss," the Sikh driver said.

I woke to dappled morning sunlight spilling in through the cab windows, and I massaged a kink in my neck. I'd had dreams about Evan before—most notably, the ones with a special guest appearance by

Andy. But like the dream I'd had on the sofa last night, this one had a special, disconcerting quality. The edges of the images had been blurred white, like the burnt out colors in an overexposed photograph. Nanny calls those dreams "the sight," because she's Irish and also because she's a massive drama queen. She claims to have dreamed John Kennedy's assassination in great detail two weeks prior to the event. None of my dreams are ever that clear-cut.

The night before I learned about my cancer, I'd had one of the rare white-around-the-edges dreams. In it, Scott and I were on board the sailboat his Uncle Carlton had given him. The sky went black, and the little boat pitched and yawed. When a massive wave hit us, I got thrown over the side. I clung to the rail for dear life and called out for Scott, who never answered. He simply wasn't there anymore. I know, I know. Clearly, God likes tired metaphors almost as much as he likes cryptic, useless messages. Most of the time, they're way too incoherent to give me any useful information. I'm left with the knowledge something bad is about to happen, and I'm powerless to stop it.

I sat up in the taxi and smoothed my hands over my hair. My face had been smooshed against the back of the seat and now it felt like my hair was severely flattened on that side.

"I'm sorry," I mumbled.

"That is all right, Miss." The cabbie smiled into the rearview mirror as I fumbled for some money. The meter read $19.

"I only have a twenty. I'm sorry it can't be a bigger tip."

He waved a hand back and forth, as if to say, "Don't worry about it."

"Was I talking in my sleep?" I asked.

"Oh no, Miss," he answered, a little too quickly. He turned to face me as I held the money out to him.

63

"Are you in need of help?"

He had lively, intelligent eyes. They were nearly as dark as Evan's.

"None that you can give me," I told him with a polite smile.

He considered this deeply. "Then I will pray for you. The Wonderful Lord—he is all good, Miss. All will be well for you if you do not despair."

"I hope you're right." I stumbled most ungracefully to the curb in front of my condo building.

Only after my Sikh friend had pulled into traffic did I consider what a stupid move I'd made. No doubt my home was swarming with cops and gossipy neighbors and probably even television crews. *Bloody double murder in upscale waterfront condo! Film at eleven!* But nothing could help me now. I had no money left—nothing but the clothes on my back and the knowledge that one Federal agent wanted me arrested and another one was probably still walking around town with my stinging handprint on his cheek. If I lived through this mess, I would definitely have to take one of those public relations courses on how to win friends—because I sure wasn't doing much of that right now.

I stood on the sidewalk outside the imposing concrete-and-glass structure I called home, wondering what I should do next. The idea that I might walk in the front door and be immediately arrested sent a cold bead of sweat down my spine. Maybe I'd get to make a call to a lawyer, maybe my name would be cleared, and maybe this would all be part of an interesting story to tell my niece and nephews. Yeah, right. The papers were full of stories every week about people who'd spent years in jail for crimes they didn't commit.

I strolled a few yards away from the building's entrance, heading toward the harbor. Gems of white light glinted off the murky brown waters, and I squinted as I drew closer. My condo building was in an exclusive complex containing the high-rise in which Scott and I lived, an array of townhouses, a marina, a restaurant and a coffee shop called Barista. As I approached the water, I passed Barista, quiet now that the initial morning rush had passed. If I had some money, I could go in there. I allowed myself a few seconds of satisfying self-pity, and then I was back to business, the now weirdly familiar business of trying to stay alive.

I could run again. I could try going to the office, a short walk from here. On a weekday morning, the place would be occupied and unlocked. Once there, I could shut myself in my office, call our lawyer, talk to Jess about everything. That idea brightened my outlook considerably.

Jess and I had met as interns at Weitzel, Baum & Tollmayer, a good fifteen years ago. Now we were two women kicked in the teeth by life at a time when our friends were settling down to empty nests, vacation homes, and a regular schedule of minor cosmetic procedures. Jess was a few years older than I, with a daughter in college. Her ex-husband had left her for her daughter's first college roommate. Boy howdy, that had been so ugly, it had made being a thirty-eight year old single woman with breast cancer seem like a cakewalk. For her, helping me get through my treatment had been an almost welcome diversion from the shambles of her life.

When I was battling cancer, I'd spent a lot of time in Jess's guest bedroom. My mom came to stay with me for a while at the condo, and then my sister Angela. But they both had jobs, and Angie has little kids, so neither could stick around for long. And of course, Scott did his best to not be around at all during those times. He arranged numerous business trips, and I suspect he even went and stayed with local friends sometimes, just to get away. Jess's home became my refuge, and Jess became my coach, forcing me out onto the wooded trails around her house and walking with me every morning, giving me pep talks and reciting statistics about how likely I was to survive. Talking to her now would fix everything. Jess would take me home with her. I would even borrow some clean clothing from her daughter's closet, since we were close to the same size.

I turned away from the waterfront, moving back toward the main entrance to the complex. On my way out, I stopped outside Barista. My condo building stood across the street, about half a block down. Uniformed police officers milled around the front of the place, and a steady stream of men in bad suits processed in and out of the main lobby. No scary yellow tape cordoning off the area, so they must be trying to keep it low key. Or maybe they'd used up all the freakin' tape inside the building and had to order more. The sight of a TV station van pulling up in front of the main entrance stopped me in my tracks. The concept of surrender—strongly linked to the concepts of sleep and food immediately following said surrender—had flitted through my head for the briefest of moments. I put that notion to rest at the sight of that van's little satellite dish whirring into action.

"Hey," came a boyish voice next to me.

I glanced over my shoulder to see the waiter from Barista standing in the doorway. His name was Louis, and he was a twenty-two year old grad student at Hopkins. Sometimes on slow days, he and I would chat. Truthfully, I had a bit of a Mrs. Robinson fantasy going on with the unnaturally beautiful Louis. Meeting him had been a moment of startling and unwelcome epiphany—he was stupendously hot, and yet it was mathematically possible for me to be his mother. Even the Mrs. Robinson analogy offered only minimal comfort, since she'd always seemed pretty creepy in my book.

As I turned, Louis flashed me his male model smile and then frowned. "You look like you've had a rough night."

"I was in a car crash," I explained.

"Oh."

I turned my attention to the TV van. "I'm thinking more of those will be showing up soon."

"Oh."

I was thinking hot doesn't always equal brilliant conversationalist when he said, "Do you want to hide in here? I don't have any customers right now."

"Why, yes, Louis." I nodded. "That sounds like a good idea."

I followed him into the coffee shop and sat down at a little table in the back. Without a word, he brought me a tall mocha espresso. I was surprised he remembered, and I guess it showed in my face.

"I always remember it because it's my favorite, too." He ducked his head down as he spoke, like he was having a hard time making eye contact.

I didn't know what to say.

"That's the first TV crew to arrive. But the cops have been coming and going all day, ever since I came in at four to open up." He sat the coffee mug down in front of me. "I don't know what happened, but I know it must be bad."

I nodded. "People are dead."

"Wow. That is bad."

I sipped my espresso.

"Did they hurt you?" he asked. "Do you need a doctor or anything?"

"What I need is a map book. Do you have one? I need to find a cemetery somewhere around Boston Street."

"I don't have a map book, but hey, my new cell

phone has a GPS navigation system built right in."
He pulled the phone out of his back pocket and held
it out to me. Laptops, cell phones, GPS. I was
starting to hate technology.

"GPS doesn't help unless you already know
where you're going, Louis," I told him.

"Sorry." His shoulders sagged a notch as he
tucked the phone into his pocket.

"You sure you don't need a doctor?"

"Do I look bad?" I laughed, already knowing the
answer.

"You look—" He hesitated. "Disheveled? That
sounds like a good word for it."

"Like ten miles of bad road, that's how my dad
would say it."

Dad. Why hadn't I remembered him sooner?

"From the way you've been pacing back and
forth on this side of the street and not going in
there," Louis said, "I'm guessing you don't want
them to find you.

"I think they might arrest me," I admitted.

"Do I want to know why?" He sat down at the
table with me, all ears and youthful enthusiasm for
the unknown.

"Of course you do." I grinned at him. "Why else
would you ask?"

He smiled back at me and toyed with one of the
little menu placards on the table.

"I hit a Federal agent, for one thing. A guy from
Homeland Security."

"Wow, when you mess up, you mess up big." He
sounded almost awestruck.

"There's lots more, but I don't think I have time
to share it with you," I told him. A little regretfully,
because I'd just discovered Louis found me almost as
interesting as I found him.

"No?" A crestfallen expression darkened his
handsome features.

"No. Can I use your phone after all?"

He stood up and pulled the razor-thin phone from his hip pocket. I took it and dialed my dad's number. When Dad had retired about ten years ago, he'd been Commander of the Baltimore Police Department's Northeastern District. And though he'd been a long time gone, I knew he still had lots of friends on the force. I doubted they could do much against Homeland Security, but I might as well give it a try.

I dialed his number twice, because I always forget to dial a "1" the first time. He lives on the Eastern Shore of the state, several hours' drive from the city. The phone rang so many times, I thought no one was going to pick up. I wondered why the answering machine didn't get it, and then, just as she answered, I remembered why. Nanny O'Hara.

"Yes?" came her croaky, high-pitched, perpetually irritated voice. She hates the answering machine. Those disembodied voices freak her out. She's really, really old. Not that that's an explanation. All technology freaks her out and always has.

"Nanny, hi, it's Sabrina!" I yelled as loud as I could. It would be hard enough to get through to her anyway, but I heard a game show blaring away in the background.

Across from me, Louis bit his lips in an effort not to laugh. I could almost laugh at me, too. My life and freedom were hanging by a thread, and everything depended on a crotchety, half-deaf ninety-year-old former barmaid who'd spent way too many years sampling her own wares.

"I don't know any Katrina. And there's no need to shout, young lady," she shouted.

"Nanny, it's Sabrina Meghan!" I ignored the part about not shouting.

"Oh!" Her voice softened so I could almost hear

the faint traces of her native Irish brogue. "Lovely! How are you, dearie pie?"

"I'm fine," I said automatically. "Well, no I'm not. Nanny, I'm in some big trouble."

"Trouble? You're in trouble? Don't all you girls use birth control these days?"

I sighed. "Not that kind of trouble. Nanny, I need to talk to Daddy right away. It's urgent."

"Is that little witch coming after him for child support again?" Sometimes she gets confused about what year it is.

"Nanny, pull yourself together and listen to me!" I ordered her. I swear, sometimes it works. "Turn off the game show and listen."

The phone clunked on a table, and I heard rustling and shuffling. Then the room went silent.

"What is it, dear?" she asked when she came back on the line.

"I need to talk to Daddy."

"I can give you his phone number at the hunting lodge."

Oh, hell. The hunting lodge. When my parents separated, my mother didn't make it easy for my dad to see us girls. She moved us all back to her home state of Arizona, and that was a long way for Dad to come for birthdays. He'd call and send a gift to each of us, but he'd go and spend our birthdays on hunting or fishing trips. When Angela and I came to see him for a few weeks in the summer, we'd celebrate our "un-birthday" with him. Angela hated it, but I liked that second, private party, so he and I maintained the quirky tradition. Sadly, that meant he was probably out of reach for at least the next day or two. Cell phone reception was usually spotty in places rich in big game.

"He's in Colorado, dear." Nanny's perky voice intruded on my inner ramblings. "He's chasing elk. I'm not sure why or where he'd put it if he found one."

"What's the num-"

"Pssst!"

I followed Louis' gaze out the big glass window of the coffee shop, and I felt a chill run down my back. A man in a suit and a uniformed policeman were heading straight for Barista. And behind them came a snappily dressed woman with starched blonde hair, walking alongside a cameraman. A detective, a cop, and a news crew headed straight for my pathetic little hideaway.

"Nanny, I'll call you back."

"All righty. Don't forget about the birth control, dearie!"

I shook my head and handed the phone back to Louis. "I'm going to have to get out of here. I'm going to go see a friend and call my lawyer."

"You could call him from here," he suggested.

"Thanks. But I should get away before that gang comes here looking for a bite to eat and stumbles over me instead. I don't have any money." I looked at the half-empty cup of coffee, and felt my face grow warm. I'm an accountant, for crying out loud. I'm not used to traveling without money.

"It's on me." He flashed a pearly smile that set off his cornflower blue eyes and the bleached blond hair. Then he went to the cash register and brought back the big tip jar that sat beside it. He fished his hand around in it—the mouth was narrow, and I worried he'd get his hand stuck—and then he started pulling out ones.

"What are you doing?"

"You'll need money!" I think he was having all sorts of heated visions about helping the gangster chick escape from the law.

"Are you an English major or something?" I asked.

"Yeah." He stopped fishing in the jar. "How

could you tell?"

"A lucky guess. I hope I make a good story."

"Hey, you will when I tell it," he boasted.

I pushed his hand away when he held out the money. "I don't need it. I'm going to my office, and I'll get help from my friends there."

"Aw, take a few bucks for a cab, Miss O'Hara."

I took ten and thanked him.

"You can go out the back door," he said. "Then walk down behind the back of the café and the restaurant and get to the entrance that way."

"I really appreciate this." I followed him through the kitchen to the delivery entrance.

"Be careful, Miss O'Hara," he said as we stood together in the rear doorway.

Not wanting to ruin a young man's fantasy, I put on a bravery I didn't feel.

"Call me Sabrina. And don't worry. I always land on my feet."

Then I gave him a quick kiss on the cheek. I couldn't wait to see the fictional version of that. "Send me a copy of my story when you write it."

"I will." He pressed his hand to his cheek.

We waved good-bye, and I hurried past the backs of the buildings, out of sight of the police, the media, or anyone else who might show up. At the entrance I stopped when the light changed, waiting to cross the street.

A dusty, black pick-up truck turned off Key Highway and into Harborview's entrance. As it cruised past me, I glimpsed the driver's long black hair, his dusky brown skin, even a flash of an earring. He focused his attention in front of him, eying the other cars inching through the turn and scanning the area for a parking space. He had nothing left over for gawking at short pedestrians patiently waiting on the curb beside him. For a moment, I was so close, I could have banged on the door and surrendered to him right then and there.

In retrospect, that would've been the smart thing to do.

A lot less blood would've been shed, that's for sure.

Seven

The morning rush had dissipated by the time I arrived back at 100 E. Pratt, the building where I'd started all this trouble for myself by mentioning the laptop to Evan. As its nondescript name might imply, 100 E. Pratt is an undistinguished, boxy concrete structure. Its only unique feature is a weirdly pointless metal frame that sits atop the building's roof. I guess if someone hasn't spent much time around boats, but has spent way too much time in architecture school, then the series of metal ribs might conceivably look like a row of sailboats. At least, that's my theory. Maybe they aren't supposed to look like anything at all.

Weitzel, Baum & Tollmayer, Certified Public Accountants occupies several floors near the top of the building. Going to WB&T would be risky—the Feds might easily have staked out the place—but my options were limited, so I took the gamble. After all, once my absence was noticed, the various law enforcement agencies had probably wasted time yelling at one another and placing blame. It appeared I was right, because no one stopped me going into the lobby.

Although the crush of morning arrivals had passed, a steady stream of visitors continued to plague the guards at the front desk, and that was good news for me. They were both too busy signing in people who didn't work there to notice how crappy and unprofessional I looked. I kept my head down and hurried to the elevators. There I lucked out again, because I managed to get an empty car and closed the doors before anyone else caught up to me.

Walking through the front doors of our suite of offices took a little more nerve. WB&T occupied three floors, but as luck would have it, my own office was located on the same floor as our reception lobby. I couldn't pass the front desk unnoticed, since I was known for being well groomed most of the time. Even on casual Fridays, dirt-streaked jeans and a lopsided pink blouse would not be my look of choice.

Iris was on the phone when I walked in. Her eyes went round, and her mouth gaped. She ripped off her headset and leaned across the front desk, laughing.

"Boy, that must have been some birthday!"

"You have no idea." I approached her desk and leaned down. "I am not here. Do you understand?"

I guess the urgency of my request came through, because she nodded silently and sat back in her chair.

"What happened?" she whispered, catching my wariness.

"Can't tell you now. It's big, it's scary, and I'm right in the middle of it. Homeland Security is involved."

She thought I was laying it on thick, playing her, possibly even setting her up for a practical joke—but that's what I wanted her to think. Like most receptionists, Iris is an enthusiastic snoop and a gossip. I'd debated what to say to her on my way up in the elevator. Then it had occurred to me—tell her the truth! It's so nuts, she'll never believe it, and so she won't repeat it to anyone. She's a lot more wary ever since she got caught repeating a fake rumor that Jeremy Tollmayer had crabs. I admit, Jess and I were the ones who fed her that one, so she tends to be especially suspicious of the two of us.

"You don't have to be nasty, Sabrina," she sniped. "I learned my lesson, okay? That's a lot of work to go to, to make a fool out of me. If Tollmayer sees you dressed like that, you'll be in trouble."

"That's why I'm not really here yet, Iris. Where's Jess?"

She told me Jess was in the copy room, but I worried it would be too risky to go looking for her. People tended to hang around there in the morning, pretending to work but really discussing last night's reality show. I heard Tollmayer's voice down a corridor behind me, so I hightailed it into my office and shut and locked the door. Then I telephoned the copier room. Fortunately, Jess answered on the second ring. She was laughing at some remark someone else had made, and I could hear a low buzz of conversation in the background.

"Don't say my name," I told her.

She chewed on that for a few seconds. "Okey-dokey."

"Say I'm Leslie."

That was her daughter's name.

"Leslie! Um. How's college, honey?"

"I am hiding in my office," I answered. "I'm covered in dirt from someone's grave and two guys from Homeland Security are after me. And I hit one of them in the face."

"Oh!" Jess replied. "Oh. Oh."

For a few seconds, I was afraid she'd passed out. Then she spoke again, her rich southern belle voice full of spirit. "Now, honey, I know boyfriends can break your heart, but you have to calm down. Honey, let me put you on hold, and I'll go back to my office."

She cut me off, and I was stuck listening to Pachelbel's Canon in D Major. When I heard a tap on my door a few seconds later, I hung up the phone.

"It's me," Jess whispered.

I threw open the door, yanked her into the room, then quickly locked the door behind us.

"What the hell?" Jess said to me by way of

greeting.

"I love you, too."

"What the hell?" she said again.

I told her everything. Well, not about Evan kissing me in the parking garage, but pretty much everything else.

"So Evan Garcia's not really your personal trainer, he's like a *spy*?" she practically squealed at me. "Ohmigod! That is soooo sexy."

I rubbed my temples. Since Walt left, Jess reads an awful lot of romance novels, the ones where the apparently ordinary guy turns out to be a fantastically ripped, dead sexy, super genius secret agent. And here I'd thought they were unrealistic.

"Jess, I'm serious." I gripped her by her chubby upper arms. She's a little on the *zaftig* side. "People are trying to kill me, and other people are trying to arrest me. And I'm not even sure which group is worse. Dead is dead, I can handle that. But these Feds are from Homeland Security. I doubt I even get a phone call if they get hold of me!"

Jess rolled her eyes at me like I was being a big baby.

"I'm sure there are still rules they have to follow, sugar," she said. "You're an American, not some terrorist. Maybe you should call them and turn yourself in?"

I sputtered and flapped incoherently like an angry, wet duck.

"I am *not* turning myself in to anybody!" I finally managed to say. "I didn't do anything! I am not getting arrested because Scott turns out to be an even bigger jerk than I suspected."

Jess walked me over to the chair behind my desk and sat me down.

"Breathe. And think."

I always liked it when she did that stern mother hen thing. She was only three years older, but I guess having a grown child had made her mature a lot faster.

"So you think this stuff about Scott is true?" She stepped away from me and moved some files out of the client chair next to my desk before sitting.

"No! I mean, not all of it. I'm thinking he didn't mean any harm. Maybe he was just trying to help some well-meaning folks cut some red tape. That makes perfect sense, doesn't it?"

Jess didn't answer. She leaned an elbow on my desk and used her fingers to pinch her lower lip. That was her thinking pose. At least she doesn't stick the tip of her tongue out when she's thinking real hard, the way Tollmayer does.

"I could see that happening. Someone approaches you and tells you about these poor orphans who need homes, if only they can get the girls to the States."

"And how would he know once they're here that the people who allegedly adopted them had mistreated them?" I demanded, like an attorney in front of the jury. "After all, he's a lawyer, not a social worker. Am I right?"

Jess half-shrugged, then bobbed her head up and down as she conceded the possibility.

"But what about the affair Evan mentioned?" Shallow of me, I know, but the idea of Scott cheating on me hit much closer to home than the idea of his helping to traffic sex slaves.

Jess hemmed and hawed a bit, and I remembered belatedly she was the wrong person to ask such a question, considering the way her husband had ended their marriage.

"Okay," I said. "Of course you believe that bit, because you think all men are lying, two-timing pricks now, don't you?"

"You mean they aren't?" she retorted. "Walt was, and my dad was before him. What about your dad?

Didn't you tell me your parents broke up because of infidelity?"

I had indeed said that during a drunken moment of commiseration with her, and I'd done my best to never say anything further about it afterwards. "It was my mother who cheated, not my dad."

Funny how adultery always sounds so much worse when it's the woman. Like we should be better than that—purer. My mom sure wasn't.

"That's why we were split up. Angie and I went with my mom, but my brother Tim refused. He was the one who walked in on my mother and her lover. So Tim asked the judge if he could stay here and live with my dad."

Jess blinked a few times. "Wow, now I see why your brother's a priest."

I floundered for something else to say. I'd had a bad night, and I was becoming entirely too maudlin.

"What do I do about Scott?"

"Have you called him to ask if any of this is true?"

Funny, that hadn't even occurred to me. "No, I never had the opportunity."

She whipped out her nifty new cell phone, incredibly small and sleek and flat. It had been her daughter's recent birthday gift to her. Now she handed it to me.

With clammy fingers, I keyed in Scott's mobile number. "Say, do you have a map book?" I asked as I dialed.

"A map book?"

"Yeah. It's a book. With maps in it. Got one?" I drummed my fingers on my desk and listened to Scott's phone ringing.

As with most moments of great anticipation, I was quickly and completely let down.

"Scott Bennett is on another line or temporarily

out of range," said a mechanical feminine voice. "Please leave your message after the beep, and he will return your call as soon as possible."

"Scott—" I paused, almost at a loss for words. "Scott, something is wrong here, and there are Federal agents asking strange questions. Call me. I'm using Jess' cell phone, but I don't know how long I'll be here."

I repeated her number before hanging up, then shrugged helplessly at Jess.

"Now what?"

"Now," she said, like a professor proposing a hypothetical problem for the class. "If you won't turn yourself in, what can you do instead? And don't say continue hiding in your office."

"Can I hang on to the phone?"

She nodded, her heavily frosted bob jiggling.

"You can have my car too, if it helps." She leaned against the corner of my desk. "I can take the commuter bus home tonight. But where will you go? Do you want to go back to my house?"

"What good would that do? At some point, they're bound to start looking at places like this and questioning my friends. I was thinking of calling Leo Penn."

Jess frowned. Leo was my lawyer, but he was Scott's lawyer, too, as well as his lifelong friend. I could see the wheels turning in Jess's head, because they'd already turned in my own.

"Who else should I call—a public defender?"

Jess shrugged. Her fount of motherly advice ran more toward pep talks about battling deadly diseases and good-natured lectures about safe sex. Avoiding prosecution for a Federal crime had never been a part of her repertoire.

"Leo's good," I said. "He's very good."

In truth, he was a better lawyer than Scott, which was why Scott worked for the government pushing papers and avoiding actual arguments in a courtroom. He didn't have that all-important theatrical streak that set the best trial lawyers above the rest. Leo had that by the bucket loads.

He also had a reputation as a womanizer, but I didn't think that issue affected me. Even before my surgery, he'd treated me differently from other women—more respectful, almost reverent. In fact, we'd gone out a few times before he'd introduced me to his old buddy Scott. In an uncharacteristic burst of ego, I sometimes believed he regretted making that introduction.

"He likes me," I said softly, and we both knew what I meant.

Jess gave me a look that would freeze a toasted marshmallow.

"I wouldn't be using him!" I answered the objection she hadn't made. "Anyway, he's a grown man with plenty of slutty girlfriends to ease the pain. Do you have a better idea?"

"Of course not," she admitted. "Even if you surrendered to the police, you'd be better off with a lawyer beside you."

"A good one. One like Leo." I stood and paced a bit. "There's no reason why he can't represent us both. It's not like we're going to be ratting each other out under torture. Assuming Scott is guilty of anything at all, it's probably more like falsifying federal forms."

"Is that a crime?"

"Hell, I don't know. I guess he could be guilty of taking some bribes. But messing with paperwork and taking some cash under the table are a far cry from human trafficking. Anyway, I'm sure Leo could make sure we're tried separately. Couldn't he?"

We both jumped when the telephone on my desk gave two short buzzes—an internal call. I sagged, disappointed that it wasn't Scott automatically dialing my office phone.

Jess looked at me and then picked it up. "Jess McClintock." She listened for a moment, and her brows knit themselves together in consternation. "You have to stall them!"

She slammed down the phone, and I knew things had gone bad sooner than I expected.

"That was Iris. She's in the copier room. There's an African-American man at the front desk, and he's asking about you. He showed her an I.D. card that said Homeland Security. She said this is either really scary or the meanest practical joke we've ever played on her."

"Is that all she told you?" I asked, remembering Jess's last words before she'd hung up.

"What? Ohmigosh!" Jess leapt to her feet.

"What?"

"When she said you weren't here, he asked to talk to one of the partners. He's with Tollmayer right now, and Iris said she heard him ask about searching your office."

"Oh, Holy Mary Mother of God!"

Jess threw open my office door, then grabbed my hand and maneuvered me down the hall in front of her. The offices on this floor wrapped around the center core of the building in a U-shape, meeting the wall of elevators at both ends. There was the main receptionist's entrance, but there were also two doors at either end of the U, so people could get out quickly in an emergency or slip out to the bathroom without having to go through the lobby area. No one could come back in that way, because the doors were set to lock from the outside. A little insurance against surprise visits from disgruntled clients, bike messengers, and other crazy people.

Jess and I scrambled around the corner to one of those side doors, stopping briefly in her office to get car keys. "You be careful." She embraced me, then placed the keys in my hand.

I gave her a big hug back and ran out into the hallway. I heard Tollmayer's voice again—he had a loud, deep voice even in one-on-one conversations, and it positively boomed when he was trying to impress someone, which he was clearly doing now.

"Miss O'Hara's never given us any trouble," he was saying. "Always responsible, always ethical. Might I ask what this is about?"

"No," came the clipped response.

"Oh. I see." Tollmayer harrumphed. "I'm concerned as to whether this is related to her work for us."

"If it were, you'd know about it," the unfamiliar voice replied.

"Go!" Jess gave me a shove toward the side exit. "Get out of here!"

"Wait. Maps?" I reminded her.

"Don't need 'em!" She grinned. "The phone has..."

"GPS, I know. Thanks, that'll be helpful."

****

"Hi, is Leo Penn there? This is Sabrina O'Hara."

I held a red phone and sat in a tiny red sports car, and I felt ridiculous. First of all, red was totally not my color, and second, as I told Jess when she bought it, this was such an obvious mid-life crisis car. On the plus side—and it was a big one—no one in America would ever think of looking for Sabrina O'Hara in a sporty cherry-colored convertible. Even my silver BMW sedan had surprised most of my friends with its wild extravagance—it was only a 325, but my pre-cancer car had been a used Chevy Malibu. Live a little, I had told myself when I bought the Beemer. Apparently, the key words there had been *a little*.

"Sandy, this is Sabrina O'Hara," I told Leo's secretary. "Is he in the office?"

83

"No, he's not." Her voice was that perfect blend of friendliness and distance that not enough assistants have. Mine sure doesn't.

"Is he in court?"

"No. He's at home all day today. Waiting for the contractor."

"Contractor?"

"The deck?" she prompted. "Surely you have heard about the much lauded roof deck?"

How could I possibly have forgotten? He'd been raving about it last week. Leo lived in a beautifully restored townhouse on Federal Hill. A few months ago, he'd decided what he needed to make his life complete was a rooftop deck complete with hot tub.

"I can see Camden Yards Stadium from my roof," he boasted. "I could be in a hot tub, having sex, and watching the O's game all at the same time!"

Sometimes he sounded remarkably like a fourteen-year-old boy. Sex and baseball at the same time, what could be better? I had pointed out that in order to follow the game, he'd need a telescope. The logistics of trying to look through it while boinking his bimbo of the week might prove difficult to arrange. He'd laughed at the time and called me a wet blanket.

I marveled at my own willingness to put my life into the hands of such a man, then remembered he'd gotten two guys set free who surely had murdered their nephews—with witnesses on hand. Maybe his goofy personal life was how he made peace with being the best damned criminal defense attorney in the state. So, I thanked Sandy for her information, disconnected, and dialed again.

"Leo?" I said when he picked up.

"Bree!" No one outside my father has ever called me Bree, and he only started doing it to aggravate my mother.

"Lee!" I returned. He never got the sarcasm, or if

he did, he ignored it.

"What's up with you?" he asked. "Isn't Scott out of town?"

"He is. But I'm having a legal crisis."

"I don't handle tax stuff," he cautioned me. "But I can talk to our tax guy for you."

"It's not work-related. It's personal. And it concerns Scott, too."

He paused. "Oh?"

"Scott, um, seems to be in trouble for doing something—I don't know, for breaking some rules at CIS or something. And the Feds seem to think I know all about it."

"Feds?" Leo repeated. And then he chuckled. "The Feds? Are you watching too many crime dramas on TV, Bree?"

"Well, okay, Homeland Security, damn it. Some agents from Homeland Security want to question me and possibly arrest me in connection with whatever it is Scott might have done."

He stopped laughing at that point. "Jesus, you're serious."

"Yes, I am. And I don't know where to go or what to do. I'm afraid to turn myself in without talking to a lawyer because I'm convinced I'll disappear from the face of the earth and die in Guantanamo."

"They don't put Americans in Gitmo, you chucklehead," Leo retorted.

"Whatever! Can I see you?"

"Do you need someone to come get you? Where are you? I take it you aren't in the custody of these Federal agents?"

"No. Well, not anymore." I heard him groan on the other end of the line. "I have Jess' phone and car—"

"That's good, then they can't track your cell phone's GPS signal," he replied.

"What, they can do that?"

"Oh, yeah," he assured me. "Why don't you come straight to the house, and we'll sort this out. I'll try to get in touch with Scott."

"I did that already," I answered hastily. "He was out of range. But listen, Leo, I want to talk to you before you try to reach him. Okay?"

Silence like a solid wall issued from the tiny phone in my hand.

"I've known Scott since I was thirteen, Sabrina."

I think that meant he was angry with me. He'd never called me anything but Bree.

"Please, Leo, I'm not saying he's a criminal. But there's a good chance he bent some rules and doesn't know how big a deal it was. Don't call and panic him until I can give you all the details."

"Fair enough."

Another issue almost too stupid to bring up entered my mind. I felt like the skankiest girl who'd stayed too long at some frat party. I wanted to get out of my filthy clothes and clean up, but Jess lived far in the opposite direction, a good hour drive from the city. I didn't have time to go raid her or her daughter's closet.

"Leo," I asked. "Do you have any women's clothes in size 6 at your place?"

Somehow, I wasn't surprised when he said yes.

Eight

I had neglected to consider the women's clothing a guy like Leo might keep on hand. There were nighties and bathrobes, a French maid costume, a scary vinyl dominatrix get-up I so didn't want to know about, and enough sexy lingerie to open a Federal Hill branch of Victoria's Secret. But there were no cotton undies and comfy sweats which was all I really wanted at that point. Of course, I also wanted the stuffed bear my dad had given me before the divorce and a big mug of hot chocolate. I wasn't getting those, either.

I wound up with a short but well-made black leather skirt and some pointy-toed snakeskin heels. Leo had laid them out in his guest bedroom, along with a mercifully loose-fitting grey silk sweater and some black thigh-highs.

"Pantyhose slow me down," he said, when I asked about them. "Why would I let any of my girlfriends wear pantyhose?"

My mouth fell open and stayed that way.

"Bree, I'm pulling your leg." He gave me a little wink. "This is all Jenna's stuff, and she never wears pantyhose. You'd have to ask her why."

Jenna was a junior partner in Leo's firm. He'd taken one look at her chest and decided to be her mentor. I didn't ask whether the vinyl outfit was hers as well.

In the end, I took one of the stockings and used it to stuff my bra cup, leaving the other one behind on the bed. I would've liked to lie down on that bed, and I hoped that once we thrashed out my statement—or whatever we had to do—I'd get a chance to rest. If not in that bed, then somewhere. Even a jail cell cot was starting to have its attractions.

The room that's in the basement in most houses in the suburbs—the fun room with the big-screen TV and a pool table—that room was on the top floor at Leo's townhouse. So when I finished dressing, I headed upstairs. Leo was there, thumbing through a news magazine. His grey eyes flicked over me, and he smiled approvingly.

"Why, you sure do clean up nice, ma'am," he said in an exaggerated Virginia drawl.

I dropped a little mock curtsy, no easy feat in such a tight-ass skirt.

"If you gave me a beret, I could pass for Bonnie Parker."

Leo's mouth lifted at one corner, and he glanced down at the magazine.

"I wouldn't joke about your current status," he cautioned. "Escaping from a Federal agent is not small potatoes."

"Tell me about it." I crossed the room and sat down beside Leo on his buttery soft Italian leather sofa. More black leather. I guessed it was a bachelor thing. Scott had wanted to replace my suede sofa with leather when he moved in, but I had vetoed it. You get stuck to it in hot weather, and it's chilly in winter, but guys think it's the epitome of cool. Especially guys like Leo.

"How about telling me all about your problem?" From a table beside the sofa, he pulled out a yellow legal pad. Then he picked up an expensive silver pen lying on the glass coffee table in front of him.

"I don't know where to start." I sighed.

"Begin at the beginning," he said. "And go on until you come to the end; then stop."

I wasn't expecting Lewis Carroll, but it was a

happy little surprise, reminding me of the stories my mother used to read me when I was a kid. It comforted me, and I eased into talking about what had happened. I began with the break-in, seeing no reason to tell Scott's best friend about my little infidelity in the parking garage. I explained Evan had been posing as my personal trainer and now claimed to be an agent with ICE. I told him about the Mendozas and the human trafficking charges. He put his lips together and made a loud razzing noise at that one. "I don't know what to believe," I said as I concluded my story. "But I sure wasn't waiting around for that Tyrese guy to come in and arrest me."

"On the whole, I can't argue with what you did. Depending on what they're accusing Scott of doing, they could easily have invoked the Patriot Act, and then you could have waited a long time before getting access to a lawyer."

"I'm almost afraid to talk to Scott about this, Leo," I confessed. "I can't help but think Evan sounded pretty sure of his facts. But he's a little bit scary, too."

"How so?"

I told him about the graveyard, Ben getting shot, and then Evan beating that other man until he'd covered himself in bloody spatters. I told him because I wanted to give him something to latch onto, and latch on to it he did.

"He's a cop. They're good at projecting self-assurance. They're also good at intimidating people and running roughshod over them."

"Hey!" He knew my dad had been a cop.

"Of course, not every cop is like that, Sabrina. But a lot of them are, an awful lot. You don't succeed at a job like that unless you take a certain pleasure in roughing people up and waving a gun around."

I didn't want to hear this. It sounded too much

like my mother's habitual belittling of my father's work, and I told Leo as much.

He shrugged. "It's frequently true. And another thing almost universally true is that officers of the law tend to fixate on one suspect pretty quickly. And when they do, they stop looking for other answers. Now, I think Scott is probably an ambitious, young agent's dream. From what you're telling me, there's a good chance he did bend a few regulations to get some girls into the country illegally. Probably believed he was rescuing them from a life in an orphanage or on the streets. But nonetheless, let's say he breaks some rules. And oh! Look at this! His uncle is Senator Carlton Chase Bennett IV! Gee, let's turn this tedious probe into a sexy political corruption case! Win some front-page coverage, get ourselves promoted. Scott is what I call a sexy suspect, Sabrina. One the media is going to eat up. And I'm sure your agent knows that and knows how much it could help his career to bring down someone from a powerful political family."

"You think?" I wrinkled up my nose. "Evan doesn't strike me as a glory seeker."

"Look. Why don't we find out what sort of agent he really is? I can call in some favors and have this guy's personnel record up on my computer within the hour."

"Okay," I rose from the sofa and nodded. "Okay, that sounds smart. Know your enemy, right?"

"Atta girl," Leo rose, too, and patted my back.

Downstairs I heard a door close and some rattling and shuffling. I tensed, but Leo hadn't had the same twelve hours I'd had. He barely noticed.

"Mr. Leo?" a voice wafted up the stairs. "It is I, Rose."

I stifled a giggle. She sounded so stiff and formal, and she was probably so proud of her careful enunciation. Rose was Leo's housekeeper, an older woman who'd emigrated from Chile many years ago, after her husband and son disappeared. Even after all that time, her accent was thick, and sometimes I had trouble knowing what she was saying.

"Hello, Rose," Leo called as he clambered down the steps with me trailing behind. "Miss O'Hara's here for some legal advice."

We came to the bottom of the stairs and entered the kitchen. There were front and back stairs in Leo's house, but only the back ones went all the way to the top floor. They'd been servant's stairs when the house was built, and that's why they came out at the kitchen.

"Hi, Rose," I nodded to her, and she did the same.

"We'll be in the office," he told her. "If the contractor comes, feel free to interrupt."

As we passed out of the kitchen, we headed back toward a glassed-in conservatory space. Leo had added this room when he bought the place, and it now served as his library and office. It looked out on a little rear courtyard, beautifully landscaped with wildflowers and brick pathways. Leo didn't do any of the gardening; he hired people for that, too. He liked to look at pretty things, he told me once.

He walked over to his desk, a big antique mahogany thing facing out into the room. The monitor that sat on top was aimed at the back wall, away from the door, so no one could see what he was working on if they walked in unexpectedly.

"I'm going to call my friend Jeff at the Department of Justice. Why don't you see if Rose can feed you?"

I understood that to mean he didn't want me to overhear his conversation.

"When you're done, can I make a call, too?" I asked. I still had the childish belief that talking to Daddy would fix everything.

"Oh, you don't need to wait. I have a second line. Ask Rose to show you."

I ducked out of the room and came back to the kitchen.

"You look nice today, Miss O'Hara." Rose arched an eyebrow significantly as she spoke. I was sure she recognized the clothes from her boss's own guest closet. Maybe she'd even seen them on Jenna. She'd never been too fond of me, and I doubted her impression was improving. Between the clothes and the request for food, I knew she'd think I had been here all night. Hunger seemed preferable. I skipped straight to asking about the phone.

"Leo's making a confidential call. But he said I could use the second line."

"Of course, Miss." She lifted the handset from a sleek, black wall phone and pushed a couple of buttons before passing it to me.

I dialed Daddy's cell phone first, but as I'd expected, he'd turned it off. I left a message anyway, my name and Leo's number, no details. Rose peered at me like a hawk eying its dinner. In an effort to avoid her, I foolishly called the home number again.

"Oh, hello, dear!" Nanny exclaimed. "I talked to your father a few minutes ago. I told him your good news."

"Good news?"

"Why, about the baby, of course!"

"The baby?" *Oh, for heaven's sake.* "Nanny, when I said I was in trouble, I didn't mean that I was—"

I cut myself off, noting the severe arch of Rose's eyebrow. Her meaty arms were crossed over her chest in a rather threatening way.

"Now, dear," Nanny O'Hara squawked. "Don't be shy about this. Why, a woman your age—this is quite a blessing from God. You're like Elizabeth in the Bible, dear!"

I stepped as far from Rose as the room would

allow, which was a distance of several yards. "Nanny," I whispered, "I had cancer, remember? I can't have babies now!"

"Cancer?" she said. "Are you sure? No, that was Angela. Oh my, wait, my memory isn't quite what it used to be."

Talk about a news flash. "Look, Nanny, did you tell Daddy to call me? I tried his cell phone, but it transferred me to voicemail."

"Yes, he said that would happen." Her voice chirped with oblivious good cheer. "When I told him your news, he said I shouldn't call the cell phone again because he was turning it off."

"Why?"

"He said he didn't want to cuss so much he scared away the elk. I didn't understand what that had to do with anything. He shouldn't be cussing at all, especially at the poor elk."

A lecture about cussing was rich coming from Nanny. After sixty years in bars and restaurant kitchens, she knew more dirty words than a sailor and wasn't afraid to use them. When I was little, my classmates would come to the house and eavesdrop on her phone conversations to learn new bad words. I gave this conversation up as pointless, as my father had probably done earlier in the day.

"Nanny, I'll talk to you later."

"Fine, dear. Remember to drink lots of milk; it's good for the baby!"

She hung up, and I growled at the phone and stamped my foot. Rose pursed her lips and gave her head a tiny, almost invisible shake.

"She's kind of senile," I said. "Do you understand what that is?"

Rose kept staring at me, her brows knit together in a single solid line.

"Um, could I have a drink, please? Ice water, juice. Anything."

"Of course, Miss."

She brushed past me in a narrow aisle between the kitchen island and the massive stainless steel fridge. As she reached out to grab its handle, her fingers brushed against mine. She spun sharply and glared at me. I reeled backwards from an almost palpable wave of anger. Suddenly, the most vivid picture burst into my head, a picture of a much younger Rose scrounging in a garbage can for food. This felt like one of my weird dreams, yet I was awake. But it was like those dreams in its vividness, colors bleeding into one another like an overexposed print. Had that really happened to her? I wanted to ask, but I didn't dare.

"What must you think of this big refrigerator and all this food for one man who's almost never home?" I asked instead.

Her expression softened, and she removed a bottle of pineapple juice from one of the shelves. Then she silently poured it into a cup she'd taken from a nearby shelf.

"Thank you." As I took it from her, our fingers touched again. I looked up to discover Rose staring at me with big saucer-shaped eyes.

"Rose? Are you all right?"

"*Sangre*," she said. "*Sangre en sus manos.*"

I hadn't lived with a guy who speaks Spanish for two years without picking something up. I sat the cup of juice on the counter and flipped my hands back and forth, examining them. Then I looked up at her and grinned, making light of it.

"Nope, no blood. You must have been seeing things."

"Not now," she snapped. "Later."

And she swept out of the room, as though I'd somehow insulted her. I sat myself down at the kitchen table and guzzled the cup of juice in a few quick gulps. Surely this mess would be resolved soon, I'd be out on bail, and we'd be preparing for a trial. Or better yet, Leo would intimidate them into leaving me the hell alone, and I would go home and go back to my peaceful little life. Although maybe I wouldn't want to stay in that particular condo anymore...

Since I was alone, I took the opportunity to check the refrigerator again. I came out with a leftover slice of pumpkin pie, which I was eating when Rose came back into the room.

"That is not a good breakfast for you," she said sternly. "Too much sugar."

"I know." That and the juice together had been a bad idea. Already I felt jittery and a little queasy.

"Mister Leo has the cholesterol, or I would fix you a proper breakfast of eggs and sausage. He should not even have the pie. I tell him, what is life without pie? If you cannot even eat my pies now, you should have the heart attack and be dead. Silliness." She clucked under her tongue at the insanity of modern medicine. "Do you want a bagel instead?"

I shook my head.

She shuffled past me, muttering something about eggs and sausages again.

I started to drool a bit.

"Yo, Sabrina!" Leo called from the conservatory. I rose and came into the room.

"Close the door."

I did, then turned back around, and approached his desk. But I could already see the picture on his monitor from where I was standing. He'd turned the monitor slightly, to make it easier for me to see. It took a while to realize the man in the photo was Evan, albeit with much shorter hair.

"Is this your agent?"

I nodded and pulled a straight-backed chair from a table and dragged it to the desk.

"Brother, we hit the jackpot with this one," Leo

muttered, shaking his head.

"What do you mean?"

"Well, he's been suspended three times for excessive force."

I don't know why it should have hurt to hear that at that point, but it did.

"He was also accused by a suspect of planting evidence," Leo read on. "He was cleared of that charge. Big surprise there. These guys look out for their own."

"Or he really wasn't guilty?"

Leo snorted in derision and shook his head at me. The doorbell rang, and I jumped.

"Relax," Leo laughed. "You're going to be fine. That's probably the contractor. Jerk was supposed to be here at eight. What is it now, ten? I guess that's right on time in his book."

He rose, still laughing and shaking his head.

"I'll be back in a few, after I go over some specs with him. Then we can try to get in touch with Scott again. Afterwards, we'll contact Homeland Security, turn ourselves in, and start negotiating. At this point, it's pretty clear to me you guys are the victims of an irresponsible fishing expedition."

He left the file up on the computer, and I was sure that was no accident. Someone like Leo didn't make mistakes. He wanted me to read it, and so I did. Born in Texas. Served in the Gulf War, honorably discharged. A bunch of medals. Criminology degree from the University of California, Irvine. A few years with the DEA and then after 2001 he'd gone to work for some government agency I'd never heard of, Internal Security Administration. Now he was on loan from that department to ICE. I couldn't make out whether Internal Security Administration was part of Homeland Security, too, or independent of them or what. I gave up trying to figure that out.

I read about the excessive force charges. Two had occurred about six years ago, two men allegedly involved in the killing of a DEA agent in El Paso. Then one last year, a guy accused of operating a prostitution ring for pedophiles. I couldn't be too upset about Evan landing that guy in the hospital on life support. But still, a person would have to look at a file like his and wonder how many other incidents were never reported. Incidents like the one I'd seen in the graveyard. And what if a guy like that went off on the wrong man? What if a guy like that went off on Scott? Scott could barely even kill a spider. I usually had to do it. If a guy like Evan attacked Scott, poor Scott would probably roll up like one of those little potato bugs and get kicked to death.

I read further down the page. He'd been put on administrative leave twice after using lethal force. I knew from my dad that was standard operating procedure. A cop could shoot a suspect and be dead to rights, but once that happened, he'd be behind a desk until the investigation was over. In both cases, Evan had been cleared. One was a guy, apparently a hit man for those Mendozas. But the other person— the other person he'd killed was a woman.

I stopped reading and turned away from the desk, strolling over to the windows. Mostly I was furious with myself for feeling so disappointed at all these revelations. I barely knew the guy. He was physically gorgeous, and I'd built this whole fantasy of who he was—maybe he was an artist too, I'd thought, looking at his hands in the gym one day. They seemed beautifully cared for and so graceful. Or he could be a musician. Maybe he was a struggling musician who did the personal trainer thing to make ends meet.

But no. Not an artist, not a musician. Just a man with a bad temper and a gun—and carte blanche from some shadowy government agency in a time of war.

"Look what the cat dragged in!" Leo hollered, throwing open the door.

And behold—Scott stood there beside him. Nice, familiar Scott, with his short, wavy blond hair and his sparkly hazel eyes and his total inability to inflict physical pain on any living thing, even a creepy bug.

I ran to him. Or more accurately, I ran away from the scary man on the computer monitor.

I threw my arms around Scott, and he squeezed me tight in return. Then he held me at arm's length.

"Where the hell have you been? I've been calling and calling your cell phone. Then I came home, and they wouldn't even let me up to our floor. I was worried sick about you."

He gave me one of those quick, married-people kisses, but that was normal for us. I hadn't started playing house with Scott because I expected a grand passion. I'd wanted a nice, reliable, even-tempered guy who liked the same things I did, and that's exactly what I had.

He led me back into Leo's office, and we sat down at a small, round conference table in front of the windows.

"What are you doing back so soon?"

He rolled his eyes and laughed, an edgy, forced sound to my ears. But everyone seemed false and out to get me by that point. I despised Evan for not being the man of my fantasies, but I also despised him at that moment for planting seeds of doubt and cynicism in me. I suspected Rose considered me a whore and had deliberately tried to frighten me; I worried Leo was on a retainer for the Mendozas; and now I was even doubting Scott, a man I'd known way longer than I'd known Evan.

"Oh, man." Scott shook his head. "Did I have egg on my face when I got to that meeting! All my immigration statistics were missing. And then, that screensaver of the shirtless guy popped up. Good God, the Mexican Under-Secretary thinks I'm gay now."

I blushed, but not from embarrassment. A big wave of relief flooded over me. These were normal-people problems, problems people like Scott and I should have—taking your girlfriend's computer to an important meeting and looking like a dork. Not being pursued by armed government agents.

"Anyway," he continued. "I called the office and had them e-mail me some of the more crucial stuff, but I couldn't get much work done without that data. I guess if I backed it all up on a flash drive and kept that with me, like you keep telling me to do, I wouldn't have looked so foolish, eh?"

"Well, it's sensitive data, you said so yourself. Not a good idea to have a lot of copies of it lying around, right?" I could afford to be magnanimous now. Scott was home, and no great harm had been done. Rose would be bringing me some real food soon. The universe, which I felt owed me an awful lot after last year, was finally delivering.

Nine

Leo hadn't come all the way into the room. He hung back, in the doorway, an inscrutable expression on his face as he studied the back of Scott's head. He looked older than Scott with his salt and pepper gray hair, and he dressed better than Scott, in imported Italian suits. In fact, Leo looked like a Hollywood casting director's idea of a lawyer. Although he had no reason for it, Scott always seemed a little more insecure about his looks when he was around Leo. Leo might glance in a mirror and run his hand through his thick hair and even wink at himself—I'd once seen him do it. Scott would peer anxiously into the same mirror, poking at an imaginary pimple. That had always been somewhat comforting to a woman like myself, who'd never had a high opinion of my appearance.

Even as I was thinking about this difference between them, Leo ruffled his fingers through his own hair, and Scott pinched at some invisible blemish on his chin.

"You got back right quick." Whenever Leo and Scott got together, they tended to start sounding more and more southern, lapsing into some easy, childhood cadence. I loved listening to it, especially to Leo. His voice was so mild and inconsequential. You'd never have guessed that voice could make grown men in the jury box dissolve into tears.

Now he stepped into the room and closed the door behind him. He strolled casually over to his desk. To the left of the desk was a printer stand, with a power strip mounted beside it. He flicked the switch on the strip, and the little green lights on the computer and monitor winked out, shutting everything down instantly and blanking out the file I'd been reading. Now why had he done that? Me, I'd have closed all my files and shut the machine down properly before flicking everything off, but some people are sloppy about that sort of thing.

"Scott, we should discuss what you two are going to say to the authorities," Leo said. "There's a Federal agent investigating you—Sabrina told you that much in her phone messages, right?"

Scott shook his head and flashed a disgusted sneer. "I'm telling you. Talk about the right hand not knowing what the left hand is doing, huh?"

"What do you mean?" Leo picked up the legal pad and pen, which he'd carried down from the loft and brought to the table. His stiff tone disoriented me. I decided it must be the professional Leo speaking, and not Scott's old buddy from Woodberry Forest School.

"I don't honestly know, Leo," Scott answered. "I'm assuming this is some interagency squabble run amok."

"You think so?" I liked the sound of that.

"What else?"

"Why would an interagency squabble over some sensitive data lead to you being accused of helping to traffic underage girls across the border, Scott?"

Scott frowned at Leo, clearly annoyed by his tone. "Damned if I know, pal."

Leo gave a long, shrewd nod and scribbled some notes down on his pad, but Scott still eyed him with a surprising degree of irritation. Abruptly, he turned toward me.

"Why are you here so early in the morning?"

"Honey, going home was out of the question," I reminded him. "You've seen our place."

"Yeah," he nodded. "But why here? Why not one

of your friends' places?"

I sighed. Leo responded to the insinuation with a huge, innocent-eyed grin which only made it look *more* like we had something to hide. I'd have to talk to him about that later. Scott's jealous streak was his most unpleasant quality, but I'd always considered it a sign of his affection. Granted, I would have preferred fine jewelry and a good sex life, but I was too old and scarred to be very demanding. I took the jealous displays as a compliment and tried not to give him too many occasions for feeling that way.

"Scott, I only got here a little before you did."

"But what the hell happened at our place, though?" he asked. "I'm all in the dark."

That was certainly true. He'd gone away to a business meeting and come home to find his condo off-limits, his girl being pursued by Federal agents, and himself accused of being a sex slaver. I patted his hand.

"It's been a rough night. And it all came out of nowhere."

I told him about running—but not about the kiss. I explained about hurting my knee and going home early, waking up, and finding a thief in the house.

"Then things got really weird."

He arched an eyebrow, and I went on to say that two Homeland Security agents had shown up and literally dragged me away. I deliberately avoided explaining that one of the agents was also my personal trainer. That jealous tantrum, I did not need to see right now. Instead, I fast-forwarded to the chase into the cemetery and my escape from the police barracks.

"So here I am," I concluded, spreading my hands.

For some reason, I hadn't thought to mention what had become of his laptop in the chaotic course of the night. Too self-centered to think it was important to the story, I guess.

Scott leaned forward and took my hands. He did not say, *Oh my God, honey, how awful for you!* He did say, "My laptop, where is my laptop, honey?"

An awkward pause ensued. Leo and I looked past Scott to one another. Leo shook his head and looked down at the floor. I think we both sensed something a little, I don't know—off?—about Scott's reaction.

I thought about what I'd told Jess, that maybe Scott had bent a few rules in some misguided effort to help those girls get adopted. Maybe something on that computer would prove he'd done such a thing, that he wasn't entirely innocent after all. Apparently, Leo had independently come to the same conclusion.

"I'm willing to bet I can make a case you truly believed you were helping some kids find decent homes. And you had no idea the so-called orphanage was a front for organized criminal activity. You confess to falsifying documents and breaking some regulations. To be honest, you'll probably lose your job, but you can recover from that pretty easily with your connections. The important thing is that if you give yourself up now and beg for mercy, you probably won't have to do any jail time."

Scott released my hands and stood. He paced over to the big floor-to-ceiling windows of the conservatory and looked out.

"I can't help you if you're not honest with me," Leo said.

Scott ruffled his hair and a wisp of it fell onto his forehead. I always loved to see that lock of hair fall into his eyes. It only happened when he was agitated and messed up—like when he was playing touch football at a picnic or when we were having unusually good sex. So, I hadn't seen it in quite a while.

"Good Lord." He slumped against the window. "I never meant for this to get so big."

Leo had been leaning his hip against his desk. Now his posture stiffened, and he inched closer to Scott.

"Exactly how big are we talking?"

"Oh, Scott," I murmured uneasily.

"Some Mexican businessmen contacted me a while ago."

Leo returned to the little, round conference table and tossed himself into one of the chairs. Scott and I followed.

"Their names are Hector and Rafael. They're wealthy businessmen who support a lot of charities down there, but they play a little fast and loose with the rules. Anyway, they told me they help fund a couple of orphanages, and we talked about how great it would be if the kids there could find homes here in the States."

"Did you know these girls were being used for sex, Scott?" Leo pinched the bridge of his nose and then scribbled on his legal pad. His jaw twitched.

"No." Scott shrugged. "But some of the kids brought up here were boys. Although I guess if what this agent told you is true, then the boys are being exploited, too." He sighed heavily and put his head in his hands.

"So you're saying you did know you were breaking regulations and falsifying documents?" Leo asked.

He nodded, still looking down at the table.

"But you did not know the children were being prostituted or sexually abused?"

"Absolutely not!"

Poor, good-natured Scott—always a little detached from reality. I guessed that had made him the perfect pawn.

"I wasn't the only one!" He raised his head and perked up like a puppy who'd fetched a stick. "I had help."

"We can pull those names out of our hat later, buddy," Leo told him. "They could be a useful bargaining chip. And did you do this out of the goodness of your heart, Scott? Because you were so moved by the plight of these neglected children?"

I could tell Leo didn't think that for one minute, and it made me mad. Scott was always involved in charitable work. He honestly seemed to have more of a social conscience than I did, that's for sure.

"Some money may have exchanged hands." Scott peered up at me sideways.

"Why did it happen at all, Scott?" I asked. "Did you need the money? Was it because of my medical bills?"

He looked back down at the table. "I, um, I didn't want to go begging to my uncle."

I rose from my seat and came to stand behind him, putting my arms around his shoulders.

Leo threw down his pen and stalked across the room. He looked angry, even a bit disgusted, as he threw open the door.

"Rose, get me some coffee!" He stomped back over to us and picked up his pen. Then he hovered beside the table, drumming on his legal pad and glaring at Scott with pursed lips.

"Don't be furious at him," I said. "He didn't mean any harm."

Rose appeared in the doorway almost instantly, holding a tray of mugs.

"I was already bringing coffee. It is like I am a psychic, is it not?" She glided over to the conference table, set the tray down, and gave me a long, hard glance. Then she looked at Scott. "How are you, sir? It is good to be seeing you."

Scott half-nodded and watched her take the

mugs from the table and set out a pitcher of cream and a bowl of sugar.

"I'm going to wash up." He rose and went out the door.

"Is that some Southern gentleman thing?" I asked Leo.

"What?"

"He never says 'I have to go to the bathroom.' How hard is that?"

Leo flashed me a forlorn half-smile but didn't answer me.

"Rose," he said, "Call the contractor and cancel, will you? My day's looking pretty crowded at this point."

"Are you certain?"

"Absolutely."

"Sorry about all this." I flashed a smile at Rose, trying to prevent her from glaring a couple of new holes into my head.

Leo smiled politely, but Rose's face remained grim as she finished setting out the coffee. "I hope you haven't forgotten those things I need at the store, Rose."

She paused in the midst of picking up her tray. Her hands shook the tiniest bit. I'd never noticed them doing that before. Was she getting old? Or was she afraid of Leo? His mood did seem to be veering into the ugly zone.

"Are you quite sure, Mr. Leo?" Her voice wavered as she spoke.

I agreed with her. Had he looked in his refrigerator lately?

"Here," Leo continued as if she hadn't spoken. He chewed on the inside of his cheek, scribbled something on the legal pad, then handed it to her with a stern look. "Make sure the parmigiano-reggiano is fresh this time."

She took the paper from him and stuffed it in

the pocket of her bib apron. "I will go immediately."

I got the feeling there were other things she wanted to say, and that she wanted to direct most of them at me. But she didn't, and then she bustled out of the room.

Leo folded his hands. "We should contact the appropriate agent at Homeland Security. I'm thinking maybe Jeff at DOJ can get me this Tyrese fellow's full name. Then we can ask for him directly and do an end-run around your little troublemaker. I don't want to deal with him, he sounds like too much of a loose cannon."

"I suppose so," I admitted. "And then what do we do? We turn ourselves in?"

"Pretty much. But it should be fine. Clearly, you didn't know about any of this nonsense. You'll probably be free to go after they get your statement."

"And Scott?"

"That'll be a little trickier," Leo confessed. "But he's got me, so he'll be okay. One thing that would be an immense help would be getting that laptop back."

"I can't imagine anyone will have taken it, considering where I put it." I remembered the map book and asked if he had one.

"Sure do," he said. "I love maps. I keep the old editions of the map books. It's like looking at history. You can see whole towns develop. First there'll be some dotted lines where there's going to be a road, then in the next edition there's a road. Then a few editions later, the road gets a bigger, darker line because now it's a wide highway—"

I was staring, my mouth agape, so he finally stopped talking.

"I only want to know what cemetery I was in. I don't need the history of anything."

Leo went to one of the book-lined walls of his office and pulled a thin, oversized book from the bottom shelf. "No history then. Just a nice, up-to-date map."

I thumbed through the index, then found the page with the Boston Street exit. I traced the route I thought we'd taken out of the city, then slapped my hand down. "Oh for pity's sake!"

"What?"

"There are three—wait, make that four cemeteries all in a row on that stretch of road! This could take days."

"No, it won't, Bree." Leo pressed a firm hand on my shoulder. "It will be the one with the busted wall and a boat load of cops prowling around the place. We can get the exact address when we contact this Agent Tyrese. I hope they haven't buried that poor slob yet, or we'll need a court order to dig it up."

"There weren't a lot of options at the time," I told him.

"That's okay." He paused for a long time before speaking again. When he did, his voice came low and cautious, like he didn't want anyone to hear. "Listen, I know Scott has been my friend forever, so in theory my loyalty should be to him. But this business about the money for your medical bills—"

"I don't want to talk about it." I waved my hand. "I know he was foolish. We could have cashed in investments or borrowed against the condo. I guess he wasn't thinking straight at the time. That's why I'm the accountant."

I couldn't help but think he'd taken my illness harder than I had. I'd thought only the physical stuff upset him, but obviously there'd been a big emotional toll as well. I was trying hard to find that touching and not to think of him as weak. Talking about the situation right now would not help me sort out my feelings.

"When this latest crisis is over, Scott and I are definitely seeing a counselor."

Leo got a squirmy expression on his face, that

look guys get when a woman is going to start saying incomprehensible, uncomfortable female stuff. I dropped the subject. It would be better to talk about it with Jess anyway.

And speak of the devil, her cherry red phone rang right at that moment. It wasn't mine, so I wasn't sure I should answer. But it might be Jess's daughter Leslie, and I always enjoyed talking to her. She'd get a big kick out of Aunt Sabrina's latest snafu. I'd left the phone on Leo's desk, so I walked over and picked it up.

"Hey, Sabrina!" Jess's own voice burbled.

"What's up?"

"Agent Double-O-Sexy was here," she sang.

"Oh. My. God. Did he ask a lot of questions?"

"Oh, yeah. But listen, he's sincerely worried about you, hon. And he didn't say anything about arresting you."

"Of course he wouldn't tell *you* that's what he's planning!"

"I'm not a good liar," she said. "Lying was Walt's job, not mine."

My stomach heaved.

"Jess, you didn't tell him where I am?"

"Not exactly. I told him you'd been here and were going to your lawyer's office."

"Oh, thanks a lot!"

"He says you could be in a lot of danger. Your very life. He said that to me, Sabrina, he said—'Trust me, Mrs. McClintock, her very life is in danger.' And then I had to explain about the name. How I'm *Ms* McClintock now because I went back to my maiden name and—"

"Jess!" I barked at her. Sometimes I think she has Attention Deficit Disorder.

"He said there are some big players involved here, extremely evil people."

"Yeah, I know. The supermarket of crime guys."

I rolled my eyes at Leo, and he grinned. We'd had a big laugh earlier when I'd recounted Evan's description of the Mendozas.

The possibility of Evan showing up at Leo's house distressed me. I recalled our conversation in the police barracks and felt myself getting angry all over again. He'd swagger in here—because he did swagger when he walked—and he'd sneer at Scott's prep school good looks and start badgering him about his involvement with the Mendozas. He might even bring up that stupid, ill-considered kiss if he wanted to provoke a reaction from Scott.

"Look, I'm with Leo now, and he's working out all the details," I told Jess. "We're going to pick up Scott's computer and then make arrangements to turn it in to the police. Or Feds. Or whatever. Anyway, I'll be fine. I'm not in any danger anymore."

It seemed like a completely reasonable conclusion. Scott had come clean about his activities, Leo had a plan to save us, and it wasn't even lunchtime yet. I could see myself home and in my flannel jammies with a cup of tea by bedtime. Okay, maybe not my own home, what with the yellow caution tape and the chalk outlines of dead guys and all.

"Hey, when this is over, can I come stay at your place for a bit?" I asked Jess.

"Oh, sure you can, hon. You be careful in the meantime. I'm glad Leo's looking out for you."

"Love you," I told her. As I hung up, Scott walked back into the room.

"Jess says that Federal agent is still looking for me. And Leo thinks we should get your computer so we can hand it over to the authorities when we meet with them."

"We can let them know where you left it, kiddo," Leo said. "We don't have to physically retrieve it."

"No, no!" Scott waved a hand. "I want to get it. I

110

want to personally hand it over to them." He gave a sheepish twitch of his lips. "Anything that helps clear my name. Oh, and yours too, Sabrina."

Leo frowned up at him and tossed his pen down, again. I'd have been more careful with a pen that costs that much, but I figured Leo probably bought them by the case. Between the business with the pen and the way he'd handled his computer, I had to fight an accountant's urge to lecture him about taking better care of his material investments.

"Buddy," he said to Scott, "you can be one self-involved idiot. Let's let the police retrieve it, okay?"

Scott had a few inches on Leo. He leaned down and spoke in a stern voice. "I really want to get it now, Leo. Before someone gets buried. Okay?"

Leo said nothing for a moment. He jostled Scott on the way out of his office, pursing his lips and shaking his head as if he was looking at the worst low-life imaginable.

"Fine. Come on," he muttered irritably. "Let's get this thing done."

Ten

I was in the passenger seat of a rented gold Impala. It made me feel like I was my own grandmother. Nanny O'Hara always drives one of those big, boaty American cars.

"Ah, luxury at its finest," I quipped. Scott's real car is a Swedish import, but he'd driven to the airport with a co-worker the previous day.

"At least I had plenty of room for my luggage in the trunk. Since I couldn't leave my stuff at home."

"Poor thing," I retorted. Already we were falling back into our habit of sniping and trying to out-do one another. I was the one who'd been physically attacked and chased from our home, but in Scott's universe, not being able to hang up his suits constituted a far greater inconvenience.

"I can't believe you hit a Federal agent in the face, Sabrina," he said, as if that were the reason we couldn't go home.

Okay. So it was part of the reason. But only a small part.

"Are you trying to say this mess is my fault?"

"Folks, can we not do this?" Leo murmured from the back seat.

I glanced over my shoulder and flashed him an apologetic smile.

"Sorry. I'm betting Scott's as sleep-deprived as I am at this point."

To this day, I don't know what Leo said in reply. I was busy looking past him, noticing another Impala, a white one, trailing about three cars behind us. I had seen it—or something awfully similar—

parked at the end of the block when we came out of Leo's place on Montgomery Street.

"Funny to see two Impalas so close," I commented. "I can't remember the last time I saw even one."

"We're on a highway, lots of business travelers out here," Scott answered. "His is probably a rental, too."

"Yeah." Leo frowned and shifted sideways in the rear passenger seat, taking a long, hard look at the other car. He was still frowning when he turned to the front again.

"I'm going to stop and gas this pig up before we get out onto I-95," Scott announced.

He turned left onto Key Highway and headed into the city, eventually finding his way to the divey gas station near the old railroad museum.

"Don't go anywhere without me!" He climbed out of the car, and I watched his profile as he went. His short, neat hair was cut to right below his ears, leaving the back of his neck bare and the tiny mole on the left side visible. He was a little above average height, and he'd always carried himself smoothly and dressed in perfectly tailored suits. Today he had on the designer trench coat I'd given him for his last birthday—another huge, post-cancer extravagance. He wore the coat unbuttoned, and its sides flapped around him in the breeze as he walked to the back of the car. He looked way more like a respectable government agent than Evan would ever look.

I remembered Evan's glossy long hair, the slight bump in the bridge of his nose, and the muscles that flexed in his upper arms when he moved. And then I closed my eyes and tried hard to not think about him, to not think about the things I'd read about him on Leo's computer. Leo suggesting Evan had planted evidence—I knew that was wrong. For one thing, my dad always said that sort of thing was more rare than the media and defense attorneys made it sound. *Do they think we're all walking around with a backpack full of incriminating evidence so we can happen to have something handy at the perfect moment?* For another thing, Evan seemed too damned hotheaded to coldly plan to frame a suspect. But the violence, the roughing up suspects—I'd seen that for myself, and it alarmed me.

How would he turn something like that off once he'd unleashed it? Would he be more likely to hurt people he loved if he'd had a bad day? My dad had never shown my mother any violence; their marriage had fallen apart for other reasons. What would he think of a cop with a record like Evan's? Would he defend the guy, tell me there was a good reason for him to have done the things he'd done? Or would he call Evan a dirty cop—the worst insult my father could level at a colleague.

What a lousy job I was doing of not thinking about Evan.

Fortunately, Leo gave me something new to consider instead. "Hey, Bree."

"Yeah, Lee?"

"That other Impala is here. It pulled in and parked."

As he spoke, I looked into the side mirror and saw the white car parked in one of the spaces directly in front of the gas station convenience store. There appeared to be two men inside, and the one on the passenger side emerged as I watched.

He looked like a Kodiak bear without fur. He had Hispanic features, short black hair, and an awe-inspiringly wide body. Not fat, just wide. If someone stuck a finger in his tummy, it would not go all squishy like unbaked bread. It would stay solid, like a big, hard rock.

"Cops? Following us?"

"I'm not sure," Leo replied uneasily.

As he spoke, we watched the big bear of a man go into the Tiger Mart. Scott had set the pump on automatic and then gone into the mart a few seconds earlier.

"Do you think he's going to arrest Scott?"

"I don't know." Leo's voice came out distant and almost daydreamy.

I started to open my door.

"Don't." His attention snapped back to me. "You can't get to Scott before he does, and you'll turn it into a public scene. If the guy brings Scott out, I'm right here, I can handle it."

We stared out our respective windows for a while, nervous and expectant. Then the bear came out of the convenience store with a can of one of those high-caffeine energy drinks and got back into his car. No sign of Scott. I heaved a great sigh of relief.

"Bree," Leo said again.

"Leo, please stop calling me that," I told him. "It makes me feel like a little kid. My father went through a phase of calling me that right before my parents split up, okay? There are no good memories with that nickname."

"Sorry." He sounded a little offended. "You never mentioned it before."

"I'm a little short-tempered this morning."

"Look—Sabrina," he resumed, leaning forward and resting a hand on the back of my seat. "I need to say something to you about the money business."

"I said I don't want to talk about it."

"Then listen. I'm not his financial advisor, so I don't think this violates our attorney-client privilege—"

Oh, I did not like the sound of that sentence. And I liked it even less as he went on.

"I'm sure it violates the unwritten Guy Code. But I can't stand a man lying to a woman, especially about something that big."

"Wait, *you* can't stand a man lying to a woman?" I snorted.

"Hey, I do a lot of things to women, but I never lie to them. I've never needed to."

He sounded proud of himself, and I was too preoccupied to explore his personal definition of honesty.

"So how is Scott lying to me, Leo?"

"Are you aware of the trust fund?"

Good thing I was sitting down, because suddenly my legs felt a little rubbery.

"What trust fund?"

"Scott has a huge trust fund his mother left him when she died. Huge, Sabrina. It's why he drives such an expensive car and keeps a sailboat on a government employee's salary. Weren't you ever curious about that?"

"He said Uncle Carlton gives him presents now and then. Money for clothes and our box seats at the symphony. The sailboat. Stuff like that. So that he can live like a senator's son would live. Because Scott is like a son to Uncle Carlton, he says."

"I don't know about Carlton, maybe he does slip him some extra cash now and then," Leo said. "But my point is, he doesn't need that. And he wouldn't need to take money from some Mexican gangsters to pay your medical bills, kiddo."

"Oh."

I sat there, staring straight ahead. I watched an old man going through a garbage can on the corner, collecting aluminum cans and putting them into a shopping cart.

"Scott never wants to take the blame for anything," Leo went on. I turned away from the old man and saw Leo staring out the window, looking lost and confused. "Even when we were kids he was like that. But it's not right for him to try and make you feel like what he did is your fault, Br—Sabrina. That's—it's—it's not what a man does."

I continued to say nothing. What could I say? *Oh, it's okay. I don't mind Scott pushing his guilt off on me.* I did mind. I minded it whenever he did it. I minded it when we were late to a concert and he told people I'd taken too long with my make-up—usually it was because of his dithering about which suit to wear. I minded when he would come home late and tell me he couldn't call to let me know because he'd been in a confidential meeting. No one has that many confidential meetings. But this was guilt of a different magnitude entirely, and I would not have it laid at my feet.

"Don't let him know I told you this!" Leo cautioned.

"Why the hell not?"

"Trust me. We want to keep that to ourselves for a bit. I'm speaking as your legal counsel now. Don't say anything to him about this yet."

His tone startled me. Very definite. The professional Leo voice.

"Okay," I agreed. "I'll keep it to myself for now. But remember when I was talking about going to counseling with him? That is totally off now. When this is over, we are over."

"I think you might be happy with that decision, Sabrina."

I heard the rustle of leather as Leo leaned back to look out the window.

The white Impala pulled away, and he let out a sharp, almost mournful sigh.

Scott came out of the store then, smiling at me and carrying a little plastic bag. He tapped on my door, and I rolled down the window.

"Sustenance for the journey!" He handed me the bag before going back to put away the gas pump.

I looked inside. There were some bottles of

water, and I passed one back to Leo. Then I found a Tasty-Bite cherry pie. This was the good thing about being with someone for a long time—they knew things without asking. When I'm depressed, there's nothing that will cheer me up like a Tasty-Bite pie. That's always been my thing for as long as I can remember. I ate a lot of them when my parents split up, which is how I'd come to be such a chubby teen. Those things have more grams of fat than a fast food burger. In fact, I hadn't bought one for myself in over a year. Only Scott bought them for me, apparently oblivious to the fact that Tasty-Bites are not a part of a low-carb diet plan.

So this was also the bad thing about being with someone a long time—the way he assumed things without asking. Assumed that I was depressed, assumed that I would want a Tasty-Bite, assumed that I would eat the little fat bomb and be grateful. A new man would not make those assumptions. A new man would have to learn who the new *me* really was, something Scott couldn't be bothered to do.

I handed the bag back to Leo as Scott got into the driver's seat. "You can have this if you want."

"Don't you want it?" Scott frowned and sputtered at me.

"I don't think it would sit well on an empty stomach," I lied.

After Scott got back in the car, he consulted Leo's map book. Then we drove to I-95 and then took Exit 57 past the Toll Plaza. I hadn't seen any more of our friends in the white Impala, so I'd put the whole thing down to coincidence. Leo still looked fretful and preoccupied, but I believed that was because he expected me to go off at Scott at any minute.

I had a hard time remembering all the twists and turns I'd taken the night before. The area around us looked different in daylight, a ramshackle stretch of rundown homes, taverns with iron bars on the windows, and trash-strewn sidewalks.

"That's it." I gestured at the road ahead.

We turned away from a highway exit onto O'Donnell Street, and I finally spied the low stone wall. In the glare of daylight, I could see the entire wall was flimsy and in poor repair, with many of its stones chipped and loose and whole sections missing. That explained why we'd plowed through it so easily, instead of crumpling up when we hit it. Ben and I must have been traveling incredibly fast because we'd slammed into that wall almost as soon as we got off the highway.

The cemetery we'd been in was the first of three, all stretched out side by side on the same side of the road. We pulled up to an open gateway, and Scott eased the car through it and into the cemetery. Off to the left, I saw the shattered remnants of the wall, with caution tape and orange cones around it. More tape marked off the area where Ben had fallen, but there were no signs of police. I guess they'd finished processing the scene soon after I'd been taken away, and now the place was back to business as usual. Scott's car crept down the curving central lane that ran through the middle of the property. As we progressed further into the graveyard, I noticed the signs of neglect and disrepair throughout. Some of the tombstones were sunk far into the ground, others had toppled forward, and the grass had been left to grow long and unkempt around the perimeter of the property. It must be an old graveyard and nearly filled by now. Who would be getting buried in that grave where I'd hidden? Some old person, most likely, who'd bought the plot decades ago, when this had seemed like a cozy, homey place to spend eternity.

"Is that it?" Leo looked off to the right of the central lane.

"Can't be." I shook my head. "Wrong side. It has to be over here."

I pointed to the left, and Scott inched past a few more rows of headstones. Beyond the cemetery lay another wooded field, and I remembered trees near me. "I must have been over near the edge of the cemetery. Over that way."

Scott stopped the car. "Let's get out and walk up and down the rows. If it's been filled in, it might be harder to spot from here."

With that happy prospect in mind, we filed out of the vehicle and began pacing through the cemetery. No one bothered us, no cops or caretakers or mourners. The sky was appropriately overcast, and an occasional hard wind whipped itself around us, stirring up empty fast-food wrappers and other debris.

We'd gone through about four rows when I saw the mound of dirt piled near a wall beside the woods, way at the back.

"There it is." My heart beat a little faster as I approached the site.

With their longer legs and lack of spiky heels, Scott and Leo easily outpaced me. They peered down into the yawning hole in the earth, then Scott turned to glance back at me. "Dang. That thing is pretty far down there. That's got to be more than six feet."

"It's a double depth grave," Leo said. "You dig it extra deep and put the first casket in and then later, when someone else dies—usually it's a spouse—you put the second casket on top."

I tilted my head at him and frowned.

"What? My family owns a couple of funeral homes and cemeteries around Lynchburg. I used to dig graves on my summer breaks. You could say dead people paid for my education."

"Not all of it." Scott gazed at Leo accusingly.

"No." Leo inclined his head in acknowledgement.

"Scott's Uncle Carlton took an interest in me and paid for some of my college expenses. I had a partial scholarship, but he paid for the rest."

I could see it had nearly killed him to admit that, and I marveled at Scott needing to bring it up in front of me at a time like this. I shifted the subject back to the matter of graves.

"Grave digging sounds like hard work. Didn't think you had it in you, Leo." I'd pictured him having a slightly more patrician background—gentlemen farmers, politicians, something more like Scott's ancestry.

"Wasn't nearly as hard as embalming. I had to help out with that too sometimes. Hated it."

"How deep is it?" Scott asked.

"At least ten feet."

"I'm not climbing down in there to get that thing," Scott muttered.

"We shouldn't climb down and get it at all, Scott." Leo planted his hands on his hips as if he were about to deliver his closing argument to the jury. "I should call the police right now and have them meet us here. Or I can call the agent in charge of the case at Homeland Security. Either way."

"Neither way." Scott took his eyes off the grave long enough to glare at his old schoolmate. "I want it back, regardless of your professional opinion on this one, buddy. Anyway, you're my lawyer, you work for me, right?"

Leo thrust out his chin. "I do indeed. And here's some more professional advice: climb down there and get it your damn self."

"Sabrina—" Scott began.

"Evan helped pull me out last night." I spoke without thinking. "You guys could do something like that. Form a chain."

"Evan? The gym rat was here with you last night? Why?"

121

"Oh, for God's sake, Scott. He's a—"

"We should focus on the problem at hand." Leo cut me off abruptly, a note of urgency in his voice. He squinted hard at me. Either he was trying to convey some message telepathically, or he'd left his glasses at home. "Sabrina, let's save the jealous scenes between you two for later."

Scott looked at me and bit his lip. Even though he hadn't opened his mouth, I could hear him explaining why I should be the one to go down there. After all, I weighed the least; I'd be the easiest to pull back out.

"Don't even think it," I said. "I meant for you guys to help each other get it. Leave me out of the plan."

He shrugged, obviously unwilling to get dirty.

Leo stood apart, regarding both of us with a look of rising aggravation. He crossed his arms over his chest and opened his mouth to speak again when Scott gave a short clap of his hands.

"I know. There are wire coat hangers in my garment bag. We can twist them together and hook them around the strap on the carrier bag." He pulled out his keys and tossed them to me. "Here, go get the hangers for me."

I wasn't sure if he were acting like this because he blamed me for putting the laptop down there in the first place, or because I'd riled him by mentioning Evan in such a familiar way. The trying to boss me around thing generally went hand in hand with the jealous fits. Usually I would laugh it off and ignore whatever he'd asked me to do. This time, I went along with it. Partly, I feared he'd try to talk me into jumping into that grave again, and I had an almost superstitious dread of that. But also, I needed to get away from him for a minute. I'd been quietly seething at him ever since Leo's revelation, and biting my tongue is not my forte.

I took the keys and strolled back to the car at a leisurely pace I was sure would annoy the hell out of him. When I got to our car, I glanced out across the cemetery and looked toward O'Donnell Street. That's when I saw the other Impala again, parked on the grass outside the cemetery wall. Fine, damn it, let them come and arrest me. I threw open the trunk of Scott's car and shifted a carry-on bag out of the way. The garment bag had slid to the back of the incredibly deep trunk, and I almost fell as I reached inside. At last catching hold, I unzipped the bag and tsked-tsked at the mess. Scott had clearly thrown his stuff together in a panic. The pocket where he usually kept his toiletries was unzipped and little bottles and packets had slipped out all over the interior. Fortunately, nothing had leaked and ruined his suits. I started replacing everything in the compartment, tightening lids as I went—I can be a little compulsive about organization, it's an accountant thing.

I gathered up a handful of those little packets of aspirin and antacid and started to toss them into the compartment, too, when the feel of one of the packets stopped me. I separated it from the others and stared at its familiar blue and white label for the longest time, running my fingers over the rubbery ring shape inside the packet.

Trooper Blondie echoed in my head. *Maybe he wears a condom with the other woman, so he figures you're both safe.*

I started rummaging through all the compartments of his luggage. I found more condoms—they rarely travel alone, after all, and I guess since he'd returned so quickly he hadn't had time to use them all up, the poor thing.

Then I found the passports.

When I found them, I knew it was all true, every word that Evan had told me.

123

Eleven

The passports belonged to Mark and Ann Atwood. I discovered I was Ann Atwood. The picture inside was me before cancer, with long, dark auburn hair. Now my hair was short and wavy and, thanks to my hairdresser, strawberry blonde. The real hair had come in mostly gray when it returned, and I couldn't handle that.

That stern blond man in the photo of Mark Atwood, I didn't know him at all. He looked exactly like this guy I'd been living with for two years, but I didn't know who he was. Mark Atwood was the sort of man who had a million dollar trust fund, then blamed his girlfriend's cancer for his decision to take bribes from gangsters. Mark Atwood was the sort of man who lied to his girlfriend and even his best friend about what he did when he was in Mexico and whom he did it with. Mark Atwood was also, most likely, the sort of man who would know those kids being shipped up from Mexico were being used as prostitutes and worse. For all I knew, Mark Atwood even participated in that sickness.

They say hell hath no fury like a woman scorned, but apparently Scott didn't get the memo.

****

The only number I had for Evan was a home number he'd given me as my personal trainer. I didn't know if the number would still work now that his cover had been blown. I hoped it would still ring in some satellite office of Homeland Security. Maybe it was even a real number. After all, he had to live somewhere.

I'd clipped Jess' silly red phone onto the waistband of Jenna's skirt back at Leo's house. Now I pulled the phone out and dialed. Of course I got voicemail. No one ever talks to a fellow human being anymore.

"It's Sabrina," I rasped in a loud whisper. I told him I was calling from Jess' phone and gave him the number. "I'm at the cemetery. The one from last night. And Scott's here, and we're getting the laptop. Only now I don't think I should do that. I think maybe he's lying to me about some stuff. I mean I know he is. There are condoms and a false passport. Mark Atwood. There's one for me, too. I swear I didn't know anything about it, and the picture is from before the C word. Before—before I had cancer. It's a picture of me before I had cancer. So he must have had these things for a while, right? I think he's dangerous. I can try to stall him, but I don't know how long we'll be here—"

"Not long at all," said an unfamiliar voice.

A big brown hand with stubby, wide fingers reached over my shoulder and grabbed for the phone. I turned to see the big bear from the white Impala.

"No!" I protested as he snatched the phone out of my hand and tossed it away like a piece of trash. Then I let out a loud, blood-curdling shriek. I knew no one nearby would come. In this neighborhood, people learned the hard way to keep their heads down and not get involved. I wanted to go on record as going down fighting. And maybe the call hadn't disconnected; maybe Evan would hear it when he checked his messages. Pray God he'd be checking his phone every few minutes for possible leads in the case.

The bear clamped a hand over my mouth and wrapped his other arm around my torso. He lifted me up bodily and carried me toward the empty grave as I kicked and writhed. Another man loomed up behind him, a skinny guy with kinky-curly Harpo Marx hair. The new arrival slammed the lid shut on the trunk of Scott's car and trudged along beside us, glancing frequently from left to right. He kept one hand in the pocket of his shabby-looking windbreaker.

"Scott, you need to take better control of your woman, man," the big bear said in faintly accented English.

He put me down on the ground but kept his arms around me.

"Get me some rope." He jerked his head at Harpo.

The blond ducked his head in assent and hurried away.

"Sabrina, honey, what did you do?" Scott's face was all tender sympathy.

"I made a phone call."

His eyebrow shot up.

"To Jess, for crying out loud. Because I found your stash of condoms, you two-timing rat bastard."

"Scott, what the hell is this?" Leo demanded.

The big bear-like man shifted me sideways in order to free one of his hands. Naturally, he pulled an automatic pistol from under his jacket. I recognized the gun's style because my dad had taught me to shoot using a similar one. Light and plasticky, they both looked like toys. But this one resembled a much bigger toy than the one Daddy used.

"You don't ask questions." He waved the gun at Leo. "You do what you're told."

"Like hell I will," Leo answered.

I wanted to say, *Atta boy, Lee, you tell 'em*.

"Miguel, put the gun away." Scott gave a tired sigh.

I got the feeling this was something he had to

say a lot, and I didn't find that reassuring.

"Where is it, college boy?" Miguel demanded.

Oh, great. Now I was stuck in the middle of some gangland class war between these two bozos.

"Down there." Scott jerked his head toward the grave.

"Handy!" Miguel nodded. "You climb down there, senorita, and after you toss the computer up to me, I can shoot you in the head right where you stand."

I stared at him, hoping he couldn't hear the pounding of the blood in my veins. I know I could hear it. "I'm not climbing down there in these heels."

Miguel flashed a crooked grin.

"Sabrina, this isn't a time for humor," Scott informed me. I was glad to have him clear that up.

Then he returned his attention to Miguel. "I don't want her killed. I don't like unnecessary killing."

What did Scott consider necessary killing? I decided I'd ask him some other time.

"You're Hector's golden boy now because of this blackmail scheme." Miguel spat on the ground. "When that changes, I'll be waiting for you. You understand me?"

"Oh, please, even I understand you, Miguel," I said. "Can you two hold your pissing contest later?"

Miguel made a smooching gesture at me with his lips. *Muy caliente. I like that.*

Harpo returned with a length of rope and a truly frightening knife, several inches long with serrated edges. "Hands and feet?" he muttered at Miguel without looking up.

"Just hands. I don't wanna have to carry her to the car."

The blond moptop cut off two pieces of rope and tossed the third bit on the ground.

"You." Miguel waved his gun at Leo. "Get down

there and get that laptop."

Leo thrust his hands on his hips and opened his mouth to protest.

"Look, my man, we don't need you," Miguel said to him. "And you aren't pretty, so even if you are his friend, I might not always do what College Boy here tells me to do. You wanna find out the hard way?"

Leo wore a leather bomber jacket over his polo shirt and khakis. He stripped off the jacket and folded it neatly. He handed the jacket to Scott. "I gotta tell you, buddy, you've done some stupid, self-centered things before, but this takes the cake. I am sorely disappointed in you." Then he jumped down into the grave.

When he did, Miguel tossed his head at Harpo, gesturing him over to us.

"Put out your hands," Harpo demanded.

"No."

"He can tie your hands in front of you or behind your back. Put your hands out now, or we'll do it behind the back. That gets uncomfortable fast."

"Miguel, do you think you need to do this?" Scott asked.

"Why, yes, Mr. Bennett, sir, I do."

Even if Scott couldn't see it yet, I could tell it wouldn't take much for Miguel to turn on him completely. "We can tie her up and take her with us, or I can shoot her. You said no shooting. Yet."

Scott nodded to the curly-headed man. I presented my hands, and he wrapped the rope around my wrists in a criss-cross fashion, before securing it with a knot at the underside—where I'd have a harder time getting to it with my teeth. Assuming they all looked away from me long enough for me to attempt such a thing.

"Anybody up there want this damned thing?" Leo called.

Miguel shoved me toward the blond, who caught

me around the waist and leered at me. Scott stood by, obviously displeased with the way things were going and how insignificant he had become to the situation.

Miguel knelt down, holstering his gun for a few seconds. He retrieved the laptop and handed it to Scott. Then he took out his gun and pulled back the slide. Oh, that was such a bad thing. Clearly, he meant business. He meant to hurt someone.

"No!" I shrieked.

"We don't need extra baggage." Miguel aimed his weapon at Leo.

"If you hurt him, I—" I stopped. I'd what? The other men all looked at me expectantly for a second, waiting for me to finish my threat. I said a little prayer to Jude again, and it came to me in a flash.

"If you hurt him, I won't tell you what I did with the backup copy."

I should probably go to church more often. The effect was immediate and impressive. Miguel lowered his gun. Then he leapt to his feet and got right in Scott's face.

"There's a backup copy?"

"Of course not." Scott laughed uneasily. "I know how sensitive this stuff is."

"I made a copy," I told them.

Scott rolled his eyes. "That's not even a good bluff, Sabrina. How would you do that? It's password protected."

My turn to roll my eyes. "I got Andy to help me." Scott had met our accounting firm's resident computer wizard a few times and disliked him intensely. Apparently white slavery and consorting with hit men was okay in Scott's moral code, but being gay wasn't.

"Why would you do that?" he asked.

"I was trying to do you a favor. I knew you'd need the information for your meeting, so I figured we'd copy the whole hard drive onto a flash drive, and I'd express ship it to your hotel. It seemed a little easier than mailing the whole thing. Also, safer, because I figured you'd get upset if the machine got damaged or lost—but it would be no big deal to lose a backup copy."

Miguel and Scott exchanged stares. Scott spoke first. "I don't believe you."

Miguel returned his attention to Leo and raised his gun.

"What about you, Miguel?" I strained to break free from the blond as his partner turned in my direction.

"Do you want to trust that I'm lying about this? Do you want to kill him and piss me off? For all you know, everything on that laptop is on its way to the FBI right this second. Do you want to take that chance? You seem more practical than my ex-boyfriend here."

The big man pursed his lips and holstered his gun again. Then he reached down and helped Leo out of the grave.

As soon as Leo was above ground again, Miguel grabbed another length of rope. He began binding Leo's hands as he talked. "Okay, sweet thing. Tell me where it is."

His voice sounded hopeful, and I don't think it was because he wanted me to cooperate. I gave him his wish.

"Look, Chico. Anything you or Harpo want, you'll have to beat out of me."

"I was hoping you'd say that," he grinned. He secured Leo's wrists and spun around like a tornado. As he did, the blond released his hold on me, like he knew what was coming and wanted to get out of the way. Miguel backhanded me so hard I staggered and landed flat on my back on the ground. I pressed a clammy hand to the burning spot on my cheek.

"That's going to leave a bruise."

"Hey! Lighten up, Miguel!" Scott shouted. When Miguel's eyebrow lifted, Scott spoke again, in a voice designed to soothe a rabid dog. "Listen, Chris is meeting us at the airpark. He's a persuasive guy. Why don't we let him talk to her?"

Miguel sneered at Scott as the blond dragged me to my feet and clamped his hand around my waist again.

"Fine." He turned to face me. "We're flying out of here this afternoon. If you tell us where the backup is before our plane takes off, I leave you two alive at the airpark. If you don't, I shoot you both and dump your bodies from the plane three states away. Over woods or a lake, that'd be good. It will take weeks, maybe months, for anyone to figure out what became of you two. By then, I'll be drinking rum and coke in Cozumel, and remembering you fondly."

He flashed something that was supposed to be a smile but was entirely devoid of humor.

"Since remembering fondly is about all you can do with women lately," Scott muttered, continuing some earlier argument of theirs.

"Listen up, college boy." Miguel lunged toward Scott. "If you want her alive, you better stop talking like that. Okay?"

As Miguel dove toward Scott, Leo also moved in that direction, with his head down like a bull about to charge the matador. Caught in a rundown, Scott didn't know which of them was a bigger threat, and his panicked eyes darted back and forth. But since Miguel had the gun, he won the bid for Scott's attention. Scott took one hand off the laptop and gave Miguel a hard shove backwards, staggering as he did so. Leo was beside him by then, and with his bound hands, he wrenched the handle of the laptop bag away from Scott. Then he turned and ran toward the stone wall, tossing the laptop over the side. He leaned his hands on it and sprang over easily, grabbing up the laptop and heading toward the wooded field beside the cemetery.

"You go, Leo! Run!" I shouted after him.

Miguel tore his attention from Scott and took off after Leo, vaulting over the wall.

"Scott, he's your friend, you could help him." I wasn't sure how, but surely he could do something.

Out of left field, he asked, "Why were you even home last night, Sabrina? None of this would be happening if you'd been out like you said you'd be."

His blue eyes burned into my own, fierce and a little desperate.

"Um, I was home because I live there? We've been over this. I hurt my knee."

"You're not acting very hurt today."

"I'm coasting on the adrenaline rush of sheer terror, thanks to you and your fine new friends, Scott."

"I told Hector you'd be out late, so he got in touch with a friend and had him send someone to our condo for the laptop. Hell, I figured you'd never know anything had happened."

"I did hurt my knee!" I gestured to the scraped and bruised area on my leg. "And some other things went wrong, too. So I came home early. That's the truth. All I knew was that I surprised a burglar, and believe me, no one's sorrier than I am."

"Did you bring that gym rat home with you?"

Here we go again. I opened my mouth to scold Scott again and to explain about Evan. But then I realized Scott hadn't been there when I'd told Leo who Evan really was. He'd heard me talking about an agent, but he had no idea who the agent was. To him, Evan Garcia from the gym and Agent Desmond from Homeland Security were two entirely different people. Maybe that would be useful in some way. Now, if only I could stay alive long enough to figure out exactly *how*.

"What if I did bring him home?" I laughed. Right there in a cemetery, surrounded by criminals with guns and knives, I laughed out loud. "I hope you aren't going to give me a speech about infidelity?"

Our latest squabble ended with the loud bang of a gunshot.

Twelve

I flinched against Harpo and gasped. Scott clasped his head in his hands and paced around in a tight circle.

They came back within a minute. Miguel handed the laptop to Scott, who retrieved it from him. Then Miguel put his hands down on the wall and vaulted over it again. Leo had to sit down on the wall first and swing his legs around like an old man. Miguel waited beside him, looking for all the world like a polite young man who wanted to be helpful. A bright bloom of red blossomed on the shoulder of Leo's tan polo shirt. He staggered toward us, legs shaking like a newborn colt's.

"Let's get out of here before some unfriendlies show up," Miguel muttered.

He caught Leo by the uninjured arm and dragged him along the path, toward the Impala that waited in front of the cemetery.

****

"I am so sorry, Leo," I said.

His head leaned against the cool glass of the car window. I was squeezed between him and Miguel, with Scott and the blond seated up front.

He clutched at the injured shoulder, where the bloodstain on his clothing slowly grew bigger. I'd taken a closer look at the wound when they threw me in the car, peeling back the neck of Leo's shirt. I was no doctor, but I felt sure Leo would be all right.

"I don't see any big holes or anything. There's a thing on your shoulder that looks more like a cut or burn or a little of both."

"Ah," Leo chuckled, "A mere flesh wound. I always wanted to say that."

He closed his eyes and spoke again. "Believe it or not, you aren't the first client to land me in a situation like this. I dodged a bullet once, but I guess I'm slowing down."

"Or Miguel is a better shot than you're used to."

"Quiet," Miguel replied.

"Aw, and here I was paying you a compliment."

We drove down O'Donnell, a dingy, old industrial thoroughfare in this dingy, old industrial part of town. I assumed Harpo was looking for the on-ramp to the interstate. As we slowed at the red light, a black truck came up the wider street in front of us and turned, heading back down O'Donnell in the direction from which we'd come. It may not even have been Evan's truck, but I didn't care.

I squirmed around and started pounding on the rear windshield, screaming for help. Miguel caught me around the chest and yanked me way down in the seat, pulling my hair back until my eyes watered.

"Stop this!" he snarled. "Do you want to die right here?"

I struggled against him, but he held me fast. After a while, he loosened his grip and buckled the seatbelt over top of my bound hands. I craned my head over my shoulder. The truck was far in the distance now, nowhere within earshot. I was on my own.

"You should calm down, Sabrina." Scott peered over his shoulder at me. "No one's going to hurt you if you tell them what they want to know."

Did he seriously believe that? Maybe he did, maybe his gift for denial was even greater than I imagined.

I, on the other hand, had no such delusions. Once they got me to this airpark and figured out there was no backup, they'd kill Leo and me. At this point, I only hoped it would be quick. But I doubted that would be the case.

Under my breath, I cursed God for giving me an extra year for nothing. A year since the last round of chemo with nothing to show for it but a nicely toned body that didn't compensate for the mutilated breast no man would ever want to see. A year of remission with nothing at the end of it but a death that would probably be so unpleasant, it would make cancer look like a happy alternative.

We merged out onto I-95 and then almost immediately slowed to a crawl.

"Hell," Scott mumbled.

Every lane was practically at a standstill. The only people getting through were two motorcyclists who were weaving in and out of the stalled traffic. It took us a good ten minutes to travel a few yards. At that point, Scott spied the exit for the Beltway that circles the outskirts of Baltimore and pointed it out to Harpo.

"We're bailing out," he said. "We'll take another way there."

"Where are we going?" I asked.

"We're heading to the airpark near Jess' house. There's a plane waiting to get us out of the state. After we get to Chicago, we switch to a regular passenger plane and go home."

"Home?" I countered. "What home do you mean?"

"Veracruz," he told me. "Home for a while anyway. By the way, if anyone asks, you're Ann Atwood."

I said nothing about the passports I'd seen.

"I assume you're Mr. Atwood?"

"Yeah. We're investment bankers, and Miguel and Tony are our business partners."

"I'd say I'm pleased to meet you," I told Miguel.

"But it wouldn't be true."

Then I glanced up front at the blond guy they called Tony. "You'll always be Harpo to me."

"Sabrina, I appreciate your spunkiness, kiddo," Leo mumbled. "But can it before you piss someone off, okay?"

"Sorry."

He closed his eyes again and gathered himself up against the window.

"Are false identities necessary?" I asked Scott.

"It's a precaution. It slows the other guys down because then they're looking for the wrong people. Anyway, it's how Hector wants it done."

"Hector. Hector Mendoza?" My voice was so cold and so steady I surprised even myself.

"How do you know about the Mendozas?" Scott turned sideways in his seat and exchanged a glance with Miguel.

I licked my lips. My stomach rippled around in my abdomen before settling back into place. What was more nauseating? That now he knew I was aware of his real employers; or that he made no attempt to deny it?

We made good progress since it wasn't rush hour. North of the city we stopped at a fast food place so I could use the bathroom. Scott went inside to get himself a soda, like he was on an ordinary business trip. Harpo stayed in the car with Leo, not that Leo needed much guarding in his present condition. Meanwhile, Miguel boldly barged into the women's room before letting me enter, checking for windows and the like. Just my luck, at this place, the bathrooms were out in the foyer, away from the dining area, so no one saw him. No one saw us at all, as far as I know. I asked him to untie my hands, and he laughed. He was a merry murderer, a man who seemed to enjoy his work.

"Figure out how to do it with your hands tied, or

137

I'll come in there and help you, Beautiful."

I had some notion of writing a message on the bathroom mirror in soap, like people do in the movies. Of course, that requires an actual bar of soap, not liquid. And a mirror is helpful too, something this divey place lacked. A sign on the wall read "Pardon us while we remodel." Great.

When we came out, Miguel took the wheel, and Scott climbed into the back beside me. I suppose they had some notion I'd be more forthcoming with information if Scott tried to talk to me. He didn't ask me anything, only sat there in grim silence.

We traveled north on Route One and kept going, no police trying to stop us.

Scott sighed and laid his head back against the seat.

I'd come back in search of him—in search of my plain vanilla boyfriend and my plain vanilla life. I'd come back to take him to his damned computer and go back to being the old me, something I had stupidly been trying to do ever since the first doctor had said the C word to me. I'd come back this morning, convinced that at worst Scott was a hapless idiot, as much a victim as myself, and that Evan was exaggerating things in order to add me to an undoubtedly long list of female conquests. But now, I found false identities, a private jet, and a man who knew exactly who the Mendozas were and didn't even bother to deny it.

"What did you think was happening to those girls being transported up here?" I asked.

"Honestly? I didn't think about it. Hector assured me the girls were pros and addicts. Look, some girls are like that, Sabrina—they'll do anything for money or drugs. Nice girls like you can't imagine some of the things girls like that will do for the right price."

"Oh, please," I snarled. "Is that your excuse for

cheating? You think I don't know how to give a man what he wants? That is lame, Scott. Maybe you don't know how to please a woman. Maybe that's why you have to pay them."

Miguel chuckled to himself.

"You shut up." I pointed a finger at his reflection in the mirror.

"Ooh, *besamé, mamita.*" He puckered his lips and blew a kiss.

"Do you pay the one you're seeing in Mexico now?" I demanded of Scott.

"Sabrina!" Scott's face blazed bright red. "Will you stop it? In case you hadn't noticed, we aren't alone."

"Do I care? Is she paid help, or is she a freebie from this Mendoza guy?"

"How did you find all this out?" He shifted sideways and glared at me.

"Chemo made me psychic."

"There!" Scott pointed an accusing finger at me. "This is what makes me crazy now. You aren't the same girl anymore. It's not the breast either, although I admit that is pretty damned upsetting to have to look at."

"Oh, you poor thing." This was beginning to sound like nearly every conversation we'd had in the past year.

"You're different inside too," he went on. "You used to be soft, easygoing, and agreeable. You went along with things. If I wanted to go to a football game, you came too, even though you don't like football. Now you say no, and you stay home and read or go to the harbor and sketch."

We stared at one another.

"I tried to tell you about all of this months ago." He lowered his voice to the merest whisper. "I believed you could help me—I don't know, figure it out. But then I decided you'd pick on me and make me feel like a fool. Kind of like you're doing right now."

"Only because you are one." I pursed my lips together, glaring defiantly at him. He'd played the blame game once too often.

Scott leaned in close to me and pressed his lips up right against my ear. "Sabrina, I'm in over my head at this point. I didn't expect them to send *Miguel* back with me. I'm scared, too."

I didn't know whether to believe him or whether it was some ploy. I felt like saying, *It's about time, you stooge*, but I bit my tongue instead. Despite all I knew, I felt a stab of pain. We'd shared a lot of years and a lot of common interests—he'd always been the guy I called when I wanted company at the symphony or the art museum. My Scott had been smart, good-natured, and prep school handsome. I was looking right at him and missing him already.

"I can't help you, Scott." I went back to gazing out the side window.

He leaned closer and laid his hand on my arm. I was about to shrug it away when we heard the siren looming up behind us.

****

"Sir, do you have any idea what the speed limit is here?"

The trooper leaning down to speak was young and tall, with big shoulders that strained at the seams of his uniform. His dark hair was shaved to a severe buzz cut, but on him, it looked cute. He was so young; another one probably young enough to be my son if I'd ever had one. At any rate, he was someone's son, and for her sake, I devoutly wished he had stopped some other car. I bit my lip, waiting for Miguel to whip out the ugly cannon he'd flashed in the cemetery, but it didn't happen.

"Officer, I am so sorry," he said. "I admit I was not paying attention. My friend and his wife back here were getting into a heated discussion, and I guess I got distracted."

What the hell? Where was the gunhappy gangster? Suddenly, he even looked different. He'd bowed his shoulders forward a little so he looked smaller, meeker. Next, he laid his head against the steering wheel, looking as if he was going to burst into tears. Meanwhile, Scott had poked his tongue into his cheek and rolled his eyes at me.

I chanced a glance at Leo, who pried open one bleary eye and returned my gaze with an expression I can only describe as one of guarded hopefulness. His eyes closed again, and he huddled deeper into the leather bomber jacket. Miguel had forced him to put it on back at the fast food place, to cover up the gunshot wound. Now I understood why.

"The limit's fifty, and you were close to eighty, sir." The young trooper peered over the rims of his smoke-tinted shades. "Can I please see your license and registration?"

Miguel motioned to Harpo, who opened the glove compartment as Miguel reached into the breast pocket of his jacket. I could feel the trooper's tension. It rippled off him in wave after wave—all these people in one car, Hispanic guy at the wheel, semi-conscious guy in the back—drunk? Something wasn't adding up. I knew he could see that, but what could he do about it? More importantly, what could I do about it?

"I'm sorry, officer." Miguel passed his license out the window. "The car's a rental, so I'm not used to it."

"We're all carpooling to a business conference, and we were already running late thanks to my wife here," Scott piped up. "And then we hit a huge traffic jam on I-95."

"Yeah." The trooper nodded in sympathy. "A tractor-trailer overturned, and all the lanes were closed for a while. They're hoping to open one of the northbound lanes in the next half-hour."

"We're sorry about this, aren't we, honey?" Scott said to me.

I scowled at him, and the trooper stifled a chuckle. "Fortunately, you two lovebirds aren't my problem."

Miguel handed him the registration from the glove compartment and then sat still, his hands gripping the steering wheel. Clearly, he'd decided killing a cop in broad daylight on a busy road would not help him complete his mission. I was surprised he was that smart.

"I'll be right back." The trooper gave a curt nod and strolled back to his squad car.

Now we'd get somewhere. He'd check Miguel's ID and recognize a fake. I grinned at Miguel's reflection in the mirror, but he met my look with a smile of his own.

"Don't get cocky, beautiful. I'm not a sloppy operator. That's why the boss sent me to keep an eye on your sweetie there."

I looked down first, trying to catch Leo's eye again. I couldn't tell whether he was playing possum or had taken a turn for the worse, but his eyes didn't open.

The trooper returned and handed Miguel his license and papers.

"Your record looks good, Mr. Castillo." He sounded a tad bit surprised. "I'm going to let you go with a written warning."

He began scribbling on his notepad. Could this be happening? I was being abducted at gunpoint, and a cop was standing barely a foot away from me. Was the universe truly that wickedly ironic?

"Hey, excuse me, officer!" I leaned forward and rested my hands on the backs of Miguel and Harpo's seats. Faint red marks replaced the ropes. Scott had scrambled to remove them from Leo and me the second he'd heard that siren. Now, they lay coiled on the floor next to my feet.

I almost blurted out the truth. But if I did that, Miguel and Harpo would go into severe damage control mode. The young trooper would probably be the first to go, and I couldn't live with that on my conscience.

"Yes, ma'am, what is it?" he asked, his voice weary with a day already full of unexpected weirdness.

"Do you work at the—"

What the hell had Evan called those barracks? There could only be so many state trooper barracks in eastern Baltimore County, after all.

"Golden Ring! Do you work at Golden Ring?"

I could feel Scott's gaze boring into the side of my head, but I absolutely didn't look his way, lest I lose my nerve. I felt Leo shift on the other side of me and saw him straighten up and open his eyes.

"Er, yes, I do," the trooper answered me. His pen froze in mid-air, poised above his notepad uncertainly.

Really?" I just about started bouncing up and down in my seat. "Do you know Gloria Petty?"

The cop lowered his notebook to his side and grinned.

"Gloria? Yeah, I know her."

"What a small world, isn't it?"

"Er, yeah, I guess."

Miguel's eyes caught mine in the rearview mirror, and I turned my head away in haste, fixing my gaze on the young trooper.

"You have to tell her you saw me!"

"Ah. And you are?"

"Sabrina O'Hara. We're great friends. Ask her if she's still dating that bounty hunter."

"Sabrina, the officer is busy, honey, and we are

already late." Scott laid a hand on my sleeve, and I flicked it away.

"Now, this won't take a minute, Scott," I said. "I haven't seen Gloria in—well, in a good while. Officer, please tell her I said hello, will you?"

"I'll do that, ma'am." He resumed writing the warning notice for Miguel.

"Ask her if she still has that drawing I made of her the last time I was at the barracks?"

"You've been there?"

"Oh, yeah," I laughed and waved my hand in the air. I wanted him to see the rope burns. I prayed he'd notice them. His head was cocked at a quizzical angle, but that might mean he thought I was wacko.

"I'll certainly let her know I saw you, Miss O'Hara." He handed the notice to Miguel. "But we should all get on our way now, ma'am."

The trooper returned to his squad car, and Miguel pulled back into traffic.

"I cannot wait to punish you, you little bitch." He leered at my reflection in the rearview mirror.

I leaned back in my seat. A burst of sweat trickled down my spine and chilled me. Leo closed his eyes and smiled. "Good try, kiddo."

"You shut up, or I'll kill you without even stopping this car," Miguel snarled at him.

I glared back at his reflection. "Not if you want that backup copy."

Thirteen

A soft autumn mist coated the car windows. We'd been driving in a sullen silence for a half-hour. We'd come off Route One and were well beyond both the city and even Baltimore County. I was confused and then downright uneasy as we merged onto Route 24, the main highway near Jess's house. We were coming into the mostly rural county of Harford, and I knew we were maybe ten minutes from the airpark Scott had mentioned. Ten minutes left until my bluff ran out, along with my life and Leo's.

We stopped at a red light, and I could see the Park 'n' Ride lot, where Jess and I would wait in the morning when I stayed with her. On the opposite side of the street stood a nondescript strip mall— mega-grocery store, hair and nail salon, bad Chinese restaurant. Suburban culture at its finest. Next door to the strip mall stood a shabby old storefront that had been converted into an antiques emporium. They sold surprisingly nice stuff. Once, near the end of chemo, Jess had taken me into the place and bought me a beautiful Japanese tea set I'd admired. It occupied a place of honor in the china cabinet back at my condo, and I wondered whether I'd ever see it or my home again.

When I'd thought I might die, I'd made a list of prized possessions and who should get them. Scott would keep my books and CDs, because we had a lot of the same tastes, and my clothes would go to my sister Angela for the same reason. I knew my mother would want the old paintings and sketches I'd made, but I'd left a note to give at least one of them to my dad and to let him choose. I hadn't owned the tea set when I made my list, and thinking of it now, I hoped someone would give it back to Jess. If, as I suspected, a bullet in the brain was what awaited me at the end of this ride. Not right away, of course. No way would I be that lucky. First, they'd want to question me about the backup's whereabouts, inflict a little pain and fear. They could inflict all the pain they wanted, but I was not going to give them the satisfaction of showing fear. I'd already made my peace with the prospect of death last year, I wasn't afraid of it. Now all I had to do was convince my racing heart that the mode of death made no difference.

We passed the strip mall and then another one. A little further along, the vista opened out on either side, and I glimpsed a couple of cornfields in the distance. Then came a cluster of old Victorian houses, the remnants of an old railroad town. In the midst of them, we turned and cruised down an empty two-lane road. More corn fields to one side of us. But opposite the fields lay a sprawling business and industrial park. Row after row of ugly squat concrete buildings housed a propane company, a furniture warehouse, and a plumber, among other things. Their hulking, grey exteriors blended perfectly against the deepening metal color of the clouded sky.

Miguel found a driveway I hadn't noticed and turned down another road running behind all these buildings. The road curved in a semi-circle, and we followed it around to a low, cream-colored building, some sort of hangar or workshop. Small private planes were parked at various angles on a wide tarmac, and an orange windsock waved from the roof of a taller building in the distance. Miguel slowed the car to a halt and got out. He opened the car door and Scott emerged, offering me his hand with a gallant flourish.

"No thanks." I pushed past him hurriedly, thrusting a hand at his chest. They hadn't bothered to retie us after the incident with the trooper, rightly trusting Leo's injury and my fear to keep us in check.

Miguel scrambled around to the front of the car and halted in front of me. He reached out and yanked me closer to him, nearly spinning me off my feet. I honestly thought for a second he'd dislocated my arm. It looked like payback time was upon me.

Leo emerged from the car next, his face pale and splotchy. He kept his right arm folded up against his chest and took deep breaths when he walked. I couldn't tell whether his pain came solely from his shoulder wound, which looked relatively minor, or whether he'd maybe hurt something else in vaulting over that stone wall.

The air had changed in the hour or so we'd been in the car. A cold front had washed down from the north, and I wasn't dressed for it at all. The wind whipped itself around us, and I folded my arms over my chest, tucking each hand into the opposite sleeve of my thin sweater. Miguel tightened his hold on my upper left arm and forced me forward. I could feel my arm already beginning to bruise.

"Will you lighten up?" I snapped. "Do you think I've got a machete up my sleeve or something?"

He flashed his evil smile in my direction, but he didn't ease his grip. I decided I'd better shut up, since he enjoyed my temperamental displays entirely too much.

Scott moved ahead of us and threw open the side door of the metal building, leading us into a repair facility. An engine sat on one end of a long metal table in the center of the room. A big overhead door filled one wall, but it was closed right now. The other walls were covered with pegboard and tools hung from every available hook. One of those big red toolboxes, like my dad has in his garage, stood to one side of the door. An array of wrenches and screwdrivers were laid out on top of it. Miguel caught me looking at them and jerked me away from them. The only light came from rows of bare fluorescent panels suspended from the ceiling. There were no windows.

Scott laid his laptop on the metal table, then moved to a far corner of the room. Leo followed him, slumping to the floor in a clumsy heap. He leaned his head back against the big overhead door and closed his eyes.

"Does it hurt much?" I asked.

He shook his head, but he didn't speak. I wasn't sure if he meant, *No, it doesn't hurt* or possibly *Can't talk now, busy bleeding to death, kiddo.*

I kept telling myself I wasn't afraid, and one death is much like another. In fact, there's a big difference between the prospect of lying bald and weak in a hospice bed, surrounded by family and friends, versus the possibility of being tortured and shot, left to bleed on a greasy concrete floor with no one to hold your hand.

"Scott, what's going to happen next?" I asked.

He paced back and forth in his lawyer pose, hands on hip, trench coat and suit jacket thrust back. "I'm sure we can all come to an understanding."

The door opened behind us, and a freckle-faced man stole into the room.

"Chris says to tell you he'll be here soon." His voice was surprising in its mildness. "He's talking to Hector."

Scott nodded and continued to pace after the freckle-faced man left us.

"Can you stop squeezing the life out of my arm if I promise not to overpower you with my incredibly crafty feminine wiles?" I said to Miguel.

He flung me into the middle of the room, letting go of my arm as he did so. He pointed to a bench beside the table.

"Sit."

"What a gentleman." I studied the paint-speckled bench for a few seconds, not wanting to sit down if that paint was wet. Then I remembered I looked like crap by now anyway. My fashion statement consisted of an oversized sweater and a hooker skirt, and not one drop of makeup on my face. What the hell was the big deal about a little grey paint on my ass? It wasn't even my skirt.

As I turned and sat down, Miguel caught my chin in his hand, squeezing until I felt the bones start to grind. Then he smothered my mouth with his own. I flailed at him with fists that felt tiny and childish next to his huge bulk.

"You can tell me where it is now." He chuckled as he disengaged from me, and I knew he was looking forward to the moment when I admitted I didn't have a backup. I guess you couldn't succeed in his line of work unless you took some pleasure in it.

I wiped the back of my hand across my mouth and then spit on the floor.

"I'll tell Hector Mendoza. Why don't you call him for me?"

Behind me, Scott spluttered.

"I don't think Hector Mendoza will bother himself with the likes of you." Miguel laughed as he turned to Harpo. "Go tell Chris to hurry the hell up. My trigger finger's getting itchy."

Harpo ran out of the workshop, the heavy door slamming behind him. They'd mentioned this Chris guy at the cemetery. Presumably, if Miguel was a sergeant and Hector was a general, Chris must be something like a captain. What did they consider Scott—another captain or a foolish traitor from the enemy army to be disposed of when their business was completed? While I was thinking about all this, Leo struggled to his feet.

"I'm feeling incredibly thirsty." He licked his lips.

"Too bad," Miguel snapped.

"Miguel." Scott glared at him. "Get him some water."

Miguel curled up his lip and walked over to a utility sink.

"No cups." He turned around and shrugged.

I got up and walked toward Leo.

"Stand still," Miguel warned.

"Oh, or what?" I retorted. "You won't kill me until you get that backup."

I walked over to Leo and took him by his uninjured arm. The whole time, I could feel the rubbery weakness of my own legs. I wondered if Miguel could see them wobble and hoped he wasn't enjoying the sight of my fear. I led Leo over to the sink and turned on the water. Then I cupped my hands under it and held them out to him.

"I am so sorry I got you into this, Lee," I said.

"Me too. Bree." He managed a mischievous little grin. He tried to wipe his mouth with the back of his hand, but his injured shoulder stopped him.

I did it for him, remembering a time when my little brother was sick, and I had done the same thing for him. As I finished up, Harpo burst into the room.

"Chris says, 'she wants to talk to Hector, let the little lady talk to Hector.' He says bring her to the plane. We'll take her right to him."

Miguel and Harpo shrugged at one another—their look said that Chris, whoever he was, might be startlingly crazy, but no one dared to disagree with him.

I didn't like this development at all. I'd expected

more negotiating, possibly even some pistol-whipping, which I had decided I could take. I had been stalling, hoping against hope someone would find us and break up this little party. I didn't want to get on some plane with a bunch of armed men, for God's sake.

Harpo stalked across the room toward me. He grabbed Leo by his injured shoulder and pulled him away from me.

Leo let out a horrible sound, half-whimper and half-growl. He stumbled against the wall beside the sink but didn't fall.

"We're gonna have us a lot of in-flight entertainment, if you get my drift." Harpo got right up in my face and leered at me.

Leo reached out a shaking hand and caught Harpo by the shoulder. "Leave her alone!"

Miguel started across the room, tugging his gun from its holster.

"Now, wait a minute," Scott started to say. He didn't understand yet how utterly unimportant he'd become.

Miguel paid him no mind as he curled his finger around the trigger.

I didn't know what else to do—I dove forward and head-butted Harpo. People do that all the time in movies, and it looks easy. I am here to tell you, it's not. I saw stars, and I heard birds tweeting, too. I groaned and clasped my head between my hands.

Harpo fell back onto the floor, gushing blood from his nose, and Miguel fired his weapon. But not at me. He shot Leo, again. Only this time, Leo stood about two feet from him—not a distant, moving target.

I started shaking with anger and screaming—no, shrieking, over and over again. I scrambled over to Leo as he flew up against a wall and then collapsed to the floor.

A thick red trail marked his path down the wall, and on his left shoulder below the collarbone, a dark splotch appeared almost instantly. Blood sprayed out at the back of his shirt this time, the huge wound nothing at all like the one on his other shoulder. His mouth opened and closed a few times in silent surprise.

"Damn." His fingers twitched as he tried to reach up to touch the wound, but the damage done by the bullet prevented him from raising his arm. He slumped forward, and I reached behind him, laying my own hands over the back of the wound in some panic-stricken attempt to hold in the blood. Needless to say, that didn't work. It poured out over my hands like water from a faucet, running down my wrists and drenching the sleeves of Jenna's sweater. The whole shape of Leo's shoulder felt wrong now, and he winced when I touched him.

"*Puta!*" Miguel spat at me. "I can keep doing that until you learn to shut up and stop causing trouble! I got eleven shots left, and I can empty them all into him without killing him right away. You wanna watch me?"

"I'll kill you myself if I ever get the chance!" I shrieked at him. "And it won't take me a whole clip."

"Miguel, stop this!" Scott demanded, but it came out sounding wheedling and pathetic. He had inched his way almost to the side door and looked ready to run away at any second. That made it a lot harder for him to sound threatening. Miguel didn't even spare him a glance. He leveled his weapon at me.

"I'm getting more than a little sick of you. A woman's like a horse, and too much spirit ain't a good thing."

Behind Miguel, the door slammed open, the steely sky casting the new arrival in a dark silhouette.

"Oh, Hell. Chris, I can explain—" Scott began to

grovel, actually covering his face with his hands.

But the new arrival ignored him, instead stepping forward and pressing a gun to Miguel's skull.

"Put it down," said the shadowy figure. Evan stepped into the blue glow of the fluorescent lights.

Miguel squatted down and laid his weapon on the floor. Then he rose and laced his hands behind his head. Harpo crawled away from Leo and me. The last I saw of him, he was hiding under the big table with the engine on top of it.

I scurried forward to pick up Miguel's gun, but that head-butt had knocked me for a loop. When I tried to stand, I fell forward on my knees instead. Evan darted his eyes in my direction, and Miguel used that split second of distraction to spring backwards and elbow him in the ribs.

I grabbed the gun and followed Harpo under the table, but he'd kept on going, I didn't know where. I came out the other side and found myself next to the toolbox. Slumping against it, I watched Evan and Miguel fight it out. At first I was too dizzy to do anything, and then I was afraid. Yeah, I know how to fire a gun, but that's a long way from knowing how to hit what you're aiming at. I could aim for Miguel and hit Evan instead. That was not a chance I wanted to take.

I shook my head a few times, laid the gun on top of the toolbox, and then hauled myself up by hanging onto its sides. I felt a little better once I was up on my feet again, although my head still throbbed.

On the other side of the table, Leo had gotten to his feet too, and I took that as a good sign. He managed a few steps and then slumped forward, his upper body flopping across the tabletop.

I picked the gun up again, careful to lay my finger along the side of the barrel. *Your finger is your safety*, Daddy said. *You don't put it on the trigger unless you mean to pull.* Hah. Who the hell was I fooling?

As I looked on, Evan caught Miguel in a fierce headlock. The two swung around the room again and again in an eerie silent dance.

Scott had flattened himself against the wall beside the door, apparently waiting to see who came out on top before throwing his support to anyone.

Evan and his burly opponent waltzed each other into the center of the room. Miguel hurled himself backward, and Evan slammed up against the steel table so hard he went down. He seemed conscious but dazed.

Miguel leaned over Evan, attempting to get hold of his gun. But Evan wasn't as addled as he'd pretended. He yanked the big bear forward by the collar of his jacket and flipped him backwards onto the floor. I could see black metal glinting between them, and I knew Evan's gun could go off at any second.

"Scott, make them stop!" I pleaded.

Scott stared at me like someone who didn't even speak English, and his eyes were so round, he could've been a cartoon character. If he'd stopped Miguel, I could have forgiven him a lot of things. But he didn't. He didn't try to help Evan, and he didn't even try to help his own companion. He cowered and waited to see who would win.

"Damn you." I ran forward with the gun grasped in both hands, ready to act.

"Get away from him!" I yelled.

Miguel spied me out the corner of his eye and rolled onto his back, flashing a contemptuous grin. He laughed and babbled a string of obscene endearments as he reached out to grab my ankle with one hand. He'd caught the grip of Evan's gun in his other hand, swinging it away from him toward me.

I put my finger on the trigger. Killing a man is entirely too easy. It seems like it will be hard to pull the trigger—physically hard—but it's not. It's like pressing the lever on a bottle of pesticide. That's about all the strength anybody needs.

Miguel was maybe a foot away from me, and his head exploded all over the place. No doubt he'd loaded the gun with some extra-deadly ammo, which had turned out to be bad news for him. A fine shower of red splashed over me—my hair, my face, in my eyes and on my lips. I was shouting *No!* over and over again and still pulling the trigger. Evan scrambled to his feet and caught me around the waist, dragging me backwards.

"Enough, babe, that's enough," he murmured.

My grip relaxed suddenly, and Evan caught the gun before it could bounce onto the concrete. I'm not sure how many times I fired, but I do know I kept my promise to Miguel: I didn't need to empty the clip in order to kill the guy. Lucky first time, I guess.

Evan pushed me down on the bench beside the big metal table.

I looked at my hands, which were painted red and sticky with Leo's blood—maybe Miguel's, too. They didn't feel like a part of me anymore. Beside me, Miguel lay flat on his back, the vacant stare of his one remaining eye fixed on me. Dimly, I became aware Evan was speaking again.

"Where's the skinny guy with the curly hair? And your fiancé?"

He made a circuit of the room, but Harpo was nowhere to be found. Neither was Scott.

"They're going to come back with reinforcements," he muttered. "Damn." He whipped out a cell phone and punched a button. "Chuck, where the hell are you, man?"

A short pause.

"Two minutes away isn't good enough! I'm in

155

here alone, and I'm going to be badly outnumbered soon. Yeah, she's all right."

His eyes roved over me in a way that seemed neither professional nor detached. He reached forward and brushed something from my face, and his hand came away bloody.

I remembered how I'd looked at him last night in the cemetery, how the sight of his face and hands speckled with blood had repulsed me. If he felt the same way looking at me now, he hid it much better than I had done.

Two of them got away," he continued. "I already talked to the airpark manager. That's what I was doing when I heard the screaming. Nothing's taking off from here."

"Three," I put in softly.

"Hang on." He spoke into the phone. "What?"

"Three. Three got away. They kept talking about waiting for someone else, someone who'd been ordering the rest of them around."

"Four," Leo added. "That guy with the freckles."

We both shrugged at Evan, as if the number of bad guys was our fault.

Evan relayed this news to his associate as he paced around the workshop. He fell silent and listened for a few seconds.

"If that's what Tyrese wants me to do," he said. "No, she's not hurt. A safe house? Do we have one around here?"

"Can you walk?" He spared Leo some attention.

Leo nodded. He was looking paler by the minute. Evan found a reasonably clean cloth on a shelf behind us and wadded it up.

"Here, put pressure on it." Tucking the flip phone between his shoulder and his chin, Evan wrapped the cloth around the wound.

Leo emitted a funny, high-pitched, cat-like whimper, but he laid his hand over the cloth and held it there obediently.

Evan pressed his fingertips to the inside of Leo's wrist and paused, frowning.

"Okay, I'm getting them out of here." Evan returned his attention to the phone. "Anywhere. Do you have local cops closing down the road in both directions? Good. We need an ambulance, too. I'm guessing the lawyer's about ten, maybe even five minutes from bleeding out."

"I am?" Leo swiveled his head drunkenly and looked at me, as if I should know the answer.

Evan snapped the phone closed and jammed it into his back pocket, trying to help me up. I shook off his touch and covered my face with my hands, disregarding the bitter copper smell of blood.

"We have to get out of here fast," he said.

"I can't." I swallowed the sharp tang of bile in my throat. When I wobbled to my feet, I wound up on the floor on all fours, gasping and choking.

"Baby, you have to get up. There are more of these goons around, and I don't have any back up. Come on."

"You'll want this," Leo murmured. He'd been leaning his weight against that metal table. Now he straightened up, weaving from side to side as he did, and I discovered he'd been covering the laptop with his body.

"Good man," Evan said to him, looking a little surprised.

To tell the truth, I was surprised, too.

"Hey, I defend criminals, but I do have standards." Leo smiled. "I don't help anybody who hits women. Or shoots me. I'm funny that way."

"I didn't mean to kill him," I said.

Evan knelt beside me and put an arm around my back. "Have your moral crisis later. Now let's go."

He pulled me to my feet, then left me, and

picked up the laptop. He put a hand on Leo's back and propelled him to the door.

Outside, the falling drops had become a little bigger, a little more emphatic about definitely becoming real rain. Ash-colored clouds obscured any remaining evidence of the sun. The cold rain felt good, snapping me back into the present. Droplets of blood trickled down my face, the rain sending them down the front of my sweater in a thin rust-colored rivulet. I held out my hands, but the blood on them was too thick to be easily cleansed. Evan led me to a black truck, the same one I'd seen earlier in the morning. He hoisted Leo into the back seat, then he tried to help me up into the front, but I grabbed his arms and clung to him.

"It's all true. Everything you told me about Scott." I held onto him for a several seconds until I heard what sounded like a goose honking. I found myself sobbing all over his shirt and swallowing down great mouthfuls of salty tears and snot. I opened my mouth to speak again, but he pressed his fingers over my lips and shook his head.

"We need to get away." He practically lifted me into the seat, then closed the door, and went to the driver's side.

"Seat belt."

I nodded vacantly. He reached over, as Ben had done yesterday and strapped me into the seat like a little child.

Fourteen

As we high-tailed it out of there, several county sheriffs' cars arrived, along with a couple of unmarked vehicles. The deafening wail of sirens swirled around us, making conversation impossible. Evan sped down the two-lane road we'd used when we'd arrived at the airpark earlier. As we approached the intersection with the state road, I saw an armada of sheriff's cars and a couple of waiting ambulances.

"How did you find us?" I asked him.

"For one thing, your friend Jess—she's a real weak link, you know that? She gave up your lawyer's name in a heartbeat, so I went to his office where I found someone named Rose. The housekeeper?"

"Rose?"

"She'd gone to see your secretary Sandy," Evan said to Leo. "Rose thought you guys might be in trouble."

"How would Rose know?" I asked.

Leo's voice came out faint, as though he was about to doze off. "She's like that."

I looked down at my hands, currently dripping blood onto one of the floor mats.

"Yeah," I remembered our exchange in front of the refrigerator. "I guess she is."

"Also," Leo rasped, "I gave her a note for Sandy saying I was in trouble."

"The grocery list!"

Leo chuckled proudly, but it degenerated into a wheezy noise that ended with a little whistle. Evan glanced in the rear view mirror with an expression of alarm and drove even faster.

Evan noticed the way I held my hands. "There's a towel under your seat. It's a little greasy, but it's better than nothing."

I leaned down and pulled it out, but after wiping for a while, I had to admit I couldn't possibly get all the blood off without soap and hot water. I settled for wrapping my hands up in the towel to dry them and keep them from messing up his truck.

"Did Gloria Petty get my message to you?" I asked, mostly to distract myself from the mess and from the funny noise coming from Leo.

"Yeah. That was the next break. After your little shout-out, her trooper friend radioed Gloria at the barracks to let her know something was up. Then he followed you guys at a distance until the car exited onto this road up ahead."

Was it incredibly petty that I bristled when he called Trooper Blondie by her first name? Yes, I suppose it was. He was still explaining how he'd found us, so I wrestled the little green-eyed monster into submission and listened to him speak.

"Chuck—he's another agent—he looked at a map, and we figured you guys were either heading for the airpark or a dairy farm. I flipped a coin, and it came up dairy farm. Lucky you, I ignored it. How you holding on back there, Penn?"

Leo answered with a wheeze, followed by a spasm of disturbingly wet coughing.

"He shot him in the shoulder," I said to Evan. "I didn't think that would be serious."

"You watch too much TV," he answered. "There are a lot of blood vessels going to the lungs in that area. And the lung itself might be collapsed at this point."

Well, golly. I guess the part about having been an Army medic was true, anyway. He swung the steering wheel hard to the right, and I became distracted once again trying to stay upright in my seat during a sharp turn. His tires screeched as he pulled the car to a halt in the parking lot of an abandoned gas station. More sheriffs' cars were blocking access to Route 24. I knew the road in front of us ran past my friend Jess's house to the south of the airpark and that it continued north, past farmland and forests and on into Pennsylvania. I assumed the cops had blocked the opposite end of the road behind us. The only things getting through were their own black and whites and a whole bunch of unmarked police cars. One of these turned into the lot and ground to a halt beside Evan's truck. Paramedics dashed from the back of one of the ambulances I'd seen earlier.

"Looks like your ride's here, Penn." Evan got out of the truck, and I did, too, because I wasn't sure what I was supposed to do.

The cold rain wasn't as welcome this time. It chilled me right away after the warmth of the truck interior, and I started to shiver. Maybe that wasn't because of the temperature.

Leo remained in the truck, smiling faintly, his gaze distant and foggy. A sheen of sweat coated his doughy-white face.

The paramedics rushed toward us, and Evan opened the rear door of his truck for them. They made Leo lie down, and they scooted him out and shifted him onto a gurney. He lay back and let them, a tight, determined grin fixed on his face.

Leo—with all his casual sex and glib self-centeredness—Leo had been the better man. When he'd guessed how far into this Scott was, he hadn't even hesitated about choosing sides.

"Thank you for everything, Leo." I squeezed his hand. "You're a good person. A really good person."

I tried not to sound too surprised, but he heard it in my voice anyway.

He opened his mouth to speak but wheezing seemed to be the only sound he could make anymore. He kissed my hand as they wheeled him away.

"He'll be all right." Evan laid a hand on my shoulder. "He made it this far."

"Can I go with him?"

Two men had emerged from the sedan parked beside us. The first looked like a younger version of my own dad, built wide and low with a round, bald head. Unlike my dad, however, he added the fashionable accessories of a reddish-brown goatee and a windbreaker emblazoned with ICE on the back.

"I don't think that'd be a good idea, Ms. O'Hara," he said.

"And you are—?"

"I'm Special Agent Chuck Neville. And this is our supervisor, Senior Special Agent Tyrese Campbell."

Ah, the dreaded Tyrese. He was surprisingly good-looking. I'd expected someone frumpy and out of shape, but, in fact, he was a slender African-American man with skin the color of milk chocolate. He was clean-shaven, with neatly trimmed hair. He looked like a Federal agent is supposed to look, nothing at all like Evan. He also looked like a man who follows all the rules. There are a lot of those guys in accounting, the guys who think there's a right and wrong way to do everything. One of the partners at our accounting firm even believes there's a right and wrong way to staple a document, and it's not straight across the top. That's the way the copier does it, so of course that's wrong. The secretaries have to staple everything by hand when they make copies for Mr. Weitzel. I could look at Tyrese Campbell and sense he'd get along famously with Mr. Weitzel.

"Okay." I stuck out my hands. "Go ahead and

cuff me. It's got to be better than the rope."

He arched an eyebrow and blinked a few times. "I'll reserve the right to do that later, if Evan turns out to be wrong about you."

I lowered my hands.

"The FBI has a safe house north of Baltimore we can use." He turned his attention to Evan, in effect dismissing me from consideration.

"So you decided they're in on this, after all?"

"Yeah," Tyrese's tone was grudging and irritated. "They deserve to be included, I suppose. Especially Pete."

"Ya think?" Evan said, clearly resuming some earlier challenge to Tyrese's authority.

Tyrese huffed and frowned but didn't answer his comment directly. "You can contact our satellite office and get the exact address from them. Get her there, and FBI will provide security, at least for today. And provided she doesn't run away from you again, of course."

A muscle twitched in the side of Evan's face, and Tyrese thrust out his chin. You could almost smell all the manly hormones in the air.

"Here." Evan thrust the blood-encrusted laptop at his boss. "You'll want to get this up to Philly and see if they can recover any of the data."

Tyrese took the computer and eyed its condition with some dismay.

Before he could speak again, Chuck opened his mouth. "Ty, we should move closer to the site. Make sure our agents are rounding everyone up."

Tyrese ducked his head in agreement. He pointed a finger at Evan before climbing back into his vehicle. "I'll talk with you later."

Chuck climbed into the driver's seat, raising a hand in farewell, and they headed down the road toward the airpark.

"Let's get you back into the heat." Evan laid a

hand on the small of my back and walked me around to the passenger seat.

The temperature had been dropping steadily, and the whole time Tyrese talked, my teeth had been chattering. I was eager to climb back into the truck.

Evan was wearing jeans and a turtleneck and a black leather jacket. Unlike me, he'd apparently had a chance to listen to a weather report today, and I briefly resented him for that luxury. I pictured him waking up in his own apartment or house or wherever he lived, eating breakfast and watching the morning news while I was sleeping in a cab and being threatened by a bunch of leering strangers. But he'd come after me anyway, even after the things I'd said in the garage and in the police barracks. Even after the slap in the face.

"I didn't think you'd be looking for me," I confessed. "I figured I'd pushed my luck way too far with that slap."

He smiled quietly, walked around to the cargo box at the rear of the truck and opened it. "Go ahead and get inside where it's dry."

I did, and in a minute he came around to my side of the cab and laid an old plaid blanket over my legs.

"Better?" he asked, and I nodded.

He closed my door and then climbed into the driver's seat. All around us, cops milled to and fro, speaking on cell phones and walkie-talkies. No one paid us any attention. I was out of immediate danger, and Evan had his orders. But instead of putting the car into gear right away, Evan leaned his head back against the seat and spoke to me.

"It did piss me off at the time. A lot. But I know what you're going through. Once I learned something ugly about someone close to me. I understand wanting to lash out at the person who delivers the news."

"What made me angry was you not believing me," he said quietly. "I don't know why either. I'm used to people getting defensive when I tell them things they don't want to hear about their darling family members. I felt so sure you'd believe me. Because we had such a rapport from the first day you walked into the gym. Or I thought we did, anyway."

"I'm sorry I disappointed you." I fiddled with the frayed hem of the old blanket.

"You didn't disappoint me. Scared the bejeezus out of me, definitely. But you didn't disappoint me." He massaged his forehead, and then he began to laugh.

I frowned at him.

"You're amazing." He turned in his seat and studied me, his face all boyish admiration and his eyes gleaming.

"Me? Why?"

"Mainly because you're still alive, and you're free," he said. "Not many people can say that when the Mendozas make up their mind to come after them."

"Yeah, but an awful lot of my still being alive is because of your help," I reminded him.

"You were holding your own in that apartment when I got there last night. And you coped okay in that hangar. In fact, I owe *you* my life this time around. I do like a girl who doesn't fold up under pressure."

He stretched a hand out toward me and brushed back a strand of my hair again. It must have looked horrible, with flecks of dried blood and God knows what else, but he didn't mind. He tipped my chin up to him. I shifted a little uneasily, extremely conscious of his hands touching my face. They were firm and a bit hard, but not rough. My eyes closed, and I breathed deep, absorbing the spicy, woodsy smell of his aftershave. The lush scent was almost strong enough to cover the bitter scent of blood.

"Sabrina." He cupped my face in his hands and then said it again, like he simply enjoyed the sound of my name on his lips. I know I enjoyed it immensely. When he leaned forward and kissed me ever so lightly, he tasted all minty and clean, like he'd just brushed his teeth. A picture of him flashed in my head for a second: Evan in front of a mirror, brushing his teeth and combing back his hair and thinking about me as he tied it up in a ponytail. Evan being nervous and self-conscious—was that even possible? And because of me?

A tingly warmth blazed up from deep in my stomach, like that feeling that comes after drinking an expensive, aged scotch. I dropped the blanket onto the floor of the cab, and I clasped my reddened hands around his neck, hugging him closer to me. I'm not sure whether I wanted him near me, or whether I wanted to block out everything else that had happened to me. Maybe both.

"Hush," he whispered in my ear, and I heard myself making those goose noises again. His hands were all tangled up in my hair. Now they slipped down a bit, massaging my back. His fingers stroked me through the thin sweater, unintentionally brushing over the outline of my bra strap. He held me tighter and kissed me again, more earnestly this time.

I had a vague notion I should warn him away from something, but I couldn't think what exactly.

Then he stopped kissing me and spoke, and everything came back to me. "When I picked up Gloria's message, I got yours too, babe. The one from the cemetery."

"I didn't know who else to call. My dad's away."

"Oh, man, Sabrina." He pressed his forehead

against mine and sighed. "I thought I'd never see you again in this life."

And that was too close. In entirely too many ways.

"No, no! Don't!" I cried in a panic, my dream rushing back over me like a tidal wave. "Let me go!" I squirmed free of his arms and jumped out of the truck.

Two cops a few yards away glanced up at the sound of the slamming door, then went back to talking to one another.

Evan's expression betrayed how badly I'd hurt him. He emerged from the driver's side of the car, gave his door a ferocious slam, and grimaced at the ground as he came around to my side of the vehicle.

"I'm sorry." He'd taken me to mean I wasn't interested in him in that way, and who could blame him?

But I'd only meant no to touching me, no to the experience of another man turning away in disgust. "You don't have to be sorry about all of it," I told him, wringing my hands.

He shook his head slowly, still not looking at me. His soft laugh hung between us in the cold rain, a little puff of white frost.

"You're confusing, did you know that?"

"I'm hoping you like that in a woman?"

He didn't answer me directly, but I saw the ghost of a smile flutter over his lips.

"I don't know if you've noticed," I said. "But I'm kind of going through a difficult time right now."

This time he laughed out loud at me. "Yeah, you are. I really am sorry. About all of it."

"It's okay."

"Come on, it's cold out here, get back in the truck," he urged me. "I won't try anything again."

I opened my mouth, then stopped myself. What could I say? *You can try anything you want with me*

167

if you don't touch my chest? Talk about a mood-killer.

"Anyway, I need to get you to that safe house. I'm already off the case. If I mess up a little thing like driving you to that house, Ty will probably throw me off this task force completely."

"Off the case?" I repeated as I climbed back into the truck. "What do you mean?"

"What I said." He shifted the truck into gear. "Tyrese was thoroughly fed up with you and me both after you escaped from those barracks. Right now, he's hovering between still being fed up with you but also being pretty impressed by your ability to elude both Homeland Security and the Mendozas. But he's still plain fed up with me. So officially, I'm off-duty. I went looking for you on my own time. That pissed him off, too. But that happens a lot when we work together. It goes both ways for us."

"What's his problem?" I demanded, having already established a firm dislike of the guy in my mind. "Were you his rival for the girl of his dreams?"

"Not quite. Actually, I killed the girl of his dreams."

Fifteen

My jaw dropped. No wonder they had a personality conflict. In my line of work, arguments turn on whether to use the cash or accrual method. I couldn't imagine having to work with someone who'd killed your girlfriend.

Evan pulled out of the old gas station and back out onto Route 24, heading south toward the city. "She got in the line of fire by mistake. We were pursuing someone else—a former agent who works for the Mendozas now. And this girl, Tyrese had grown fond of her—more than fond of her—was our informer, and she got in the way. Things happen fast."

He squinted out the window, careful not to meet my eyes.

"My father killed a suspect once." It seemed important to let him know I understood. "The guy was practically a kid, only seventeen. Dad had a hard time with it. I think that was part of why my parents broke up. My mom didn't see how he could do it, and he couldn't make her understand. Then he got all withdrawn and angry. I understand better than I would have a couple of hours ago."

"Yeah, I suppose you do." Evan nodded slowly. "This time around Tyrese has been worrying I was making the same stupid mistake he made, getting involved with the wrong woman. Especially when you disappeared. So he took me off the case and told me to take a vacation, go visit my family in Texas."

"Are you going to go?" I asked.

"Does it look like I am?"

We headed onto Route One, back toward the city.

"I'd take I-95. It's a lot faster. But Chuck said an accident shut down all the lanes. That's part of what slowed them down."

"Yeah, it slowed Scott and his friends down, too. What happens to me now?"

He sighed heavily and didn't answer at first. "We'd like to keep you in protective custody."

"What exactly does that entail?"

"Putting you in a safe place and keeping you guarded." I could tell from the way he talked there was way more to it than that.

"For how long?"

Silence.

"Evan? How long?"

"At least until we lock up Scott Bennett and his companions. Possibly longer. If you're required to testify at a trial, you'll need protection until it's over. Or longer."

"How much longer?" My breathing became fast and shallow.

We'd come up to a red light, and now he turned his dark eyes on me. I couldn't be sure, but I thought I detected pity in those eyes.

"Possibly for the rest of your life. If that's the case, we'd probably have to give you a new identity, move you to another state."

"Oh, God!"

"It might not happen." He looked away from me, fixing his gaze on the traffic light that swung in the wind.

"This is what you were trying to protect me from? This is why you didn't tell me who you were, and this is why you ignored Tyrese's orders. This is why you didn't want me to be an informer for you guys."

He shifted gears and drove forward, still

avoiding my gaze. "I'm sorry I couldn't keep you out of it."

Somewhere, the wonderful Lord must be having quite a laugh at my expense. My life played like one black comedy moment after another these days. Surely he could go find some other badly lapsed Catholic to torment?

"Will my parents know what happened to me? My sister? My niece and nephews? What about my brother—he's a priest, they're good at keeping secrets—could I at least confess to him where I'm going?"

"You're getting ahead of yourself," Evan said. "It may not come to that. And anyway, it's always a choice. We don't force people into the program."

I turned my face away and stared out the window at the pelting rain.

"The alternate choice being to stay where I am, who I am, and wait for them to come and kill me?"

Evan made a lame attempt to reassure me. "The east coast isn't the Mendozas' usual base of operations. They may cut their losses on this project and go back home."

"Right. What would cutting their losses involve?"

"Hard to say. But if I sold life insurance, I wouldn't sell any to your fiancé right now."

"Can I please point out he never gave me a ring, and we never actually settled on a date?" I interjected, but not because I wanted to advertise myself as available. More because I wanted to put as much distance between Scott and myself as I possibly could at this point. A bit mercenary, perhaps, but by now it should be obvious I have a strong survival instinct.

"I'm clear that yours was an ambivalent relationship even before I showed up." Evan flashed a cocky little smirk.

"I don't want him to die at the hands of those people though."

"No, I don't want that either." Evan spared me a quick glance and a nod. "I wouldn't want a rabid dog to be left in their hands. Especially since killing it would be the least awful thing they might do to it. We'll do what we can, Sabrina, but getting out of this mess is ultimately up to Scott."

His telephone began trilling loudly, and he flicked it out of his pocket, checking the screen as he did so.

"Hey Chuck." He listened a little while, tossing in an occasional grunt of acknowledgement. Then he said good-bye and slipped the phone back into his pocket.

"Chuck says they've got two men in custody—one's the pilot and one is a short guy with freckles."

"I remember him, but I hardly saw him at all."

"Oh, he's a fountain of information now. Obviously not someone willing to take a fall for anyone else. That's good news. And the airpark manager said a Mark Atwood was scheduled to fly out of there around noon and land in Chicago. Presumably, they were going to take a flight from O'Hare down to Juarez."

"So now Scott and Harpo and that third guy they mentioned—they're pretty much stranded."

I felt a mixture of satisfaction and trepidation.

"Harpo?" Evan flashed another smile, one with those amazing dimples. I was sorry I'd pushed him away earlier. But rejecting before I could be rejected still seemed a little easier on my self-esteem than the alternative.

****

The safe house turned out to a big old Victorian, slightly shabby and in need of a paint job, but otherwise picturesque. A low hedge surrounded the front yard, and a chain-link fence enclosed the back.

It stood on the corner of a quiet street in a solidly respectable middle-class neighborhood in Baltimore.

"I was expecting it to be a little more isolated."

Evan parked his truck in the adjoining driveway. "Like that cabin in the middle of nowhere that they always go to in suspense movies, right?"

I nodded.

"Sometimes it's necessary to park someone in Cabbageville, but being near the police department, a fire station—and our own satellite office—those are good things."

He climbed down out of the cab and came around to help me out. The rain had continued steadily during the whole drive, and I shivered when he threw open the door. He reached out to me, and the rain-moistened blood ran down my hands and onto his own. I grabbed the towel from the floor and passed it to him. He shook his head.

"We'll do a better job cleaning up inside. Come on."

We hurried up the driveway and across a path up the front steps. To one side of the front door, a porch swing hung idle. How nice it would be to sit out there on a summer night and watch the world go by.

"Don't your neighbors wonder about this house?"

"Nah. Periodically, the FBI sends some cadets or rookies through to make it look lived in. That's what my FBI contact told me once. The public story is it's a halfway house for people with drug and alcohol problems. Believe me, nobody in the neighborhood wants to get to know the folks here."

Oh, Jim Dandy. Now I was a gangster's girlfriend with a drug problem.

We came into a small entrance foyer with a narrow turned staircase to one side and a short corridor running parallel to the stairs. The corridor opened onto a small living room, a bigger dining room, and a kitchen toward the back. The furniture throughout looked serviceable but bland, a bunch of bargain stuff from a thrift store most likely. The dining room held a table and some chairs, but it also housed two desks with computers and both were up and running. Two strangers, a man and a woman, were standing in front of one of the monitors.

"Hey," they both said casually as Evan strolled ahead to meet them. Evan returned the greeting and then held his arm out to me, coaxing me forward.

"Sabrina, this is Liz and Pete."

Liz held out a hand, and I raised my own, warning her away. She put her hand down and frowned. "Looks like you've had a bad morning."

"I'm not sure yet," I said. "I can't decide which is worse: chemotherapy or shooting a guy in the head."

"Oh, definitely chemo."

Hah. Easy for her to say.

"The guy probably deserved that bullet." Liz continued. "Why don't I help you get cleaned up while Evan and Pete talk shop?"

"Are you an agent with Homeland Security too?" I asked as we climbed the stairs.

"No, I'm FBI. So is Pete. We don't always play nicely together, but your guys needed a safe house, and this one was closest. Also, we're all part of a joint task force, and each of us is working different angles of this same sordid scam. Pete is one of the agents who broke this case."

"Broke it how?"

A large bathroom lay at the top of the steps, and Liz led me into it, pulling towels out of the cabinet as she talked.

"He was investigating the disappearance of a thirteen-year-old girl down in Montgomery County. We'd had a similar case one year earlier. Eventually, he found out both girls had been living in the household of a local corporate bigwig. We built a case against the guy, and then we offered him a deal if he'd tell us who the girls were and where they'd come from."

"What kind of deal?"

"No death penalty. Also, that we'd charge him with something else, something that didn't involve raping children. Other prisoners can be pretty hard on the ones who hurt kids. So we charged him with assaulting a Federal officer and multiple counts of kidnapping instead."

"That's—creative." My mother's liberal skeptic voice was howling in my head about abuse of civil liberties and the shredding of the Constitution. Or something strident like that. Liz seemed to hear her complaints.

"He was relieved." She handed me a bar of soap. "He sure didn't want it to become headline news that he'd sexually abused and probably killed not one but two underage girls. He claimed he and his wife had adopted them through an agency in Mexico. When we found out who was behind the agency and the size of the operation—then our assistant director insisted we bring Homeland Security into it."

And Scott—my Scott, the man I'd shared a bed with for two years—that man had been one of the people who had arranged these *adoptions*. I found myself gagging, and I ran over to the toilet barely in time.

Liz leaned over me and handed me a cup of water. "I guess there are more similarities between chemo and killing a guy than I remembered."

She was older than me, late forties, maybe even fifty, with a thin angular face and short salt-and-pepper hair. I sat back on the floor and swished the water around in my mouth as I gazed up at her, waiting for an explanation.

"It's the left one." She pointed to the left side of her high-necked sweater.

"Did he ask them to send you here on purpose?" But no, I'd heard Evan on the phone, and he'd never said anything about someone named Liz. We'd only come here because he'd been told to bring me here.

"That depends on which 'he' you mean." Liz smiled. "Could be Someone upstairs had a hand in the arrangements."

I shook myself, trying to collect my thoughts.

"Are you married?" I asked, quite suddenly and without regard to my rudeness.

"Yes, I am."

"He doesn't mind?"

She patted me on my back. "A real man isn't going to dump a woman over this anymore than he'd dump her for losing a leg."

Liz stretched out a hand and helped me up off the floor.

"You have a nice hot shower. Maybe I'll get a chance to talk to you when the shifts change. Until then, I'll be in the cable TV truck parked in the alley behind the house. Pete will be in a car parked across the street."

"You won't be in here with me?"

"No." She smiled. "Evan will probably be around for awhile though. I have a feeling he won't want to leave right away."

And she winked at me as she closed the door.

I held my hands up to the showerhead so that the pulsing stream would loosen the dried blood caked beneath my fingernails. The hot water pelted down on me for a long time before I even bothered to pick up the soap. It loosened muscles I didn't even know were stiff. I soaped the area around my scar gingerly, even though it was over a year old now. The scar still seemed pink to my eyes, though nowhere near as bad as it had immediately after the surgery. I usually told people I'd had a lumpectomy because they don't treat you so delicately then. They still look at you like you're normal. They think it's like getting a mole removed, so they don't ask as many questions. Before the cancer, I'd had perfect breasts—high and even and very full. Everything that women pay thousands of dollars to get from surgery, I'd been gifted with naturally. Somehow, that had made it impossible for me to think about plastic surgery to make myself look more aesthetically pleasing after the event. It wouldn't be *mine* anymore, so why go through the pain of more surgery?

And truthfully, a part of me liked looking at that scar sometimes—being forced to remember what I had survived, not allowing myself to pretend I was the same woman. It had been a hard decision for Scott to comprehend. What I saw as a stark, empowering honesty, he saw as me wallowing in self-imposed martyrdom. Now I thought of how often he'd nagged me about cosmetic surgery. We Irish can be contrary. I suppose I might not have fought reconstruction so hard if he'd been less vocal on the subject.

I stepped out of the shower and toweled off. I felt quite literally like a new person. Or at least, like a newly awakened person. The unreal quality of the last twenty hours of my life had been a bad dream. Now I was waking up. Or else I was getting used to a certain level of insanity in my life. Liz had the right idea—Miguel had asked for that bullet. No sense beating myself up over what had happened. What was done couldn't be undone, as my platitude-loving Nanny would no doubt tell me. I wrapped a big towel around myself and headed out into the upstairs corridor. There were three other doors, all opening onto modestly furnished bedrooms. In the one right next to the bathroom, I saw some clothes lying on the bed.

"This must be the place," I said to myself. I walked into the room, and I was about to close the door and drop the towel when I heard someone clearing his throat.

I turned, and Evan stood at the top of the stairs.

"I'm going to go get us some food, okay?" It was cute how careful he was to look only at my face.

"I guess." The idea of being alone in this strange house disturbed me in the extreme.

He picked up on my mood. "Liz and Pete are outside if you need anything. There are alarms on the doors and windows, alarms on the front and back gates, a driveway alarm. You'll be fine."

I nodded stupidly.

"There's an intercom downstairs in the kitchen, too," he added after an awkward pause. "You can use it to buzz them directly at any time. Not that you'll need to."

"Is the house bugged?"

"No, babe, it's not. Sometimes people have to live in places like this for months and months, so we try to make it as normal as possible."

"Months and months?" I had missed the original point of his remark completely, finding another, far scarier one.

"Months and months."

"Will you be here the whole time?"

He was the nearest thing to a friend in this place. Maybe Liz could be a surrogate friend too, if they let her come in from the rain now and then. But I guessed that other than bathroom breaks—if then—she probably stayed outside.

"I'll be here as much as I can. Let me go get some food now. You'll thank me later. And we can talk more then."

I inclined my head then backed into the room and closed the door. The clothes on the bed were my own clothes—I recognized my old Maryland Institute sweatshirt and some black sweatpants, also some nice cottony panties. Someone female—Liz?—had picked the underwear for me. I saw a couple of bras along with the enhancer shells, and then I knew she'd been the one who'd brought the clothing here. The fact that someone wanted me to get comfy here—that was not good news. I went to the closet, threw open the door and found more of my own things. Jeans, shirts, a couple of dresses. Enough for an extended stay.

"Well, welcome home, Sabrina." I sat down on the edge of the bed and pulled on the Jockeys and the sweatpants. Then I scooped myself into the bra and tucked in the obnoxious little piece of foam padding. I had tried not bothering with it, but then the bra cup would get indented and look lopsided. So I put it on and then pulled on the old shirt.

The mattress beneath me was soft, a cozy old double. At home, Scott and I shared a massive king-sized bed. We just about had to swim the English Channel to get to each other in that thing. I ran my hands over the plaid coverlet and it felt so very, very soft and inviting. I hadn't slept since those few stolen minutes in the taxi ride back to Harborview. Now that I was clean and warm again, nothing in the world seemed as important as laying down on that bed. And so I did.

****

The path immediately before me was clear, black gravel, but only a few feet ahead, it disappeared under a carpet of fallen leaves, fiery orange and gold. Once it had been a railroad line, but now it was a suburban walking trail.

At this time of day with sunset approaching, the trail was completely deserted and therefore a little creepy. To one side of the path lay a flat expanse of land covered with tall marsh grasses. On the other side, between the path and the cluster of McMansions where Jess lived, lay several yards of dense woods. How different it looked from those sunny mornings during chemo, when Jess would hustle me out for the daily pep talk.

I crossed over a wooden bridge and paused to look at the gurgling branch of the Bynum Run a few feet below. The stream was a tributary of the Susquehanna, but here beside the trail it was not much more than a shallow, slow-moving bit of scenery.

Jess's house was the last on a cul-de-sac that backed right up onto the woods. A visitor could walk about a half-mile around to a paved path and come to the front of her house that way, but from where I stood on the walking trail, I could see a good portion of the back of her house. And it was all dark in there. No one stood on the deck waiting for me, no homey yellow lights shone inside the house; and in the logic of a dream, I knew this wasn't because she was still at work. The darkness meant something bad. I cut through the soggy ground of the woods, my sneakers sucking and squishing in the wetness.

By the time I arrived at the back deck, I was sweating a bit—not from the exertion but from the fear welling up in me. Silence lay heavy all around me as I approached the steps. That was all wrong. Jess had a dog. A big, loud, barky dog. Part German Shepherd and part Border Collie, Kasey was the friendliest dog I'd ever met, but always, always loud.

I crept up onto the deck and stood at the patio door, waiting for I didn't even know what. The mysterious and dreaded "they" had been here; I recognized the signs. The rain was pissing down on me. I was cold and I was tired, and Scott was, in fact, a criminal and a cheat and my dad was far away on his hunting trip and my mom even further away in Arizona but Jess was here. Surely Jess was here, in this house waiting for me. I would go in, and she would make everything all right, the way she had when I was sick.

So, I tried the patio door, found it unlocked, and stepped into Jess' kitchen. The clouds and fading afternoon light cast everything in grey tones. The gleaming white ceramic floor, the pickled oak cabinets and table—all looked like something out of a black and white movie. So the dark streak on the floor looked black at first, not red. Until I knelt down and examined it more closely. Then, even in the twilight, I could recognize it as blood.

I glanced around the room, spying the first big splotch of red in the middle of the floor. More spatters covered the table legs and the refrigerator door. Dark finger smears showed on the decorative railing that divided the kitchen from the family room area, and a streaky trail led out of the kitchen and down the central corridor toward the front door. Where it ended in a large, furry lump of utter stillness. I sat down on the floor beside Kasey. His throat had been cut, and he was still warm and soft, but he was clearly dead.

I backed away, and as I passed the door to Jess's club basement, I noticed more blood on the doorknob. That stopped me cold. I couldn't go down there, not yet anyway. Instead, I returned to the kitchen, where I stared at the blood-spattered farmhouse table.

This table was where I had sat when I told Jess I had cancer. I didn't cry then. I swallowed it down and did the brave girl act. The only time I wavered in that act was when my mother took leave from work for a little while and came all the way from Arizona to hold my head whenever I threw up. But the rest of the time, I was all I'm gonna beat this thing! *Jess saw through that, but she put up with it. She shed many tears for me, which was probably the most generous thing anyone has ever done in my life. I would tell her the bad news, and she would cry in my stead.*

When I finally broke down and cried in her arms, it wasn't over the cancer. Well, I guess in a way, it was. I cried for the five hundred dollar designer bra and panties Scott didn't want to see. The bra and panties Evan had thrown at me the night he spirited me away. See, I'd come through cancer, and my hair was still super-short—almost Army boot camp short—but I'd started working out obsessively as soon as I got diagnosed, and I'd stuck with it as much as I could. When my treatment had finally ended, I bought the sexy lingerie set thinking it would finally get Scott interested again. I was delusional. I'd believed he was avoiding sex out of concern for me, out of fear I was still too sick or sore to enjoy it. But when I paraded my new body in front of him in that lingerie and he turned out all the lights and looked the other way—then I knew it had nothing to do with my feelings and everything to do with the fact that he was revolted by me now. That was when I went to Jess's house and cried and cried and cried. Now I started to cry again, only no one held my head this time and said Shhh.

"Don't start." I looked up to see Jess standing on the opposite side of the room, in front of the blood-spattered refrigerator.

"Hey, you're okay!"

"For now," she grumbled. "But I'm telling you, in the next life, I'm going to do a better job of picking my people."

"Your people?"

"Family, friends, spouses—you." She threw her hands in the air. "The entire universe has let me down. First, Walt dumps me for a blonde bimbo barely out of high school, and then you go and get me killed."

"Killed?"

"Killed. And by him!" She raised a finger,

reminding me of the Ghost of Christmas Yet to Come. I turned and followed the line of sight to the man who stood behind me, where no one had been standing seconds ago. Even in the deep shadows, I recognized Evan—his height and wide shoulders, the long hair pulled back, the glint of gold in his ears, the semi-automatic I'd seen him use, now pointed at Jess's face. When he fired it, the boom vibrated through me, its echo carrying the sound of certain death.

Sixteen

I sat up in the bed, my hands clamped over my ears. Outside, the rain droned on, accompanied by the occasional flash of lightning and the recurring rumble of thunder. Sighing, I stood and crossed the room to peer into a mirror above the dresser. Because I couldn't find a brush, I ruffled my fingers through my hair. But dear Liz had found my make-up case and brought it here. I popped the case open, grabbed my concealer, and rolled a little under my eyes, trying to cover the dark blue shadows. Then I slicked on some pink lip-gloss and eyebrow pencil. Being on the run from a Latin American crime family was no reason to get shoddy with my appearance. After all, I'd done my best to look good throughout my illness. If I could manage then, I could manage now.

As I descended the stairs, I heard the monotonous drone of a television. I crossed the foyer and entered the living room where Evan was sprawled on the sofa, his arms crossed behind his head and his bare feet hanging over one of the armrests. He was watching a rerun of an old cop show.

"You don't get enough of this in real life?" I asked.

Since he'd given no sign of hearing me, I had expected to startle him, But he didn't even flinch. He grinned and turned his head in my direction. "Did you have a good nap?"

"Yes." My dream came back to me then, and I shuddered. "No. I had a nightmare."

"It'll get better in time." He sat up on the couch. "You did what you had to do. Keep telling yourself that."

"No, it wasn't about that. Never mind, it was one of those weird dreams that doesn't make any sense. What will happen to me because of Miguel?"

"Happen?"

"Will I have to go on trial? It was self-defense."

Evan looked back at the television. "Don't worry about it. I'll tell Tyrese I did it."

"What? You can't do that!"

"I can." He shrugged. "To be honest, it might make the paperwork a lot easier for everyone concerned."

"That would bother me." I hugged my arms against my chest.

"Want credit where it's due, eh?" He smirked.

"No! But I—that's an awful big thing to lie about the rest of my life."

"True." Evan nodded. "I'll leave it up to you. I'll take the blame if you want, but I promise, you won't go to jail for it if you do own up."

"Then I'd rather do that."

His eyes sparkled when he looked up, and it made me uncomfortable having someone looking at me with all that obvious adoration. I'm far more comfortable with ambivalence in my men.

I noticed my pocketbook sitting on the coffee table. "Boy, you guys don't see me leaving any time soon, do you?"

"Afraid not. But that's a good thing. The cops are on the scene of the crime, and you're here, safe from harm. Hence the term *safe house*."

"I get that." I noticed my cell phone beside the bag. "Do I get to call my family?"

"Not yet."

"Why the phone then?"

"A hunch."

"What sort of hunch?"

He didn't answer again. Instead, he stood and padded into the kitchen. "You ready for some lunch?"

He saw the Mommy Look on my face. When my niece tells a lie, which happens more than it should, my sister gives her a certain look: eyebrow arched, lips cocked to one side, head slightly inclined. I gave my niece that same look once, and she announced to everyone that I had learned to do the Mommy Look. Apparently, that look worked on grown men, too.

"Okay, okay." Evan threw his hands in the air. "We had an idea that Scott might try to get in touch with you. We swept the phone for bugs, so it's clean now—"

"Now? It's clean *now*?"

He opened the refrigerator door, pulling out a pizza box. "I got pepperoni because that's pretty basic. I've never met anybody who won't eat pepperoni. I ate half, but I left the rest for you."

"What about Liz and Pete?"

"They stay outside. All the time. One inside, two outside. I brought them each a calzone and a cola, okay?"

"What time is it?"

"About two o'clock." He moved through the kitchen smoothly and gracefully, getting out a paper plate and putting two slices of the pizza on it. Then he popped it in the microwave and set the timer.

"It only seems later because the storm's making it so dark." He glanced over his shoulder and gave me a comforting smile.

"I dreamed you shot my friend," I blurted at him.

"Your friend?"

"Jess. I dreamed you shot her."

"Rest easy, then. She talks an awful lot, but I don't envision needing to kill her any time soon. I'm pretty sure she's not part of Mendoza's operation."

He pulled the pizza from the microwave and handed me the plate. Then he ducked into the fridge again.

"We've got cola, lemon-lime soda, and beer."

"Soda."

He grabbed the soda and a can of beer as well.

"Should you drink when you're working?"

"Technically, I'm not working." He popped the tab on the beer. "Tyrese made me put in for vacation time for the rest of the week, so I'm guarding you for free, right now. They'll send someone real for the next shift, around eight. I stayed because I was worried about you, and Ty had too much on his plate to argue with my offer."

I blushed and carried the pizza into the dining room, where I sat down. He came in and dropped into a chair next to me.

My last real meal had been a frozen entrée of shrimp and pasta twenty-four hours ago, but food held no appeal at the moment. In every silence, I found myself pushing aside the image of Miguel, his face collapsing and erupting in a stream of blood and bone, and I didn't want to know what else.

"I don't think I can eat any of it." I pushed the plate to the middle of the table.

Evan sighed heavily and gave me a look that reminded me of my dad. Even though he lived in the same state, over on the Eastern Shore, we didn't see each other much. He worked nights as a security guard, and anyway, he and my mother had had an ugly parting of the ways. I always felt vaguely disloyal when I spent time with him. But when I'd had my surgery, he'd braved sitting in the same waiting room with my mother—no mean feat—and he was the one who had finally convinced me to eat when I didn't want to be alive anymore. Now Evan gave me the same demanding look my dad had given me. Maybe it was because men have a generally healthier relationship with food than we women do.

"Yes, you do have to eat," he said. "You still need to eat, even after killing someone. Not eating won't undo it. And besides, it's a good pizza. Trust me. I traveled through gale force winds and hard rain to bring you that pizza, pretty lady. Eat it. Please."

I made a great show of studying the pepperonis, unable to meet Evan's steady gaze.

"Why does—why did Tyrese think I was in cahoots with Scott and his unsavory friends?"

He grew serious, presumably assessing how much he could safely share with me.

"Your fiancé—"

I opened my mouth.

"Sorry, Scott. He's been seen with Hector Mendoza, but not Hector's elder brother Rafael. When their father died recently, we assumed the leadership passed to Rafael, and that was an end to it. Now we aren't so sure. Homeland Security thinks Hector might be estranged from his brother, but we don't know yet. It could be an act, or he might have set up a rival operation. Considering how many people were after you last night, though, I'm inclined to think he's Rafael's rival now, and that both groups were trying to get that list of 'adoption' clients on Scott's computer. It's possible that one brother figures he can use the information to bring down the other brother's operation.

"Anyway, our intelligence analysts believe Hector also has a political agenda—unlike his brother, who just wants lots of money. We don't know if he hopes to run for office in Mexico someday or bribe a few high-ranking officials down there and up here in order to change policies. Or maybe he's hoping to quietly foment a bloody revolution or something. We have no clue. But because of that information, we think it's no coincidence that he befriended Scott."

"You mean, because Scott's uncle is Senator Bennett?"

"Having Scott on your payroll might be useful if you wanted to influence the Senator's vote somewhere down the road. To be honest, we have no evidence Scott's uncle knows anything about what his nephew's been up to lately."

"And you guys figured I must know what was going on because I was Scott's girlfriend? Haven't you heard the woman is always the last to find out?"

Evan ducked his head in a gesture of concession. "Hector hobnobs with quite a few powerful people in Mexico and in Europe, and he cultivates an upscale, sophisticated image. Part of that image is collecting art. A few months ago, right after we became aware of Scott's possible involvement, you went to Mexico with him."

"I remember." Ah, the foolish hope that trip had engendered. "I badgered Scott into taking me. I wanted to revive what little romance there'd ever been in our relationship. Ours was never a great love for the ages, in case you haven't guessed."

Evan smiled crookedly and took a sip of his beer.

"I wanted to give us both time to readjust after my surgery, but I knew things were bad. I knew I'd have to leave him soon if he couldn't get past the way I look now."

Evan's eyes shifted down to my chest and back up so quickly, I almost missed it.

"I suppose you people had our condo bugged?"

He didn't argue with me.

Suddenly I understood his reassurances about the safe house.

"Then you must be aware there hadn't been anything going on between Scott and me for months. I figured living alone without romance and the other stuff that goes with it would be easier than sharing a bed with someone and doing without all of it. So I was trying to make up my mind whether or not to leave. I hoped going to Mexico might give us a fresh start."

Evan cleared his throat nervously in the pause that followed.

"We haven't had your place bugged for long. Anyway, I never listened to any of the tapes. The junior guy on the team is the one who gets stuck with crap work like that. He gets to sift through it all and tell the rest of us if anything significant crops up. Work like that has its novel appeal at first, but after a couple of assignments, you tend to lose interest. Some guys will call you in and play back some juicy intimate bits, but Ben never did that. He's a good kid. He told me that if you knew what was going on, you and Scott sure weren't talking about it at home, but he didn't tell me anything else. Although he might have been more circumspect than usual because he knew it would bother me to hear about—um, the other stuff—with you."

I put my hand over my mouth to hide a little smile. Girl power—it was nice to know I still had a little bit of it, at least as long as I kept my clothes on.

"Do you remember meeting a distinguished-looking older man you had dinner with at Bellinghausen while you were in Mexico?"

"Yes." Boy, they had been watching me. What a creepy feeling. "Ramon Sonero. Scott wanted me to meet him because he owns an art gallery there. An intriguing collection, a lot of contemporary works. We had such a nice time that day. I thought if I gave it a little longer, things would work out. Scott was downright romantic when we got back to the hotel. I remember on the elevator how he kissed—"

I snapped out of my reverie in time to notice Evan's jaw twitching fiercely.

"Ramon Sonero is the dealer for Hector

Mendoza's art collection." He hurried to bring me back to the real subject. "Pete—the agent you met—was investigating two murders of teenaged Mexican girls, and he learned their killer was a contributor to Senator Bennett's campaign. We at Homeland Security knew someone at CIS was helping to get underage girls into the country illegally, but we didn't know who to suspect. Then Pete discovered that your Scott was tennis buddies with his murder suspect, and he became the focus of our investigation.

"When we looked back at Scott's meetings with other known Mendoza associates, Tyrese noticed that you were at the Mexico meeting with Sonero and wondered if Scott brought you into the fold that day."

Now I wondered, too. Is that what he had meant to do? That had been the last good day we'd had together. And a pretty good night, too. Sure, Scott had still wanted all the lights out, and he'd made me keep my bra on so he didn't have to see so much of the scar. But I'd decided that night that maybe I was being too demanding, maybe leaving my bra on for the rest of my life wouldn't be such a big deal. He'd done his best to be tender and attentive that night. I'd half-expected him to finally set a wedding date after the Mexico trip. But instead, he'd grown more distant, more openly hostile to me afterwards. For some reason, he'd decided he couldn't confide in me. Whether he wanted to draw me "into the fold" or whether he wanted me to help him get out—either way, he couldn't tell me the truth; and the fact that he couldn't had led to a cold war between us.

Evan rose and sauntered into the kitchen. I followed him, watching as he busied himself opening the pizza box, getting a slice, and putting it on another paper plate. All the while, he was careful not to look at me while he worked. I stood in the midst of the room and watched him. He had such a graceful, confident way of moving I admired immensely. Even before the cancer, I'd never been comfortable in my own body. I was the kid that got picked last for the basketball team in gym class, even after the crazy girl who talked to herself and chewed her own hair. I was that bad. Probably I would still be terrible at basketball, not being particularly coordinated, but at least I'd learned how to run and swim and lift weights. It was a start. Maybe someday grace and being comfortable with myself would come, too.

His back was to me as he pressed the start button on the microwave.

"I like to watch you move."

"You know what?" He turned around slowly. "You're starting to drive me crazy."

"I'm sorry," I replied, taken aback.

"I swear I'm no egotist. But I'm pretty sure you want me." His jaw was twitching again, and I'd seen enough to know that wasn't a good sign. "Man, you fall into the harbor, or you shriek and burst into tears if I try to touch you. Do you do that to Scott, too? Because no offense, Sabrina, but that can be a significant turn-off for a man."

"No, I don't do that to Scott. Because he doesn't try to touch me anymore. Okay?" I stalked out of the kitchen and grabbed my can of soda. I took a big, angry gulp, and the bubbles made me hiccup. I left the pizza in the dining room and carried the drink back to the sofa. Evan followed me into the living room and looked at me quizzically.

"I can't have kids." I frowned at the TV. "I don't know how much detail you have about what happened to me."

He blinked and backed up a few steps. "Not much. That part wasn't particularly relevant to the investigation. I know you had a lumpectomy over a year ago, but that's good right? It means it wasn't serious and you're okay now."

I chuckled bitterly to myself. Once cancer knocks on your door, you are *so* never okay again. Survivors don't get cured; they get time off for good behavior. One woman in my support group said to me, the only way to beat cancer is to die of something else before it comes back.

"It wasn't a lumpectomy in the end. Or not a simple one, anyway." I still wouldn't look at him. "See, they got in there, and it was bigger than they thought. I'm pretty sure they wanted to take the whole breast off but were probably afraid I'd sue. So they did this thing called a quadrantectomy. Takes too long to say, no one's ever heard of it, so I keep saying lumpectomy. After that, I had to have chemo, and the chemo induced an early menopause."

"Oh."

I glanced up long enough to see his eyes waver and shift from me to the television. He snatched the remote from the coffee table and turned off the program.

"Damn, now I'll never know whether they catch the bad guys," I muttered.

"Can you do anything about it?" Evan asked.

"About the bad guys? Isn't that your department?"

"Sabrina, be serious."

"No, I can't do a thing about it," I admitted. "The situation appears to be permanent. My doctor told me if it comes back, it's usually within the first year. And it hasn't come back. You know what I mean by *it*. So—no kids for me."

"That's too bad."

I couldn't read his face at all when he spoke.

Evan sat down on the neighboring sofa and stared at the table. I could feel him reassessing me in his head, considering whether I was worth the trouble—a damaged, aging female that wasn't an easy lay and couldn't even be used for breeding. Also, a woman with a rude tongue. My eyes felt wet, and I wiped at them impatiently.

"Um, I'm so sorry about the terrible things I said to you in the garage. About the hit man thing, and the drug cartels. And making fun of your name. And that remark at the barracks about your having to pretend to be a drug dealer a lot. I swear I'm not a racist person. I have this bizarre gift for knowing the exact thing to say that will cut someone down. Sometimes what comes out of my mouth surprises me."

"You don't need to apologize. Those were extraordinary circumstances. And I've handled you all wrong from start to finish."

He smiled one of those big dimpled grins again. "It's the Irish in me. I have such a weakness for girls with freckles."

"Irish? What, Desmond isn't another phony name?"

"None of them are phony names. It's way better if you can use part of your own name in your cover identity. That way you're more likely to answer when someone's talking to you."

"Then you really are part Irish?"

"Irish and Welsh and about everything else you can name. My dad's a horse trainer from Northern Ireland who married into a family of Tejano ranchers near San Antonio. His mother was Welsh and her maiden name was Evans. That's who I'm named for. And on my mother's side of the family, there's some Comanche blood and even a Chinese great-grandmother. My dad says we're our own United Nations."

I had to laugh at that. "Texas? I thought you were from California. You don't sound Texan. You don't twang."

"Whaddaya mean, I don't twang, missy?" And he twanged quite convincingly as he said it.

Deciding I was hungry after all, I went back into the dining room. I stood next to the table and took another huge bite of pizza.

Evan followed me again. "I went to college in California. Also, I'm a good mimic. Or so my college girlfriend told me. She was always recruiting me for theatre department productions. Hey, if I didn't like killing people so much, I'd have probably gone into acting."

"Evan!"

"Joking." More big dimples. "Sometimes that's the only way to deal with it."

"I guess I'll learn," I said. "Tell me why you went to college in California? Were you following that girl?"

"No, escaping from another one." His smile faded. "It was after the Gulf War—the first one. I was engaged to my high school sweetheart, and I came back to find she'd been sleeping with the quarterback from the school's football team. I guess if I'd had to deal with this war in Iraq, she'd have made her way through the whole team. Anyway, I felt like a fool, and so I went to California, moved in with some friends from the Army, and got recruited by the DEA. The rest is history."

"I was engaged once, too." I picked the cheese off a slice of pizza and nibbled at it, telling myself this conversation did not sound like two people on a date. "He was a nice guy, but I kept expecting more. Another lawyer."

"You like those guys in suits, huh?"

Up until meeting Evan, my answer would have been an unequivocal yes. I still wasn't sure what had changed. He'd told me early on that he was thirty-three, and I was pretty sure he had no reason to lie about that. Was I merely an aging woman looking

195

for a fling with a younger man, someone who represented some wild side I didn't know I had? Or had something shifted in me, some set of priorities I'd never even known I had?

"We were supposed to get married, but I didn't feel enough of a spark, so I called it off. Now he has a nice wife and three kids, and he's a happy man. So I did him a favor."

I slumped against the dining room chair and ran my hands through my hair. The emptiness of my life hit me all at once.

"I know you're tired." Evan misunderstood my gesture, probably putting it down to more aftershocks from the shooting. He leaned toward me and spoke in a reassuring voice. "This is all going to be over soon. And it's going to end happy. I swear it, babe."

I laughed. "Evan, even when I was in college, no one called me babe."

"I'm sure they were thinking it."

I shook my head, utterly unconvinced.

"Hey. I'm not trying to make a pass at you this time, okay? But you should know you're still pretty. It's wrong that Scott made you feel like you're not."

"That isn't his fault," I admitted. "He knew the person I was before, and I'm not that person anymore. I look different, I act different. Cancer's what defines me now. I don't want it to be, but it is. Maybe someday it won't be, when I get a few years past it. God willing. Look, I'm a good accountant, a loyal friend. I like to think I have a good sense of humor. I'm a pretty good artist, too, even though I never had the confidence to do anything with it. But now, everything seems to boil down to me being a breast cancer survivor. Scott always wanted me to have cosmetic surgery on my breast, and I hated that idea. Maybe I wouldn't have, if he had shut up about it for five minutes. I can be kind of contrary."

"Well, you are Irish. But then, so am I."

He looked across the table, sheepish and amused with himself all at once. We both laughed out loud. His eyes sparkled, so warm and inviting.

"I don't know why you're flirting with me when I've told you about the cancer and the menopause and all of it." I finished my pizza and wiped my mouth.

"Sabrina, that's not all there is to know about you." He gave me a frank, serious look that seemed to allow no disagreement. "I also know about how you cope in a crisis, how determined and resourceful you can be. I like that. Do you want that?"

He pointed at the remaining slice of pizza on my plate, and I shook my head. He scarfed it down in a matter of seconds and shrugged. "Not every guy cares about breasts, Sabrina."

I snorted.

"No, I'm serious. Take me, for instance," he insisted. "I'm way more interested in legs and—and what goes with that. You have fantastic legs, and a nice round—. Okay, look. The point is, cancer didn't do anything to the parts of you I notice first. And the rest of you's pretty cute too. Babe."

I could barely restrain myself from leaping across the room and shouting *"He said I'm cuuuute!"*

Evan licked the remnants of tomato sauce from his fingers. I stood up and stepped closer, laying a hand on his silky smooth hair.

"Don't do that." He hunched his shoulders forward. "It's difficult enough—"

Abruptly, his chair scraped across the wood floor, and he rose from the table with an almost angry haste.

"Tyrese would tell you I've never been good at following rules. But some, I've always tried to respect. Like don't take advantage of a woman in crisis. I never expected that would be such a hard one to obey."

He scratched his head, as if even he was confused by his interest in me. "I gotta go wash my hands. I'll be back." He strode out of the dining room.

I heard his soft footfalls on the carpeted stairs. I tidied up the dining room, tossing plates into the trash, and pouring the remains of my soda down the sink.

A woman in crisis. Well, yes, if any woman was in a crisis, it would certainly be me. But did that mean I couldn't think straight? Really, what the breast cancer thing had taught me was that a woman never thinks clearer than when she is in a crisis. Because she doesn't have time to second-guess herself.

After a minute, I heard the bathroom door creak open softly. So I climbed the stairs to meet Evan there.

Seventeen

"I haven't thanked you properly for finding me." My voice came out hoarse, a little bit shaky, as I approached him.

He leaned against the doorframe, his tall figure a black silhouette against the yellowy glow from the bathroom light.

"And is that what this would be then?" He reached out and took a strand of my hair, curling it around his fingers. "A thank you?"

"I don't know what it would be," I admitted. "And no, I'm not used to that problem. I never sleep with a guy unless it's serious. I'm thirty-nine—"

He raised an eyebrow. Oh, hell, of course he'd read my file.

"Okay, I'm not thirty-nine. Thirty-nine was the year I had cancer. I should let that go, shouldn't I? That's what you would say."

"Would I say that?" I heard a lilting tease in his voice.

"Yes, you would. You were so convincing as a personal trainer because you kept giving me all that peppy, up-beat, focus-on-the-future advice."

His head tilted a fraction of an inch, but in the dark upper corridor, his expression remained hard to read.

"I'm forty," I admitted. "I'm an infertile forty-year-old woman with one and a half breasts and an ugly scar, Evan. And I've only been with three guys in my whole life, all guys I'd known for several months—or even years—and all guys I believed I would marry. I was wrong every time. So I have no clue what you are to me. But you're right, I do want you."

A flash of lightning illuminated the upstairs, blue light streaking all around us. I could see little crinkles around Evan's eyes when he smiled. He took my hands and kissed the palms.

I caught my breath.

"Evan, I've never said that out loud to any man in my entire life," I told him. "*I want you.* It would be a very crippling blow to my self-esteem if you reject me now."

"Oh, I couldn't reject you." He pulled me into a tight embrace. "I don't know how any sane man could."

He took my hand and walked me into the bedroom, the one where I'd fallen asleep earlier. I fell onto the bed, and he tumbled down beside me. The bed creaked softly at the added weight. A streetlamp loomed on the corner outside the window, casting its glow on the gold rings in his ears. They made me think of a pirate.

"Are you sure this is a good idea?" He traced the outline of my lips with his forefinger.

"God, no." I laughed. "But I've spent too much of my life going for the sure thing, the safe thing. Even when I thought I was dying, I still wanted to be safe. Safe with Scott, safe with my job, safe with my body. Now—*now!*—I finally get it. There is no safety, none. So I was thinking I'd go for happy instead."

"Then I'll do my best not to disappoint you, babe." He nuzzled my hair.

"I don't know how far this should go." My nerves were getting the best of me. "I'm kind of scared. It hurts now. A lot of the time, it hurts. It's part of that menopause thing. Are you sure you want someone who's so much trouble?"

"My dad says every good thing is worth some trouble," he told me. "We'll take our time, it'll be okay."

He got me all choked up. I pulled away and sat up, wiping my eyes.

"What about—?" I stumbled. I'd never been good at discussing this sort of thing.

"What is it?" He sat up and put a hand on my shoulder.

"Um, Scott wasn't faithful. I should probably have about a dozen blood tests when this crisis is all over." I sniffled.

"Yeah, probably you should," Evan agreed. He did that nuzzling thing again, rubbing his nose up behind my ear. I shivered all over.

"I was a Boy Scout," he whispered. "I'm always prepared. We'll be okay. I couldn't stop now, even if I wanted to."

"Wait, what?" I held him off at arm's length for a moment. "Always? You're, like, *always* prepared?"

He shrugged. "Yeah, pretty much."

I blinked a few times. I know what my mother had taught me to think about a guy who always carried condoms with him. Look at Scott. But Evan was younger, so maybe that was another difference these days. Maybe now the nice guys all had long hair and earrings and—um, condoms?

"Sabrina, they don't take up much space. It's only a couple in my wallet, not a whole box." A slightly defensive edge had crept into his voice, and I suspected I wasn't the first girl to be a little taken aback by his readiness.

"Oh. Well, okay."

"Hey." His tone softened. He tilted my chin up and searched my eyes. "Do you not want to do this after all? Because I'm okay with that, too. I'll be disappointed, but it's okay."

I grinned. "Didn't you just say you couldn't stop if you wanted to?"

"Oh, baby, that was something pretty to say. A

way to tell you how much I want you. But I don't want you to feel badgered into it."

And then he wrapped me in his arms, in a warm, engulfing hug that made me feel—I don't know, appreciated. Valuable. I tugged at the hem of the turtleneck he'd been wearing. That was positively raunchy behavior for me with someone I'd known such a short time.

He let go of me and helped things along, pulling the shirt over his head without ceremony. Then he took off the wooden cross I'd seen him wearing so often, placed it on the nightstand next to us, and reached into the back pocket of his jeans. I guess I probably looked a little startled, because he paused and gave me a questioning glance again. But I wasn't worrying about what he kept stashed in the wallet anymore. I was gaping at his chest. Because it turned out he had all these tattoos. A bunch of them.

I'd already seen the tribal armband at the gym when he wore those sleeveless muscle shirts, but just above his left pec, there was also something that looked like a big blue coyote howling at the moon. And then another tattoo began beneath his ribs on his right side and wrapped under his arm, disappearing around his back.

I must admit that as I stared at his chest, I wavered. I had never been with a guy who had even one tattoo or one earring, let alone multiples of each. What the hell was I thinking?

"Second thoughts again?" He smiled as though he might laugh out loud at any second. "Do you want me to turn around so you can see the rest of it?"

"Huh?" I blinked and then flushed when I realized how openly I'd been staring. His lips curved up, looking a little condescending. He turned his back and revealed an elaborate, psychedelically colored image of a snake with wings and a human face.

"Wow," I breathed. "That had to hurt."

Evan glanced over his shoulder, his eyes sparkling.

"I didn't mind. There's a scar from a knife wound hidden in there. That hurt a lot worse than getting the tattoo. Tattoos are a good way to hide scars. My cousin Hernando did this one. He has a sideline in covering up scars for breast cancer survivors."

"Do you get kickbacks from him or something?"

"Maybe."

"Why?"

He looked momentarily befuddled. "Um, I don't really get kickbacks."

"Not that. I meant, why does he specialize in covering up scars for breast cancer survivors?"

"His mother was my Tia Elena," Evan explained.

Oh, her. He'd mentioned her when I first told him I was a cancer survivor. Whenever I tell people, they want to connect in some way. Unfortunately, they usually connect by telling me about some friend or relative who died of the disease. That was Evan's Tia Elena. His eyes lit up when he spoke of her, of how beautiful and elegant she was. She had died when he was a teenager, and I suspected he'd had a bit of a crush on her.

"He does beautiful work, your cousin. I'll keep him in mind." I reached out a finger and began to trace the pattern on Evan's back. "Is this that Mexican god?"

His flesh rippled with little goose bumps as I ran my fingernail over the serpent's head, which lay near his right shoulder blade.

"Quetzalcoatl," he said.

I leaned forward and pressed my lips to Quetzalcoatl's, so full and insolent-looking, much like Evan's own lips.

A sigh shivered through him, and I wrapped my arms around his broad chest. He raised his own arm and drew it around my shoulders, gathering me into an embrace.

"Is it okay if I leave my shirt on? Or at least my bra?"

"No," he whispered, burying his face in my hair. "Don't do that. I want to see all of you."

I rested my head against his shoulder and struggled to find the words. "I have this huge dent in my right breast now, Evan. And a hideous scar."

"So?" he said. "I didn't worry about the tattoos when I took my shirt off, did I? You don't seem like the tattoo kind of girl, but I figured you were already seeing past them to something under the skin."

Gently, he took his arm from around me and pulled up my ratty old sweatshirt. Time stopped. It would be worse than he expected. It would end like my dream. They'd taken a piece of me the size of an orange. I looked lopsided and ridiculous.

With shaking fingers, he unhooked my bra. I started to close my eyes.

"Don't." He slipped the straps from my shoulders, and I pressed my lips together, trying to keep my teeth from chattering with nervousness.

And then the bra was off, and he stared and stared at me. But not with the repulsion Scott had shown me. Evan studied it, his steady gaze reminding me of the way a surgeon would look at it. Then he reached out and gently touched it with his fingertip.

"Does it still hurt?"

"No," I answered. Scott had never, ever asked me that question. "No, it doesn't hurt anymore."

Evan bent his head down, and then he kissed the scar.

"It's not that bad," he said when he raised his head. "I kind of like it. Because it's part of who you are—a fighter. Someone who doesn't give up. A beautiful, brave woman."

"You don't mind? The scars? The weird shape?"

"No, I do not mind." He leaned into me and pressed me down onto the bed, closing his lips over my right nipple.

"I can't feel much on that side, Evan, so—"

I didn't finish the sentence. It turned out I could feel much more on that side than I'd thought. He traced a line of kisses over my breasts and my upper chest, all the way up to my neck.

"I love your freckles," he whispered in my ear, his voice all rough and husky. "Someday I'm going to count every one of them."

Oh, if I had a dollar for every lemon I'd wasted trying to get rid of those things—and now I was glad that it had never worked.

"But I like the parts where there aren't any freckles, too," he went on, his dark hands caressing my pale breasts again. "All that creamy white skin hidden from everyone but me."

Then his lips soothed a path down my heated body, tender little kisses all over my stomach and down to my belly button. He tugged at my sweatpants and eased them over my hips, along with my panties. The whole ensemble went flying somewhere across the room, and I laughed. I reached down and caught hold of the little black tie that bound his ponytail. I gave it a yank and tossed it in the same direction. His hair fell forward, casting a web of shadows over the lines and planes of his cheekbones.

"I'm not sure how I'm going to feel about being involved with a guy who has prettier hair than I do," I told him.

"I'm confident you're woman enough to handle it," he murmured.

Poets talk about love being a hunger, but I'd

never felt it until that night. I hungered for him. I needed him inside me like I needed water or food, and I pulled him snug against me and tried to speed things along.

"No. Slow, remember?"

He pressed his lips to mine, and they were soft and a little salty. Then he fluttered them over my breasts and stomach again. He bent my knees toward my chest and parted my legs, and I let him. I was so unlike myself with him. Or I finally *was* myself with him, in a way that I couldn't be with any other man.

His teeth sank lightly into the insides of my thighs, marking me. I discovered I liked that. But an uneasiness rose up in me as his tongue shifted closer and closer to—.

"Um, Evan," I said shakily. "Are you sure about this?"

"Mmm. Very."

" Scott didn't like—"

"Scott is not a part of these proceedings," he warned me. And his tongue proceeded to stroke the warm, furred space between my legs.

"But no one's done this to me in years and years." My voice climbed a couple of octaves and ended in a bit of a squeal.

"Seriously? Years?" His head popped up in amazement, and I nodded timidly.

"Then it's about time, babe."

And he was right.

I liked everything Evan did that night. He was so tender and so demanding, all at once. I liked the way he laced his fingers through mine and then pressed my hands down above my head, squeezing them tightly with each well-timed thrust. I liked the taste of myself in his mouth as he kissed me. I liked the dirty, naughty things he said, things about how it felt to be inside me, how I fit him like a glove, some things I didn't even understand because they were in Spanish. More things I could never tell another living soul because they were so rough and so sweet at the same time.

Outside, the storm raged on, and from time to time I became aware of the thunder and the hard rain. Or a bolt of lightning would brighten the room and show me the look of helpless abandon on Evan's face—his eyes flickering open and closed, and his nostrils flared wide as he hovered above me. There was a moment of ferocious pleasure, when I truly forgot who I was and saw colors I couldn't name. Now this, I said to myself, *this* is an orgasm. A really big one. When he knelt up on the bed and hugged me tight against him, he whispered in my ear, *Te amo*. I said it back to him, even though I wasn't sure whether either of us truly meant it; and then I wrapped my legs around him, sobbing as we came together and shook in one another's arms like two people caught in an earthquake.

Evan healed me. I don't know how else to say it. Either he was the best actor in the whole world, or he truly believed I was beautiful. All of me. I could feel it in the way he touched me. No one had touched me that way in a very long time. I don't think Scott ever had, even when I was whole. That tender way a man touches a woman when things between them are new, his fingers skimming over her so light and delicate, like he's afraid of breaking her—that was how Evan touched me. Over and over again.

Later, much later, he snuggled up behind me and wrapped me in his arms.

"I don't understand myself, what I just did." I fought back tears, not wanting to come across as neurotic and needy. "Is this love? I don't know your favorite song or anything like that. Shouldn't I? How can you love someone if you don't know them?"

"We know a lot of pretty important things about

each other," he answered. "I know when you make up your mind to do something, you're hard to stop. I know you can be loyal to a fault. That's why you went back to Scott—not because you're stupid or desperate. You were loyal. That's a good thing."

"This is a new thing for me," I said. "Going to bed with a guy I've only known for a few days."

"You've known me longer than that."

"But I haven't, have I? I've only known the real you for two days, and here I am in bed with you."

"Sabrina." He nuzzled my hair. "Don't think it to death. It was fantastic, it is fantastic. It doesn't make you a bad girl. In fact, you were very, very good."

He made me smile, and I cuddled closer to him. I reached back and stroked his cheek with my fingers. They brushed against his earring, and I gave it a little tug.

"Why do you wear those earrings? I mean, they're very cool, but don't you take a lot of ribbing for that?"

"Not often." He didn't say anything else for so long, I thought I'd insulted him. Then he cleared his throat and spoke up.

"I did it on a dare. I was fresh out of the Army, and my brother Christian and I were drunk and he dared me, so I did it. That's all. I keep them in memory of who he was—he was my brother, but he was also my best friend. It's corny, I know. I don't tell many people the why of it."

"Then I'm glad you told me." I turned in his arms so I could look at his face. "What happened to him?"

"He worked for the DEA—he's the one who got me my job. Tyrese was his partner. They went undercover to infiltrate the Mendoza gang—" Evan faltered. "The Mendozas took him from me."

"Oh God, I'm so sorry."

"It's all right," he whispered. "It's in the past, long in the past."

We fell into an easy silence, breathing in and out together, drowsy and at peace. My head nestled in the crook between his chin and his shoulder, and I closed my eyes, starting to doze.

"It would be something by Van Morrison," he mumbled lazily. His hair fell forward and tickled my nose, and his breath became soft as he relaxed into sleep.

****

We slept for a couple of hours, then woke in the early evening darkness, hungry for one another all over again. Evan had curled himself behind me again, and I felt the pressure of his erection stirring against me like a snake. Astonishingly, wondrously, I felt the answering wetness trickling out of me. My whole body was awake again, in a way I had thought couldn't happen anymore.

Evan's fingers traced the line of my face and glided down my arm to my hip. He pressed his hand against my belly, slipping it lower until it came to rest on the warm mound of my vulva and began massaging me there. His other hand lifted my hair, and he caught the nape of my neck in a sharp, vampire kiss.

"Yes," I whispered. "Yes, please."

His hands left me for only a moment, and without seeing it, I heard the rustle of the little foil packet. Wordlessly, he parted my legs and slipped into me from behind. That was a first. Men didn't do things like that with me. It wasn't that I refused; it was that they never even tried. I'm one of those nice girls, and guys look at us a certain way, expect certain limits with us. Missionary only was generally how Scott had looked at me, even before my surgery. I don't know why Evan didn't look at me that way or expect those limits. Probably he never

209

looked at a woman and saw rules and limits. Probably he never looked at anything that way in his entire life. For a guy like him, venturing into uncharted territory is second nature, and now I seemed to be part of that territory.

His right hand stroked my hair as the other cupped my precious, perfectly normal left breast. He began to move harder in me, and I let out a little moan, arching my hips tighter against him. I looked down and saw his golden-brown hands slip around my waist, pulling me tighter against him. The darkness of him against my pale Irish skin—it was like a perfect study in chiaroscuro and somehow that made what was happening between us even more amazing. We weren't just good together, we were a work of art. I laughed, but it came out as a long, high cry of release. Or maybe triumph.

Evan rocked against me, hard and silent except for an occasional grunt, and I found myself crying out louder. I sounded like someone in a porno movie, unreal even to myself. I worried Pete or Liz would come into the house, and I tried to rein myself in, but I couldn't. Maybe it was the incredible level of stress or the fact that Evan was magnificent in bed or how long it had been since the last time, but I couldn't shut up to save my life. If someone had stuck a gun to my head right then and told me to be quiet they'd have had to go ahead and shoot me.

Scott hated how noisy I was. Not that he got me to that point often. Never since the surgery, in fact. I had assumed something was wrong with me, that all those toxic chemicals had simply destroyed my ability to be aroused or to respond to a man. Before the cancer, there'd been a few pretty good episodes with Scott. He wasn't totally inept in that department, just more restrained than Evan. But on those rare occasions, if I started getting noisy, he'd shush me. Like it embarrassed him. Once he even put a hand over my mouth.

Evan did not do that. Instead, he answered my noises with low animal rumbles in his throat, urging me on and winding me up even more.

This is going to be even bigger than the last time. Then I got a little worried. Could you actually have sex that is too good? Maybe my heart would well and truly stop when we came this time. No wonder the Elizabethans called it dying.

In the final throes, Evan rolled me onto my hands and knees, groaning into my ear. I was so high, my injured knee didn't even hurt when he did that.

In some dim part of my brain, I could hear a steady buzzing sound, like bees swarming, and I worried again that I would die this time. Wasn't that one of the signs of a stroke, that humming noise? But oh, what a way to go.

Then some more practical part of my mind kicked in. *Doorbell. Door.* That buzzing sound was the doorbell going off. The words finally formed in my head, and I said them out loud.

"Oh, Jesus, I don't care," Evan whispered right in my ear.

We both knew that our brief respite was at an end, but we couldn't care right then. We were both frantically trying to finish what we'd begun, like two dogs on the front lawn praying the master won't turn on the hose. I reached back and pulled at his hair, and we both let out a long, barely stifled moan.

"Yo, Evan, we're here!" a man's voice called from downstairs.

"Hey, did you hear me, Ev?" The blustery new arrival bellowed up the staircase. He sounded like he was laughing as he spoke, like he knew what was happening in our room.

"Hang on a sec, Chuck," Evan answered, his voice deceptively under control. "I'm coming."

211

That was it. We both found that so brilliantly hilarious, we collapsed onto our backs in a sweaty, tangled mess of frustrated giggles.

"I hope you aren't going to make me blow open the bedroom door again, Spike," Chuck shouted in reply, and we started giggling all over again.

I laughed so hard I made a little snorting sound, and then I laughed even harder at that. "Wait a minute, who's Spike?"

Evan's face flushed bright red. "It's a nickname. And it's a long story. I'll tell you later."

I never did hear that story.

Eighteen

"Sorry it took us so long to get here. Not that you guys were missing us too much." Chuck shifted out of his jacket and hung it on a coat rack in the foyer, where it dripped puddles onto the wooden floor.

I'd expected an entire squadron of federal agents to be smirking at us when Evan and I finally dressed and came downstairs. In reality, only four greeted us: Chuck, two unidentified men in grey suits with narrow ties, and Tyrese Campbell.

He'd arrived last and hadn't said one word. He sat in the living room chair I'd occupied earlier, his elbows resting on its arms and his fingers steepled together in front of his face. He still wore his black trench coat, and he'd planted his drippy body right in the upholstered chair. He stared at me where I sat beside Evan on the couch, silently challenging me to complain about his messing up my temporary refuge. From time to time, I'd see him poke his tongue in his cheek or purse his lips like he'd tasted something sour.

Chuck cleared his throat a few times. "We couldn't find your man Scott. Or this other man you talked about, the one with the curly hair."

I stifled a tiny whimper. Hey, maybe they'd move me to San Diego, and I could open an art gallery. I've always liked the nice, mild climate and pretty view of the Pacific Ocean. Yes indeedy, witness protection—it's a good thing!

Nope. Even drunk I'd have trouble convincing myself of that one.

"They can't have gone far, Miss O'Hara. There's a high chain-link fence at the back of the airpark grounds. We figure they scaled that, and we have people searching the surrounding area even as we speak."

"Where does it lead?" Evan asked.

I got the jump on them all by answering first. "To a walking trail. It runs past the airpark and some businesses and then behind a big housing development."

Tyrese cast a questioning glance in my direction.

"My friend Jess lives in one of the houses. We could practically walk right out her backyard and come out on that trail."

Tyrese made a face that was almost a snarl.

"Does Scott Bennett know where your friend lives?"

I said nothing. The look on my face was answer enough for them.

"Give me her address." Tyrese pulled a cell phone from the pocket of his sodden coat. I did so as he punched in a phone number. He fired out his name and some identifying code, probably a badge number or something, then asked to speak with some other senior agent. He gave the agent Jess' address and suggested he send a couple of people to her house to make sure she was okay. I relaxed and leaned back against the sofa, reminding myself that not all weird dreams come true.

"They might not go to her place." Chuck leaned his meaty palm against the living room doorframe and stared into the middle distance, as if he were concentrating on some math problem. "They could have grabbed the first car they found and headed out of town, possibly north to Pennsylvania."

"They won't leave." I raked my hands through my sweaty hair, then pressed them to my cheeks. "They'll want the laptop. And the backup."

"The what?" Evan frowned.

"The backup. I told them I made a backup."

"Why in the hell did you do that?" Tyrese demanded.

"They were going to kill Leo," I snapped back at him. "I couldn't think of anything else in a pinch, okay? I told them I had a backup, and that I wouldn't let them have it if they hurt him."

Tyrese stared at me for a long time. I couldn't make out whether he considered me brilliant or a great big pain in the ass. For all I could tell, he was thinking about what he would have for dinner that night.

"You must be one hell of a poker player," I said to him.

Chuck made a little strangled sound and then hastily cleared his throat. Tyrese shot him a scolding look.

"I don't gamble."

"Mister, aren't you in the wrong line of work?" I countered.

"Not the way I do the job." A little twitch in his lips might have qualified as a smile. "Now, the way our friend Evan here does the job—that's gambling."

He gave Evan a weirdly intense look, almost tender. He was the big brother who's constantly arguing with his sibling but gets completely furious when anyone else tries to put that brother down.

"Of course, Evan's way wouldn't be so bad if it weren't for the gambling he does with other people's lives."

Chuck tried to jump in with something light-hearted, but he wasn't fast enough.

Evan scratched his forehead. "Yeah, about that—. How is Ben?"

"The same," Tyrese answered. "Critical condition. On life support. All thanks to your gonad-driven management of this case."

To my surprise, Evan lowered his head and hunched his shoulders like a little boy waiting for the smack of a belt.

"Hey," I said. "Don't talk to him that way."

Evan shushed me as Tyrese widened his eyes.

"I'll bet you've mismanaged a case at least once in your life." I thrust my hand on my hips and gave Tyrese that Mommy look that had worked so well on Evan. He was unfazed. Evan bit his lower lip, and I worried I'd hurt his feelings. "I didn't mean you've mismanaged this case! I'm sure you did the best you could."

Oh, God, that was even worse. If I didn't shut up soon, I'd never have another orgasm like that last one again. "Evan, I'm just saying we all mess things up under pressure, and Tyrese is possibly being too judgmental."

Chuck made that strangling noise again, and then it degenerated into a mad fit of coughing. I wondered if he were a smoker, then I glanced over at him and realized he was trying not to laugh.

"Young lady." I turned back to Tyrese. His eyes narrowed. The look he leveled at me reminded me of a mechanic trying to find the source of that pinging under the car hood.

"Don't 'young lady' me," I interrupted. "You aren't that much older than I am. Anyway, don't you think we both feel bad enough about what happened to Frodo? Ben. I mean Ben."

"Sabrina, this isn't your argument." Evan spoke quietly, no hint of laughter in his face anymore. He sat back on the sofa and tucked his hair back behind his ears.

"I'm so sorry, Tyrese." His voice dripped with sarcasm I'd never heard him use before. "You're right. I wasn't thinking straight. I wanted Sabrina safe and away from the scene. I let my emotions get in the way, and I screwed up. Badly. Are we even now?"

Tyrese's back went up, literally. He squared up his shoulders and thrust his chest out in a defensive posture.

"Do my mistakes in this case equal all the mistakes you made in Vera Cruz in '98? Do they?" Evan bolted from his seat and headed toward the corridor.

Tyrese looked to me like ex-military—the ramrod posture, the unreadable facial expressions, stern and unemotional. So, I was taken aback when he responded to Evan's remarks by covering his face with his hands and sagging forward.

"You guys are not doing this again," Chuck said. Evan turned in the doorway and stopped to listen. Tyrese looked up. Even the two unidentified guys in suits pricked up their ears like a couple of Dobermans. Chuck might not be the boss, but it looked like everyone listened when he had something to say. He'd been leaning against the doorframe, his posture downright slouchy and relaxed. Now he straightened and arched an eyebrow at Tyrese. "It's not Evan's fault your new man was shot." Then he pointed a finger at Evan. "And what happened to your brother wasn't Tyrese's fault either. Both of you, grow up."

"He was Christian's partner," Evan muttered. "He should have seen what was coming. He should have done something."

"You two need to forgive each other—at least temporarily—and get angry at the Mendozas again, okay?" Chuck looked from one to the other expectantly. I decided I liked him immensely. He reminded me of my blunt-spoken dad. Or even my slightly wussy brother-in-law. He reminded me of any sensible guy trying to restore order during a family feud. Then I remembered I was at least part of the reason the family was feuding.

"I'm sorry too," I said into the pregnant silence that followed Chuck's remarks. "I am truly sorry I didn't see what was happening with Scott. I was consumed with my own problems, my own life, and not paying any attention to him. Maybe I'd have figured out what was going on if I hadn't had so much else to focus on right then."

Evan crossed the room and sat down beside me again. "You're not seriously trying to blame yourself for Scott's idiotic behavior, are you, babe?" He threw an arm around my shoulders and that surprised me. I had thought he'd want to maintain a cool façade in front of his co-workers.

"You two make a heartwarming couple," Tyrese muttered. "I'm glad Ben's sacrifice proved to be so worthwhile for you, Evan."

Evan's jaw twitched, and he opened his mouth, but I cut him off. "I'm sorry about Ben. He seemed like such a sweet guy. I hope he'll be all right, honestly I do."

I started to reach my hand out to pat Tyrese's arm. He responded with a look that could freeze the water in a whistling teakettle. I guess it worked on criminals, or at least on his subordinates. It didn't do much for me. I'd seen uglier looks at Thanksgiving dinner for about fifteen years—every time I showed up without a husband.

"Oh, please. If you think you're frightening me, you've obviously never met my mother. Why don't you can this whole guilt trip about Ben, okay?" I crossed my arms over my chest and enjoyed his befuddled expression. I could see he wasn't talked to that way very often.

Tyrese poked his tongue in his cheek and gave me that appraiser's squint again. "Good God, if I'd known you were this feisty and that you had freckles, too, I'd never have let Evan anywhere near you."

Again with the freckles! Who knew they were an aphrodisiac for some men?

"The freckles didn't show up in those file photos." Evan appeared to be beaming at me as he spoke, and that scared me way more than Tyrese's scowl.

"Well, you got what you wanted." Tyrese ducked his head at Evan, as though grudgingly impressed, "Let's hope you'll be able to think straight enough to do your job now."

"Does that mean I'm not on vacation after all?"

Tyrese glanced from Evan to me and then back.

"You can probably take the rest of today off. But yeah, I'll put you back on duty tomorrow. I doubt if the secretary even processed the paperwork yet. Don't make me wish she had."

"I'll do my best, Boss." Evan unfolded his long legs and rose from the sofa. "Right now, I'm gonna get a soda. I'm thirsty."

"Can't imagine why," Tyrese muttered, but he didn't sound so angry and disapproving this time.

As Evan passed him, Tyrese reached out and grabbed his arm. "Ben's not your fault. Christian wasn't mine."

Evan gave a curt nod and left the room. After he'd gone, I leaned in toward his boss.

"Mr.—um, sorry, I only remember Tyrese—".

"Campbell. Tyrese Campbell. But Tyrese is fine."

I nodded, and then I didn't use it. He seemed too much like a 'Mister' for me to be at ease calling him Tyrese.

"Evan says I might have to stay here a long time."

Tyrese massaged his neck. "It's a possibility. The bottom line is all of this is your choice. Whether you want temporary protection from us or the FBI, that's a choice. Whether you testify against your fiancé and his associates once they're caught—that's a choice, too. Whether you go into WITSEC—witness protection—after you testify—another choice. Truthfully, if you insisted, you could walk out of this house right now and go back to work tomorrow."

"I could?"

"But I wouldn't advise it," he concluded.

"No," I sighed. "I didn't think you would."

"Now, you can certainly contact a lawyer for a more unbiased opinion."

"I don't even know what lawyer to call. The lawyer I trusted is in the hospital now. What about my family, can I contact them?"

"My advice—and that's all it is—Miss O'Hara, is that you not contact any loved ones until we have Scott and his associates in custody."

His meaning was distressingly clear. They might be listening to my family and friends' conversations; they might use them to get to me.

Evan stomped back into the room with his arms loaded with cans of soda, passing one out to everyone. The barely suppressed rage toward Tyrese was utterly gone, as far as I could tell.

"We need to figure out why so many people came after us last night." He sat down beside me but offered no additional display of affection.

Chuck spoke up, and again everyone stopped to listen.

"It looks like there's a definite split. We have some information from our source in Mexico City. She's not highly placed, but it doesn't take someone at the top to see the brothers are feuding. I'm thinking Hector sent the guys in the building, but the others in the cars might have been sent by his brothers to figure out what he was doing. Either way, both sides have to be stretched thin right now. This isn't their stronghold."

"So we're looking for Scott Bennett and who

else?" Tyrese turned to me for the answer, taking me off guard.

"Oh." I sat up straight, like I was back in school and this was a pop quiz. "I saw a skinny blond guy with curly hair. He stuck his face right in mine, and I head-butted him, so he might have a broken nose now—"

Tyrese rolled his eyes at Evan, who grinned back at him like a proud teacher.

"I'm not trying to brag," I said. "It might not be broken. But he was bleeding a lot. And Scott was there. The freckle-faced man."

"We have him and their pilot," Tyrese confirmed.

"And the other man—Miguel. He had a gun. My dad was a police officer, and he taught me how to use a gun when I was a teenager. He was going to shoot us. Miguel, I mean. Not my dad. He's on a hunting trip in Colorado. My dad, not Miguel."

Evan laced his fingers through mine. "Sabrina, you're babbling."

"We get it," Tyrese told me. "Self-defense. Phony ID, logically enough. So we're waiting on prints."

"They talked about another man. They were waiting for someone named Chris to meet us."

A chill descended on the room. All three of the men looked away from me and to one another, pursuing some silent line of reasoning I couldn't follow.

"No," Evan said after a moment.

Chuck cocked his head, obviously disagreeing with his colleague's verdict.

They must know some Mendoza henchman by that name. "Is he extremely dangerous?"

Chuck answered. "If it's who I think it is, then yes. He's insane. He likes messing with people's heads, hurting them."

Evan's jaw twitched furiously again, and Tyrese

had left the chair to pace around the room.

"It's possible the name's a coincidence. It's possible this is some local hired gun they're using." Chuck took a deep breath and clenched his fists. "It has to be."

"We'll get the locals to put out APBs on Scott, the blond guy, and we'll send them a flyer on Chris, too," Tyrese said. "So they know what he looks like. In case it's no mistake."

They talked some more, about shift changes and who else would be guarding the house. I asked them how long they thought I'd need to stay there, and Tyrese made some blustery noises without really answering me. Chuck and he got into a heated discussion about whether I'd be able to resume my old life as soon as Scott and his friends had been captured. Chuck thought Hector was a practical character, and that if his men were caught, he would simply disavow all knowledge of them and would probably also stay the hell away from me.

He sat down on the other side of me on the couch. "Once you've given evidence in this particular case, you won't matter anymore. He's hoping we won't be able to make that case in the first place, that's why he's after you and the laptop. But if he fails, he'll eliminate the people who can provide the most damaging testimony against him and his operators. And that's not you—that's Scott. Once we catch Scott and his accomplices, you become a lot less significant in the scheme of things. I'm betting Scott Bennett will sing like a canary if he thinks it will save his own ass."

"I'm pretty sure you've got that right," I admitted. "So the trick is to keep me alive until I have to testify against Scott and these other men?"

"If Scott talks, we might not need your evidence at all."

"But you don't have Scott. And meanwhile, it

can take a long time for a case to come to trial, can't it?"

"We would try to get it expedited. At Homeland Security, there are a lot of non-traditional approaches we can use."

"But how long—"

I was about to press them again for an estimate on how long I would be living like this, but the sound of my cell phone ringing stopped me. I stared at the innocuous little device on the coffee table, blithely and rather ironically chiming out The Bee Gees' "Staying Alive." Jess had reset it from "A Little Night Music" as a joke when I was going through chemo, and I'd kept it. It gave people a laugh. Although not right at the moment, of course.

Tyrese nodded to the two quiet guys in suits. They went into the dining room, and one of them picked up a headset and put it on. Then Tyrese nodded for me to pick up my phone. Obviously, when Evan had told me my phone was no longer bugged, he meant that it was no longer bugged by *the bad guys*.

"Hello." My voice quavered a bit, and I cursed to myself. That would sound even more pronounced when it came down the line to whoever was at the other end.

"Oh, hello there, dearie pie!" Nanny's voice came over so loud, I had to hold the phone away from my ear. Tyrese made a cutting gesture across his throat.

"Nanny, I can't talk now," I told her, but her shrill voice steamrolled right over me. I shrugged apologetically at Tyrese.

"Sabrina, honey, Consuelo and I are worried about you and your situation."

Consuelo was the companion Daddy had hired to help Nanny out whenever he couldn't be around.

"Nanny, I don't have a situation!"

"Consuelo is concerned at your age you might

try to get rid of the baby."

The eyebrows darted way up on the guy in the suit who was listening to my conversation.

"Nanny, for Heaven's sake, I am *not* getting rid of the baby."

As Nanny babbled away in the background, I watched Tyrese leap to his feet and glower at Evan. "You told me nothing had happened between you two!"

"It hadn't!" Evan actually flinched as he spoke. "Not until—. Hey, you took me off the case, man! Even I don't work that fast!"

"Nanny!" I spoke very carefully and very loudly. "Pay attention. I am not pregnant and never was. You are old and mostly deaf, and you get confused. Now you need to get off the phone and stay off. I'm waiting for Scott to call. He's the one who's in trouble, Nanny. He's having some problems at work, and I'm waiting for him to call."

"Well, that's all right then." She clucked. "Maybe I was thinking of Angela. That little baby machine gets on my nerves. As if popping babies out like slot machine loot is some sort of accomplishment."

And with that, she hung up. The Suit yanked off his headphones and collapsed in a heap in front of the computer. He was laughing so hard, tears filled his eyes. Even Tyrese had enormous difficulty maintaining his poker face. I frowned at them.

"I am so pleased my life can provide comic relief for all of you."

Evan threw an arm around me and grinned. "I can't wait to meet her."

Oh dear God, it suddenly dawned on me, *if we live through this, he'll have to meet them all.* My gruff, sweet dad and my self-important sister and my pious brother and my goofy grandmother and even that scary, controlling woman in Arizona I called Mom. All of them. That thought was almost enough to make a girl wish the bad guys would get her.

Someday, I'll learn not to think such irreverent thoughts. When "Stayin' Alive" played again, I whipped open my phone and shouted into it. "Nanny, I love you, but you have to leave me alone! Right now!"

"Sabrina! Hey, I've never been confused with a ninety-year-old woman before! You've left me in the lurch here!"

Scott chuckled. His voice was full of false joviality—the voice he used to explain why he couldn't come home on one of my chemo days, why he absolutely had to work late that night and might stay with a friend of his who lived in Georgetown so he wouldn't have to drive when he was so tired. Probably that was the only Scott there had ever been. Probably the funny, good-looking, artsy Scott had been the plastic wrapper on the real Scott—the cowardly, selfish, self-destructive Scott.

"I left *you* in the lurch?" I repeated.

"Who was the guy with the hair? Is that your new boyfriend from the gym? Doesn't look like your type, Sabrina, but I guess you aren't after him for his intellect, eh?"

Did he not know Evan was a Federal agent? Or was he trying to draw me out?

"Um, maybe," was all I said.

"Keep him out of this mess," Scott retorted. "I could still take you with me when I go if you come to your senses. But if you don't—then at least keep the young stud out of it."

I bristled. "He's not that much younger than I am."

"Fine. Now, listen, you still have something of mine and my friends are—Sabrina, to be honest, they're pretty pissed. If I don't get that laptop back tonight, I'm probably a dead man."

Did I care? That was the $64,000 question. I asked it out loud. "Ask me if I care."

"Excuse me?" Scott still believed I was the soft, squishy girl he'd met six years ago. To him, I was a tender bleeding heart who could easily be talked into things because I was too nice to make a scene. He still didn't understand—that person had been burned away, burned right out of my veins as the Cytoxan burned away the cancer cells. I'd only just figured it out.

"I said—ask me if I care, Scott," I told him again.

"Okay." He sounded a little less certain of himself. "You're angry right now, and I can respect that. But you don't understand what's at stake."

"Well, why don't you educate me? What is at stake? You sure aren't in this situation because you needed the money. Leo told me about the trust fund."

"Of course I'm in it for the money," he answered. "You can never have too much money. But there's more to it than that. See, we can use these perverts' weaknesses against them. We have records of congressmen, lobbyists, businessmen—people I met through my dear clueless uncle, most of them. We make money by hooking them up with our little entertainment service. But what I got Hector to see is that we can do even more than that—we can use that information against them, make them pay a second time in order to keep us quiet. We can even influence votes on immigration policy. He loves that. He has big goals, Hector does. Politics. Everybody wants to be in politics. Boy, if Uncle Carlton knew what sort of people he's been playing golf with for the last twenty years!"

"So he's not a part of this?" I asked.

Scott made an amused, razzing noise that didn't sound entirely sober.

"Of course not, that old stick in the mud. But I'm good at persuading people, Sabrina. Used to be good at persuading you. Should've been a salesman. Never wanted to be a lawyer in the first place. It's the family business."

"My heart bleeds for you." I struggled to control my voice.

"Okay, your contempt is immaterial. Bottom line—I want my laptop, I want the backup copy, and I want it all tonight. And I want the cops and the pretty boy kept out of it."

The guy in the suit who was listening stifled a grin at that last remark.

"Oh, or you'll do what?!" My dream didn't worry me anymore. Tyrese had sent agents to protect Jess—they'd be there soon, if they hadn't already arrived. And Scott hadn't mentioned her, so Chuck was probably right. They were hiding out somewhere else or on their way up to Pennsylvania.

"I won't do anything," Scott told me. "But I have this friend who has a bad temper, and he's getting pretty impatient with the situation."

I heard muffled voices, as if someone had covered the receiver, then a new voice came on the line.

"Hey, sugar," it twanged. "Your fiancé is handling you badly. No doubt you'll be more interested in what I have to say."

I kept silent. In the background, I heard Scott murmur two simple words. "Please don't." Then he added, "Leave it alone."

The best thing about Scott was that he loved animals. He was always fond of any furry thing, and as far as I knew he always treated them well. His dog had died shortly before he moved in with me, and it had upset him terribly. The poor thing was seventeen and going blind and had a tumor, but he'd hated to put it down. He might not have much regard for me, for his uncle, or for any other human being, but I knew that bit about liking animals was no act. So, when Scott said what he said, I knew where they were and that those agents wouldn't get there in time to help Jess. Or Kasey. I'd have to handle it myself, right here and now.

"Don't you dare hurt the dog." I sounded more confident than I felt.

The guy on the headset looked utterly baffled, as did everyone else. I was betting even the stranger at the other end of the phone looked a little surprised. He said nothing.

"I know what you want to do, and I'm telling you now don't do it. If you do it, you'll get nothing from me, nothing."

"I could always hurt your friend instead—or even Scott here. You choose."

Scott sputtered and babbled in the background.

"Look, if anything happens to the dog, Jess won't ever speak to me again, so she won't be my friend anymore. And as for Scott—he's not my fiancé, and I'm glad to be rid of him. I don't care what happens to him. You let him know I said that, okay?"

Tyrese jumped to his feet and started shaking his head frantically. I ignored him. He hurried into the dining room and took the headset from the guy in the suit.

Scott started protesting again, louder this time. The stranger shouted, "You heard her!" Then a sharp crack was followed by a thump. A woman screamed, and everything went quiet.

Nineteen

"I gotta say, I agree wholeheartedly with your choice, sugar," the stranger said.

"My choice?"

"Scott!" His laughter crackled down the phone line, and he sounded like a big, mirthful department store Santa. "Sugar, I didn't much want to hurt the dog either. Like 'em way better than people."

I heard something that sounded like Scott whimpering and near tears. Then he spoke, and I heard him asking—no, pleading with the stranger— to not hurt him again. Listening to another person beg is incredibly disturbing, even if it's someone you don't like anymore.

"What did you do?"

"I broke his arm." The stranger tossed out the words as if the answer should have been obvious. He sounded darned pleased with himself, too.

I couldn't think of a single thing to say, for fear of what might happen next.

"Now that we understand each other," he continued, "I want you to deliver that laptop and the backup as soon as possible. You may not care for Scott anymore, but I know you don't want him to die at our hands. Because I promise you Miss O'Hara, that would be a long, slow, painful process." He sounded downright gleeful at the prospect.

I leaned forward in my seat, propping my elbows on my knees, hunching myself up against the world. Evan laid a hand on the middle of my back.

"It will take me awhile to get to the laptop." It always worked when they said that in the movies. "I hid it."

"I'm sure you did. You're a bright girl, much brighter than Scott led me to believe."

I ignored the bait. Something about his voice nagged at me, some familiar cadence to the words. Maybe I'd met him when we were in Mexico? But he spoke perfect English, so that seemed unlikely. Had he called Scott on the phone in the past? That must be it.

"I'll give you two hours to retrieve the laptop and the backup files and get here. You already have our address, don't you?"

I had this notion that if I could change what happened to the dog, make it different from my dream, then what happened to Jess would be different, too. "I want you to put Kasey outside right now. I want him out in the backyard, barking away when I come up to the house, or I don't go inside. Do you understand?"

The sound became muffled again, and then I heard some banging and clattering—doors opening. And then he must have held the receiver out so that I could hear Kasey barking loud and clear.

"Happy now?"

"No. You can't seriously expect me to do anything for you unless I can talk to Jess."

He didn't acknowledge my request, but a rustle and swish crackled over the line before I heard her voice.

"Hey, this totally sucks," came her snuffled greeting.

"Yeah, I know. But I'll be there soon, and everything will be fine. Don't cry."

"Oh, right. Everything will end happily ever after."

"Pretend it will, and maybe that will work," I told her.

"Who the hell are these people, Sabrina?"

230

"They're the bad guys, Jess. They want me, and they want Scott's computer, so I'm going to bring it to them."

"What happened to—"

I cut her off. I didn't know who she might mention. Mentioning Leo would be okay, Scott knew about him. Mentioning Agent Double-O-Sexy could complicate things. Not to mention how ridiculous I'd feel if Evan learned about her nickname for him.

"I'll be alone when I get there. I told that guy not to hurt Kasey. I couldn't get him to promise not to hurt you."

"Thanks so much." She sounded a tad bit ungrateful, if you ask me.

"I didn't think I could get them to put you out in the back yard, too. Want me to try?"

She made a sad little noise, half-laugh, half-sob. "No. It's raining, and I'm too chubby to fit in the doghouse."

"We've both been through worse," I told her.

"I sure hope you're right."

The stranger came back onto the line. "Scott tells me you had a friend with you at the airpark, someone from your gym?"

Tyrese nodded to me.

"Um, yeah," I answered.

"Don't bring him. Don't bring anyone. Come alone with the computer and the backup, and we'll see you at nine."

With that, the line went dead.

"We need to tell those agents en route to back off." Tyrese waved a hand at Chuck. "Tell them we have a hostage situation, and they need to keep a low profile until reinforcements arrive. And we're going to need a laptop."

"What about Scott's?" I asked. "Leo kept it safe for you guys. He nearly died for that stupid piece of plastic and metal."

They all looked at each other, like a little league team that had broken a window and hoped no one would find out.

"Scott's computer is already on its way to our data analysis center in Philadelphia," Chuck said.

I must've looked pretty panic-stricken, because Evan patted my back and spoke up. "It's okay. We'll fake it. I'm sure we've got another one that looks like it. You can do this."

"Huh." I snorted. "Like I have a choice."

****

Okay, I'd said to myself last year, I'm probably going to die, and I haven't accomplished one damned important thing. Now I could die for a cause. If I could walk into that house and do something, anything—Stall? Distract? Something. If I could do whatever that something was, Tyrese and his agents might be able to get Jess out alive. I was probably a dead woman whatever happened. But at least Jess's daughter would still have her mom. That was something I could make happen. So when I snapped the cell phone shut, and Tyrese came to me, I already knew what he wanted, and I knew I would say yes.

"I'd like you to wear a wire when you go in there."

"Oh, no, no, no!" Evan jumped to his feet. He threw his hands in the air and shook his head at Tyrese.

"It's okay," I said.

"It is not. They'll be looking for that, and they'll find it!"

"Where do you put it?" I asked Tyrese. "Is it small? If it's small, you could put it inside my bra. They won't look there."

"To be fair to Evan, Ms. O'Hara, they probably would look there," Tyrese told me. "They have no honor, and they wouldn't balk at making you strip."

Evan's jaw began to twitch again, so I laid my hand on his shoulder.

"Evan, calm down." I smiled. "They won't want to strip search me, not when I say I've had a mastectomy. They'll get way too flummoxed."

"But you didn't have a—"

"They don't need to have the details, do they? I don't care how mad, bad, and dangerous these guys are. They won't want to touch me with a ten-foot pole when I say *mastectomy*. That's the kind of guys they are."

And Scott would be there to tell them all about my hideous deformity. Finally his delicate sense of beauty would turn out to be a good thing.

Tyrese stepped forward. "I think this is worth a try."

"Yeah, you would think that," Evan snapped. "You're not the one in love with her."

Talk about an awkward moment. Chuck and Tyrese found something incredibly fascinating in the dingy, early American carpet. Even I didn't know where to look. Sometimes people say *love* during sex, but it seems wise not to bring it up again later.

"I—um—thank you," I murmured, sounding rather dazed.

He spun on his heel and stalked out of the room into the kitchen.

"Should I go after him?" I asked no one in particular.

"Damned if I know," Tyrese said. "Chuck, go see Liz, and get the equipment ready to have Ms. O'Hara wired. We also need to get a computer that looks like Bennett's."

"I'll get right on it." Chuck hurried out the front door, obviously glad to have a job to do, glad to be away from all those icky emotions. Tyrese gestured at the two guys in suits.

"You guys, um, go and help him."

233

They shrugged and followed Chuck out of the room, all of them assiduously avoiding the sight of me.

Tyrese made a show of rifling through his pockets. "I'm going out to my car and gather a few things I need. I'll be back in a few minutes."

"Thank you." I seriously doubted he needed anything from his car. After he left, I stood around in the living room, trying to decide whether I even wanted to go into the kitchen. Professions of undying devotion seemed premature to say the least. And yet.

I tiptoed down the corridor and pushed open the swinging door. He was sitting with his head in hands.

"That was a surprise," I stepped behind him and laid my hands on his shoulders.

He straightened up and spoke without looking at me. "I said it earlier, or do you really not speak any Spanish?"

"I heard it, I said it back," I reminded him.

"But now that you've calmed down, you aren't so sure?"

"I can't think about it right now, is all," I smoothed my hand over his beautiful long hair, brushing it back with my fingers again and again.

"I'm sorry. Didn't mean to blurt it in front of everybody. In front of Tyrese! Christ. Did I sound like a stalker?"

"No," I knelt beside his chair. "Oh, no."

I laid my head on his lap. He bent forward and buried his face in my hair.

"If they find a wire, they'll kill you right then and there. There's no way we'd be able to get to you fast enough."

"I know." I wanted to scream with rage, but I fought it down. "It's okay. I just had the best sex of my life, what better day to die? At least I won't be bald if it happens now."

He lifted my face toward his, those dark eyes searching my face. We kissed then, slow and deep and full of longing. I started to cry, and he wiped away the tears with his thumbs, but he continued kissing me. Afterward, he released me and reached around his neck. He brought out the wooden cross he wore around his neck.

"Oh, Evan, stop," I protested.

"My grandfather carved one of these for all of us—my brothers and my sister—for our Confirmation. It's good luck."

He slipped it over his head and then draped it around my own. He fussed with the leather necklace a bit before tucking it inside my sweatshirt. Then he kissed my forehead.

"I'll save the rest of what I want to say for later," he whispered in my ear. "For when you come back."

****

The rain had stopped, but clouds still drifted across the moonless sky. Out on the edge of the city where Jess lived, everyone was snug in their club basements watching television, blissfully unaware that the Mexican Mob had taken over the house at the end of the cul-de-sac.

Agents were all around me—I had nothing to fear. But I was afraid anyway. It turned out I wasn't quite as at peace with death as I'd thought. My hands were sweaty and cold by the time I halted my Beemer—kindly brought to my new home by yet another agent earlier in the evening. I sat in the car for a few minutes, fingering Evan's cross. I don't think I was consciously praying. I had reached a level of fear so profound as to actually knock the automatic "Hail Mary's" right out of my head. That doesn't happen to a Catholic too often, even a lapsed one.

The cross bothered me, and I couldn't say why. I absolutely did not want to wear it into that house,

which made no sense. Jess was an indifferent
Lutheran, not someone who would take offense at
the sight of the thing, and if anything, maybe it
would prove intimidating to the bad guys. But what
would happen to Evan if I died wearing this thing?
Would he turn on God? Be all consumed with anger
at the Big Guy for not protecting his new lover? I
had met so many good people at the chemo
treatment center: a born-again Christian woman
with three children and a husband in Iraq; a sweet
old grandfather of about fifteen kids; a church
deacon whose frail wife depended on him for
everything. All of them were dead now. Putting
God's symbol around my neck would not keep me
alive one minute more. It might be better for Evan to
curse me, someone he'd only known for a month
anyway, than to curse God when I was gone. So I
took off the necklace and laid it on the seat beside
me, next to the laptop. I left them both there, and I
emerged from the car.

****

Scott opened the front door as I walked up the
path. His usually crisp linen shirt was rumpled and
dotted with little splashes of blood, and his left eye
was red and puffy. He grabbed me with one arm and
embraced me like I was his long-lost sister. And
truth be told, I didn't have the heart to pull away.
Over his shoulder, I saw Jess sitting in a wing chair
in her living room, hands neatly folded in her lap. If
not for the rope binding them, you'd have thought
she was watching a particularly enthralling TV
show.

I stepped into the foyer and Scott drew back,
closing the door behind me.

My old friend Harpo loomed into sight as I came
into the living room. He was sitting on the sofa, and
he had a gun pointed roughly in Jess' direction. He
swung it around and aimed it at the doorway as I

entered. His nose was purple and swollen, and I suspected he would make me pay for that later. He gave me that leering grin again.

"Hey, Harpo, good to see you again!"

"Chris wants her searched." He ignored me and spoke to Scott.

"Fine, I'll do it." Scott turned me toward him and laid a hand on my shoulder.

A quick bark of laughter issued from Harpo's lips.

"I'm sure you'd like to! But I don't think Chris and I would trust your judgment on this, Scotty."

I found the courage to laugh out loud without a trace of quaver in my voice. "Scotty?"

Scott shrugged at me, as if the nickname were news to him, too. The look in his eyes pretty much said, *These guys are scary-crazy. Look out.* I sighed heavily and stepped forward.

"Have fun, Harpo." I opened my rain slicker. Shrugging it off, I turned to hang it from the coat rack in the foyer.

Harpo grimaced and stalked toward me in three long strides. "Get your shirt off."

"Excuse me?"

Play dumb. That had been Chuck's advice when he explained how the wire worked and what they wanted. Play dumb, make the other guys do most of the talking. We want to hear them admitting to as many criminal acts as you can get out of them, and we want to stall them from looking at that laptop. Can do, I had said.

"Excuse me, you want me to what?" I laughed again, because it flustered Harpo when I did that.

"I want you to take your shirt off, make sure you ain't bugged."

"I'm not taking off my shirt. I'll take your frigging laptop and go, that's what I'll do."

"Please, man," Scott said. "She has her reasons."

237

Harpo smirked. "They always do, but I don't much care."

He lunged at me and started patting me all over. His thoroughness came as no surprise. He pried my legs apart and inched his way up to my crotch.

"I don't think I could fit a gun in there."

"You'd be amazed." He straightened up and went for my chest.

"Please, don't!" I squealed, sounding as meek and terrified as possible. But it was entirely an act. I don't know if terror had brought about a bizarre level of detachment, but I felt ridiculously confident. I had to restrain myself from kicking Harpo in the nuts. "I had a mastectomy. Please don't touch me there. Anywhere else."

As I expected, Harpo snatched his hands back like they were on fire. He eyed me suspiciously.

"It's true," Scott confirmed. "Believe me, you don't want to see it."

"That sucks." My curly-headed friend stomped back into the living room, fortunately losing all interest. Scott grabbed my elbow and ushered me in the same direction, then he sat me down on the sofa, next to Harpo.

"Good to see you again." Jess pasted a smile onto her ashen face. "Sorry I didn't have time to clean."

I grinned at her. This was a familiar routine between us, and I knew she must have been holding up all right if she'd remembered it.

"I couldn't tell." That was my usual reply when she compulsively apologized for the state of her always-immaculate house.

"So glad you could join us at last, sugar!" The disembodied voice came from around the corner. I recognized it from the telephone, but again there was that additional weird echo of something else. I should know who this guy is, I said to myself as his light footsteps approached.

And then he was there, resting his hands on Jess's shoulders in what looked liked a brotherly gesture of affection.

It was Evan.

Twenty

No, not Evan at all. On second glance, I marveled how I could have made the mistake. Evan didn't have all those grey streaks in his hair or that network of frown lines on his forehead. Nor did he have that flat, empty dullness in his eyes. But otherwise, the features—the earrings, the ponytail, the sly crooked smile—those were all my Evan.

"You're Christian," I gasped. Evan had never said the man was dead. He'd said, *they took him from me.*

"How do you know my name?" he demanded.

"Name?"

Fortunately, I was so startled by the whole turn of events, I had no trouble sounding like a vacuous little airhead.

"Oh!" I exclaimed. "Name? Your name? Is that your name? I meant, um, you're a Christian. Because of that thing you're wearing."

And I pointed at the Mesquite wood cross around his neck, twin to the one now lying outside on the passenger seat of my car.

He scowled. His lips parted to reveal a set of ugly, yellowing teeth. My sister Angela had an old college friend who wound up with a mouth like that after years of alcohol and drug abuse. "Meth mouth," Angela had called it. Had that happened to Christian? Was that the beginning of his downward spiral?

"I wouldn't call myself a Christian, exactly."

"Then why wear a cross?" That was all wrong. I was supposed to get him to admit to kidnapping and running a ring of sex slaves and here we were debating theology.

"Superstition? Desperation? Still hoping the Old Guy will come through for me in the eleventh hour?" His knuckles whitened where he was gripping Jess's shoulders.

"Oh, mean old God broke your heart, did he?" I retorted.

Surprisingly, he smiled. "Yeah, you could say that. But God's a fickle friend, isn't he? There I was at the lowest point in my life, and who'd He throw in my path? Hector Mendoza. And what a mentor Hector turned out to be. Helped me discover all sorts of hidden talents. Ask your sweetie here, he knows all about Hector."

He turned his glassy stare in Scott's direction.

"Don't you know all about him now, Scotty? How he starts with the little things—convincing you to turn a blind eye to a little lawbreaking, forgetting to file some stupid piece of paperwork you're too busy for anyway. Isn't that how it started for you, Scotty? Then you're feeling a little lonely, and he moves on to buying you a woman—oops, hope the little lady here isn't too shocked to hear that one."

He gave a sheepish little shrug, all too reminiscent of a gesture I'd seen Evan make a few times.

"And then if the woman doesn't cheer you up, there's the free drugs. Am I right?" He winked at Scott and flashed me a chilling, triumphant smile.

I glanced at Scott and found he could still surprise me. Guilt was written across his face in bright red. Drugs, too? Drugs?

"See," Christian continued, "Some people start falling and keep falling and, there's no bottom. Is there, Scotty? Scotty's starting to understand how that works, aren't you, buddy? I could order him to kill that dog in the back yard, sugar, and he'd probably do it."

Scott chewed on his lower lip and closed his eyes, fighting back tears. I wanted to hug him, and I wanted to tell him to grow a pair, all at the same time. I remembered Chuck saying stay angry with the Mendozas, so I went and hugged him.

"No, he wouldn't hurt the dog, not even for the likes of you."

"Aw, that's real sweet, sugar." Christian sounded a lot more Texas than Evan. That must be why I hadn't recognized the voice sooner. They both had a similar quality, a mellow, smoky baritone—but Evan's came out in a slow, even California drawl while Christian spoke in a sharp Texas twang. Maybe Evan had consciously adopted that other way of speaking to differentiate the two of them.

"So having my fiancé help you smuggle girls across the border illegally, that was part of his glorious initiation into your little secret club?" Scott sniveled against my shirt as I spoke—almost comically pathetic. Jess simply sat in front of Christian, silent and rigidly at attention.

Christian nodded. "That's pretty much the idea, sugar. Those girls would've wound up the same way back home. At least they got a taste of the bright lights and the big city before they met their inevitable fate."

"You're kind of bleak. Ev—"

I had started to say, *Evan's nothing like that.* "Ever consider therapy?" I amended.

"Drugs are more fun," he replied. "Cheaper too, if you work for the right people."

I shoved Scott away and strode toward Christian. Scott slumped against a wall in a dejected heap. "Okay, I don't want to hear any more about this. You're enjoying yourself way too much."

Christian cocked an eyebrow at me and stifled a crooked grin.

I tried to smile back. "You have something I want, I have something you want. Let her leave the house, and I'll get the laptop."

"Get it?" He snapped to attention, his eyes flashing with anger. "You were supposed to bring it here."

This was where I had departed from Tyrese's instructions. In some utility van somewhere on that street, Tyrese had ripped off his headphones and was having a massive heart attack. But I'd desperately wanted to get Jess out of that house. If I could accomplish that, my dream wouldn't come true. Evan wouldn't have to come in the house and accidentally shoot her in the confusion. Unfortunately, now I could see that the shooter in my dream hadn't been Evan. It had been Christian.

The whole dreams-and-premonitions thing would work much better if they weren't always garbled all to hell. The dream about Evan rejecting me when he saw me naked—that had been just plain wrong. Rose's vision of blood on my hands had been right, but so vague as to be useless. Now I could see that by trying to prevent the bad thing in my latest dream, I may have managed to put both Jess and myself in even more danger. I'd be walking her and me out of the house, right into possible crossfire between Christian and the Federal agents.

Knowing it was too late to fix my mistake, I squared my shoulders and spoke. "The laptop is outside in my car. I swear to God. I swear to the Blessed Mother. You name it, I'll swear on it. Give me your cross, and I'll swear on that."

I stepped toward him, but he raised his right arm and pointed a big semi-automatic at Jess' head, something vaguely military-looking. Insecure loser.

"We can all go outside together to get it," I pointed out. "We go out, I open the car door. You let her get down the street—way down the street—and then I hand you the laptop."

Christian nodded, as if he were carefully considering this option. "And what do you think will happen after that?"

This was the critical moment. I wasn't born in a cabbage patch. I knew damned well someone like Christian wouldn't let me walk away from this, even if I did give him what he wanted. Tyrese hadn't given me much advice on how to handle this particular crossroads, so I improvised.

"I'm thinking if I try to walk away from this, you kill me. You can't risk witnesses."

He nodded. Jess winced.

"But what if I wanted to play for your team?"

Oh, he was tremendously entertained by that, I could see it in the quirky twist of his lips.

"It's not like I get to choose the members, lady," he warned.

"You talk to your pal Hector about me." I stepped a little closer, working hard to ooze sex appeal at him, something I'd rarely done successfully even before my surgery. "Tell him I'm a first-rate accountant with a degree in Art History. Tell him I had breast cancer, and I'm living on borrowed time anyway. I don't want to spend what's left of it hiding in some witness protection program. You let her go, I give you the laptop, and then you talk to Hector about hiring a new financial advisor before you blow me away. Will you do that?"

He inclined his head, as if to say he admired my ability to do business. Whether he meant it—well, I hoped I wouldn't have to find out.

"I'll consider it, sugar. Now everybody out to the car. Here, you take this one."

He yanked Jess out of her chair and shoved her across the room to Harpo, who caught her and brought out a saw-toothed knife from a sheath on his leg. Jess's eyes darted back and forth between the two men, and a little whimper escaped from her throat.

Christian chuckled at Jess's expression of terror. "My friend likes the personal contact knives give him."

"How exciting for you, Harpo," I sniped at him. His face pinked up a bit, and I instantly regretted my action, fearing he would take his revenge out on Jess. But he only hustled her toward the foyer. Christian closed the distance between us and had his arm around my shoulders before I could protest.

"A nice suburban couple out on an evening stroll." He grinned down at me.

Our little troop surged forward, stepping around the dazed figure of Scott, who remained slumped on the floor, sobbing quietly.

"Scotty!" Christian nudged him with a booted toe. "Get your lazy ass up, and open the door for your woman."

Scott did as he was told, unable to look me in the face as he jumped to Christian's commands. He shuffled out the door on the opposite side of Christian.

We came out into the chilly night air and progressed down the sidewalk, stopping in front of my car.

"You go down the street that way." Christian gestured down the street in an easterly direction for Jess's benefit. I suspected they must have another man in a parked car down there. I couldn't imagine he would let Jess walk away any more than he would tell Hector to hire me. But we all pretended to believe each other. After she'd run a few yards, vanishing into the darkness, Christian grappled me closer. He gave a curt nod in Scott's direction, and Harpo lunged forward, pointing his knife at Scott's jugular.

Scott's eyes went wild as Harpo caught him by

the elbow. "Chris! Stop him!"

"Know what? I've never liked you, Scott." Christian's gaze was cold and even and downright inhuman. He left them behind on the sidewalk, nudging me forward into the street. We stepped around to the driver's side of the car, where I bent and unlocked the door. A black shadow shifted against the blacker night at the end of the cul-de-sac, and I prayed Christian hadn't seen it. He held me tightly against his side, pinning my arms against me. I squirmed myself around, turning in his arms to face him, as I'd done a few hours ago in bed with his brother. Now we were huddled chest-to-chest, and it was weird to see Evan and yet not see him—the webbing of tiny lines radiating from Christian's lips, which had probably once been as perfect and luscious as his brother's; the yellowy whites and the bloodshot veins surrounding the same coffee-colored irises.

"Hey." I conjured up the throatiest, most seductive voice I could imagine. "I can't help wanting to know what you look like out of that shirt."

I pressed myself closer, and he grinned a bit. He lowered his gun. Not by much, but enough that it wasn't aimed right at my stomach anymore. He tightened his embrace and pressed his own body against mine, pinning me up against the frame of the car.

"For instance." I licked my lips and hesitated.

"Yeah—?"

He didn't see the black shapes looming up out of the woods; his eyes were focused entirely on me now.

"I was wondering, since you look so much like him—do you have the same tattoo of Quetzalcoatl on your back? Christian?"

And then I shoved my knee up into his groin. He staggered backwards, as much from the shock of my words as from the physical attack. I fell away from him, diving into the street. As I rolled, I looked up and glimpsed Chuck planted firmly in front of me. I was so, so glad to see Chuck and not Evan. Mostly I didn't want Evan to suffer like that, but frankly, I also wouldn't have trusted him to pull the trigger when Christian recovered his footing and raised his own pistol to take aim. Chuck, however, had no such compunction. His first shot threw Christian back up against the hood of my car, and his second almost missed because Christian slumped to the ground so quickly.

While Harpo might prefer playing with knives, he'd kept the handgun I'd seen when I first came into the house. He yanked it from his waistband or somewhere and fired at the advancing phalanx of cops.

Scott hurled himself to the ground and laid his one good hand over the back of his head, ready for death or arrest or whatever took him. I stayed down and saw other figures surging forward out of the night, Tyrese and Evan among them.

Harpo fired at them as they advanced. Evan saw the shot coming and knocked Tyrese out of the way, turning sideways as he did so. His empty hand clutched at the air as he lost his footing and fell against Tyrese, both of them landing in a heap on the ground.

Oh, dear God, had he been hit? How was that possible? Didn't they all wear bulletproof vests? But I knew from my dad's own stories those things were far from perfect. A few feet from me, Christian struggled against the car, pulling himself into an upright position.

"Damn it, damn it!" he shouted over and over. He inched around to the front of the car, closer to where I lay, and he raised his gun and fired.

He fired above me and to the right. He fired at Harpo, whose watery eyes expressed all the surprise and confusion I felt.

"That was my brother, you idiot." Christian slipped down to the asphalt again, leaving long streaks of red on the hood of my silver Beemer.

The cops descended in force then. Tyrese dragged Scott to his feet and would have handcuffed him except Scott howled too loudly to make it worth the trouble.

Chuck squatted down beside me and patted my arm. "Good girl. You did good."

In the glow from a nearby streetlamp, I could see Chuck's wide eyes. He wasn't looking at me.

Christian had fallen only a few feet to my left. Now he turned his gun around, holding it by the barrel, and handed it to Chuck. "Long time no see." Christian's breath came in short rasps, and a little trickle of blood flecked his lips when he spoke.

"Wish we could have done this without the guns, compadre," Chuck said.

"I don't." A serene smile lit up Christian's face.

Sirens loomed louder and louder all around us, and I looked back where Evan had fallen. I started to crawl away in that direction, but then I saw him stumbling toward us.

Tyrese shadowed him with a face full of fear. He kept putting his hands out and trying to put them on Evan's shoulders, but Evan shrugged them off. Two paramedics ran toward him, but he lunged away from them and staggered closer to us.

"Christian?" He said it like he still couldn't believe it was his brother. And then he said it again, like he was genuinely happy about it. "Christian."

He dropped to his knees and started gasping for air.

I scrambled nearer to him as the two paramedics closed around him.

"No!" He protested as they started to drag him toward a waiting ambulance. "No, I want to see my brother."

His voice was weak and child-like in its intensity.

"Evan, go with the nice paramedics, buddy," Chuck said. "Don't make me carry you to the ambulance."

Evan jerked an arm away from one of the paramedics and struggled to get up. He wheezed out a slurping, wet sound. I was still several feet away, and I could hear it. It reminded me of the noise Leo had made after the second gunshot.

"Oh, for God's sake, Evan!" I shouted. "Get in the damned ambulance! Please! I'll stay here with your brother. He won't be alone. Only just go, please."

And that finally sunk in. He flipped over onto his hands and knees and pushed himself to his feet. Another medic brought a stretcher, and he waved it away, brushing back his hair and walking with the slow, deliberate care of a drunken man. The last I saw of him, he had slumped against the side of the ambulance, and the paramedics had to help him up into the back.

Christian had watched all this in silent fascination.

"Who are you? You must be important, or my brother wouldn't listen to you. And you can't be an agent. You've been with Scott since before he started working for us. And the Mendozas watch every move Scott makes. You didn't know anything about his activities, I would swear you didn't."

"No, I didn't until two days ago," I admitted. "But I guess Scott made me sound so inconsequential, no one bothered to follow me around and watch every move I was making, did they?"

Christian laughed, and it turned into a shattering, racking noise.

"Can we get a paramedic over here?" Chuck shouted over his shoulder. I caught a glimpse of his eyes in the glow of the streetlamp, and they were wet and glittery.

"Don't want one," Christian managed to whisper. Then to me he said, "You are definitely not the woman your fiancé thinks you are, lady."

"No. That woman's dead. She died over a year ago, but it took a while to figure out who I wanted to be instead."

Christian's eyes fluttered closed. "That happened to me once. But I didn't like the new man. Just as happy to let him go now."

A paramedic elbowed his way in between Chuck and me.

"You tell my brother," Christian began, then stopped.

"What?"

"Tell him, he always had better luck with the ladies." He contorted his face in a rigid, unsuccessful attempt to smile, and then he began coughing up blood again.

Chuck knelt beside him. "Talk to me about Hector and Raphael. Are they at war?"

Christian nodded. "Hey, is there a priest around?"

Chuck rubbed at his goatee. "You always have been one for the melodrama. You aren't gonna need one of those."

"Don't tell him that!" I reached over and wrapped Christian's bloodstained fingers around the cross he wore. "He'll hear you."

He shrugged his hand free of mine.

"Nah, Chuck's right." He waved a hand in the air dismissively. "It's way too late for that."

"Try not to talk." The paramedic shouldered Chuck aside and ripped open Christian's bloodied shirt.

Christian's eyelid flickered, and his pupils drifted in and out of focus. Then he wrapped a sticky red hand around the wooden cross. He tried to speak, but his voice trailed away to nothing, and his eyes closed. They didn't open again in this world.

Twenty-One

"We were all based in El Paso back then." Chuck set a cup of coffee in front of me. "We were like the Three Musketeers, man. Did everything together— got drunk, got laid, got shot. For a while, we even lived together in this big house that belonged to my uncle. When Evan graduated from college and joined the DEA, he moved in with us, too. He was about twenty-three then—he'd sailed through college in about three years. Man, he idolized his brother."

Chuck sat down beside Jess and me in the waiting room. After being set free, she'd encountered an FBI agent on the street. Now we sat next to each other on a dingy beige leather sofa while Chuck told his story.

"Christian loved a girl—sweet, pretty little thing. Her name was Jenny, and they got married. He'd been hesitant at first, because our work is so dangerous, and he didn't want her to worry about him every day and night. She was real easy-going though, said she could handle it. So they got married and Chris moved out. Tyrese and Evan didn't get along as well without Chris in the middle. Tyrese is real by the book, real meticulous in his work, and he's like that at home, too. Evan's not, to put it mildly."

Somehow, I wasn't surprised to hear that.

"Anyway, Jenny got pregnant almost right away, and Christian, he was so happy. He was walking on clouds."

"What went wrong?" I asked.

"A car crash. She was returning from church one

morning, and a truck ran a stop sign. Jenny died and their unborn baby with her. And Chris came apart. No one could put him back together. Not me, not Ty, not even Evan."

"But why would he join the Mendozas?" I asked.

Chuck shrugged. "Christian and Evan drank a lot in those days. They were real hellraisers, the two of them. I'd join them sometimes, but man, I couldn't keep up. Ty was never much on that stuff. Christian started drinking even more after Jenny died, and starting fights in bars—bad fights, send-people-to-the-hospital-for-stitches fights. Getting called in for counseling sessions at work fights. I suspect Christian had started doing other stuff too—besides the alcohol—maybe even before Jenny died."

"Didn't anybody tell him to see a shrink or something?" Jess asked

He looked at her with cynical amusement. "Lady, do we look like the kind of guys who discuss psychotherapy over cocktails? He talked about eating his gun—"

Jess looked confused and turned her face to mine. I frowned and looked away. Let Chuck explain it. I already knew what it meant. My dad had a friend who'd done it.

"Committing suicide," Chuck explained. "Christian found he didn't have it in him to take his own life, and that made him sick of himself, made him feel weak."

"That's awful." Jess said with a shake of her head.

"Yeah. Ty and Christian got assigned to infiltrate a branch of the Mendozas working in the El Paso area. It went well, a little too well. Ty was getting frightened by how convincingly Christian played his part—he was doing cocaine and amphetamines, and he was sleeping with any woman who'd have him. Yeah, he looked and acted like a rising drug lord. The Mendozas wanted to know these guys better. They wanted to bring them into their fold, which had been the whole idea. So Ty and Christian went down to Vera Cruz, to meet the brothers."

"And then what?"

"No one knows all of it." Chuck rubbed his hands up and down over the razor stubble on his cheeks. "Ty doesn't like to discuss it. They were found out and tortured.

"Ty says they both could have escaped, but Christian didn't want to come. He'd been spilling his guts to the Mendozas, naming agents, detailing operations—anything for another shot or snort or fix of whatever they happened to be offering that day. He told Tyrese that this was where he belonged now, that he hadn't been able to protect his wife, that he didn't have the guts to take his own life, and that all he wanted was oblivion. That's the part Evan never ever wants to hear, the part he never believes."

"I don't blame him." Even when he'd confided in me, Evan had made Christian sound like someone admirable, his hero.

"We'd see photos from time to time—him with known Mendoza associates, so we knew he was still alive. Finally, Evan saw him when he was working a case in Nogales. And he caught up to him. He was overjoyed. *The prodigal brother*, he said to me later. *My brother who was dead has been found.* But it turned out he didn't want to be found. Evan believed if he could get Christian home, he could get him into rehab and he'd be all better. But Christian didn't want any of that. He shot and killed Evan's partner that night and made his escape. That was a horrible bloody night. Evan killed an informer who'd helped lead him to Christian. A woman. Christian kind of—okay, not kind of—Christian deliberately pushed her into the line of fire when Evan was aiming at someone else. That was all about five, no, six years ago. And I don't know another thing about Christian until you walked into that house and said his name."

Chuck sat back and took a long swig of his coffee. We looked up, and Tyrese was standing in the doorway.

"Evan blames me. And who can argue with him? I blame me. But Christian was a loose cannon after Jenny died. Hell, he was a loose cannon *before* she died. For all I know, he'd already cut a deal with the Mendozas before we went down to Vera Cruz. Sometimes I think he wasn't tortured into becoming that person, that he was acting for my benefit, and the real choice had been made long before we went there. That's what I tell myself when I need to get to sleep at night."

"And does it work?" I asked.

Tyrese flashed a tight, bitter smile. "Fortunately, I've never needed much sleep. Any word on Evan yet?"

A surgeon in blue scrubs appeared in the corridor. Tyrese stepped aside to let him into the room.

"Your friend is out of surgery," the doctor announced. "The bullet entered under his arm— here." He raised his own arm and pointed. "It pierced one lung, missed his spine, and nicked his spleen. I was able to remove the bullet, and he's stable right now. Our main concerns are bleeding and infection. If the spleen starts bleeding again, it'll probably have to come out. But you can live a full life without a spleen."

"What do we do now?" I asked.

"We wait."

The doctor asked whether Evan's parents had been notified, and Tyrese nodded. "They're on the way. They want to claim Christian's body, too, and bring him back home to be buried."

255

"What a helluva thing this is." Chuck shook his head.

"Can I see him?" I asked the surgeon, a fatherly older man. "Please?"

He regarded me with gentle sympathy. "He's not conscious. And there are tubes everywhere. But I'll tell you what, we'll let you come to the nurse's station in the ICU. You can see him from there, but I'd rather you not disturb him."

****

For days, I came to the hospital and made my rounds. Leo and Ben were there, too. Ben had regained consciousness but suffered from aphasia and partial paralysis on one side of his body. His doctors said he would recover his speech, but they weren't sure about the use of his limbs.

Leo looked happy and relieved the first time he saw me come into his room. He remained under guard, and I remained in the safe house. But Chuck didn't think we'd need to be protected much longer. Hector Mendoza had been apprehended in Chicago, and his extremely well paid battery of lawyers argued the Feds had no jurisdiction over him. More shrewdly, he also contended that Scott Bennett and Christian Desmond had exceeded his instructions. He'd only wanted them to talk with me about a missing computer. As Chuck had predicted, Hector was going to play innocent and hang Scott out to dry. Scott, meanwhile, didn't take kindly to having his arm broken. He complained it would be the ruin of his tennis game, and apparently that made him so spiteful, he agreed to testify against Hector and his associates.

He'd been at the hospital, too, for three days and was about to be released when I finally forced myself to go to him.

"I'm glad you're testifying against Hector," I told him.

"It's not like I have much choice, do I?" Gingerly, he draped a suede jacket around his shoulders as an armed agent stood nearby.

"Can you at least go stand on the other side of the room?" Scott asked the guy, who complied without the least change of expression. His jacket started to slip on the side where his arm was in a cast. Without thinking, I reached over and caught the jacket. His good hand went up at the same moment, and it brushed mine as I pulled away hastily.

"Where will you go from here?" I asked.

"To a safe house, until I can record my testimony."

"But after that?"

"Then I go into this government program called WITSEC. Scott Bennett meets with a fatal accident. And somewhere far away, a forty-five year old man starts his life all over again. No family, no friends, not even a suit of clothes or a watch from his past life."

All I could think was *better you than me*. Out loud, what I said was hardly more diplomatic. "How could you screw up so badly, Scott?"

"I was already looking the other way on a bunch of little things, then you got sick, and I couldn't stand it. Couldn't stand watching it and knowing you would die. Because I was sure you would die. So I was drinking more and more—"

"And doing drugs." I remembered what Christian had implied and couldn't believe it.

Scott shrugged his good shoulder. "Not like real drugs, Sabrina. A few pills when I couldn't sleep, and a few pills to keep my mood up and improve my energy level. Nothing serious."

I shook my head slowly. "Are you honestly that good at deluding yourself?"

"In fact, I am," he replied with a mocking little

smirk. "But you'll be pleased to know one of the conditions of my deal with the Feds is me getting into a twelve-step program. Personally, I think that's a waste of my time and theirs, but they forced my hand."

"I hope it works out for you."

He brushed back the wavy lock of blond hair and peered down at me with a familiar mischievous gleam in his eye. Once I'd found that charming, now it only irritated me. "I'm hoping it works out, too. They told me I couldn't be a lawyer anymore, too big a risk of running into former colleagues at conferences and professional associations. So I'm hoping they give me a restaurant. Or maybe a marina. Maybe both, like that place in Northeast where I dock the sailboat Uncle Carlton gave me—the marina with that Italian restaurant. Wouldn't that be great?"

He did love sailing, and he was a fine chef when the mood struck him. He seemed downright excited about Witness Protection. Or maybe that was him putting a happy face on the wreck he'd made of his life.

What else could I say to him? All the personality traits that had made him so charming—the glib sense of humor, the ability to brush off bad news, the gift for focusing on having fun—all that had worked against him, turning him into a shallow, self-involved monster when the test of my illness had come our way.

I walked out of that hospital room without a backward glance, relieved he would be going soon, embarrassed I had ever cared for him. It's rare a girl can be sure of being completely rid of an old boyfriend—no matter how big the world is, people tend to travel in the same, small social circles. I still occasionally ran into the guy I'd told Evan about, the one I'd been officially engaged to. At least thanks to

WITSEC, I wouldn't have that problem with Scott.

****

I had one other near miss with that pesky witness protection program. Since Tyrese had opened up a bit about what had happened with Christian, I tried to talk to him a little more whenever I saw him. One day after visiting Leo, I ran into him in the hospital corridor and was reminded of something Leo and I had discussed.

"Tyrese," I began. "Are all of you part of this Internal Security Administration thing? Or only Evan?"

He looked positively stricken. For a second, his hand went up to his chest, and I fully expected him to have a heart attack right there. He grabbed my elbow, surprising me with a truly fierce grip, and yanked me away from a nearby nurses' station.

"I don't know where you ever heard of that, but don't ever say it out loud again," he cautioned me. "Not unless you want to meet with the same sort of accident your ex-fiancé's going to have. Got it?"

I nodded frantically. He released my arm and strode away, in the opposite direction from where he'd been going when I first saw him. He flipped his cell phone out of his pocket as he walked, and I had the distinct feeling he would be talking to someone about me in a moment. Call me psychic.

****

Sometimes Jess would meet me at the hospital on her lunch hour. She claimed she was trying to give me moral support, but truthfully? She spent more time talking to Chuck about his "fascinating job" than she spent sitting with me.

For a few days, the Shock-Trauma nurses let me come and stand in their station and watch Evan. Then that stopped. I wasn't an authorized person from Homeland Security, and I wasn't immediate family, they told me. They apologized a lot. I figured someone higher-up, either government or hospital, had obviously decided to crack down on the visitor restrictions.

I went back to the waiting room. Sometimes I was joined by Chuck, who tried to be sociable, or Tyrese, who did not. Other times, Evan's parents were there. His mother was a tall woman, slender and regal. She reminded me of a runway model—a self-assured, imposing woman who eyed me with obvious disdain. Evan's dad—even taller than his mom—seemed to have no similar reserve toward me or anyone else. He greeted me with a smile and a hug the first time we met. Often, he would walk into the room and say things like, "Ignacio will wake up any minute now, Mama, I know it." She would roll her eyes every time he said something like that, but eventually I noticed her smiling fondly when his back was turned. They both called Evan by his middle name all the time, *Ignacio*, and they spoke to one another in Spanish. To me, they were very exotic and romantic.

Evan's dad was what Nanny O'Hara calls Black Irish. These are the Irish who, unlike my father and me, do not have red hair and blue eyes. They have black hair and dark eyes, and legend says they're descended from the shipwrecked sailors of the Spanish Armada, men who swam ashore in Ireland after that famous Protestant Wind destroyed their empire. So, if the legends were true, that would mean both Evan's parents were Spanish. Maybe that was why they were drawn to one another in the first place—some ancient common heritage. Or I could be stereotyping again.

On the sixth day, Mr. Desmond came to the waiting room alone.

"Inez and myself, we're thinking we should start taking shifts." He smiled a little less enthusiastically than usual. He carried a book in his hands and that worried me. It meant even Mr. Desmond no longer expected his son to wake up anytime soon. He sat down next to me and I stared at his book—*Patriot Games* by Tom Clancy.

"I don't know if I caught your last name, Miss Sabrina, isn't it?"

"O'Hara. Sabrina O'Hara."

"Now that's a fine name. And are your parents from Ireland then?"

"My grandparents on my father's side are," I told him. "They came from Monaghan."

"Oh, did they?" He beamed. "I'm from Armagh, myself. Across the border. Beautiful green land it is there."

"Yes, I've been." I'd gone during a semester abroad in college. "Texas must have come as quite a shock."

"Yes, it did. Evan's father gave a cheery laugh. "I worked on my uncle's stud farm in Tipperary, and I came over with him for an International Horse Breeders' Show. Saw Inez, never wanted to go home again. Desmond men can be impulsive."

"No. Really?" I'm pretty sure he heard the heavy sarcasm in my voice.

"Loyal to a fault when we make up our minds, though." A frown darkened his brow. "Most of us, anyway. Christian was different. He was always different. Inez said once, 'it's a good thing he wasn't our firstborn, or he'd have been an only child.'"

"How many kids do you have?"

He had to think about it, his face reddening as he did so.

"Six now." All his former liveliness had disappeared from his voice. "I have six children now."

"No." I patted his hand. "You have seven. You always will."

He smiled and inclined his head a little. "I'm

ashamed to say there were times when I would tell people six even before Christian died. It was so hard to explain, and people wanted to pity me if I said he'd gone missing. So I would say six."

"You shouldn't feel bad. You didn't owe people any explanations."

"Ah, but I owe myself one, dear." His lips quavered in a sad approximation of a smile. "I always think if I'd loved him better, he wouldn't have turned out—well, like he did. Always argumentative he was, even as a baby. Cranky and difficult and hard to please. When he grew up, I thought going into law enforcement would be a good thing, make use of all that energy and anger. But things happened, and he only got worse."

Mr. Desmond shook his head. "You could never love him enough. No matter how much you loved him, he never felt like you'd given him enough. Always dwelling on the bad things, was Christian."

I considered staying silent, being diplomatic, the whole nine yards. I hadn't even been good at that before facing death twice in one year.

"You should know he tried to protect Evan in the end."

Mr. Desmond bowed his head, beyond words, beyond comprehension. "In a way, I was relieved when he disappeared. What kind of a father is this fellow? That's what you're thinking to yourself, I'm sure, because I've thought it myself often enough."

"No, sir, I don't." Who was I to judge? I'd never had a child and never would now.

"Ignacio—Evan, that is—he always looked up to Christian, dreamed of being like him. Heaven knows why. It was better for him once his brother went away. Then he became a better person. He became the man he thought his brother was."

"Christian wanted a priest at the end, too," I said.

Now he looked up, his dark eyes studying mine.

"There weren't any around, but he said an Act of Contrition. My brother's a priest, and he says that should count for something."

Okay, so I embellished. The man had lost his son, for crying out loud.

"Thank you kindly." Mr. Desmond looked at his book again, and I noticed it shook a little bit in his hands.

My own hands shook a bit, too. I didn't tell Mr. Desmond what my brother Tim had really said. I'd mentioned Christian taking hold of that cross, and maybe trying to confess. Tim had gone on a furious rant about my persistent naiveté and bad Catholics who think they can break all the Commandments and go straight to Heaven as long as they make a deathbed Confession.

"I hope you'll keep in mind, sis," he had said to me, "that at most, what that guy did—if he did it— will get him maybe a year off his time in Purgatory. Assuming he didn't go straight to hell."

"How can you be so sure?" I had shot back. Then it degenerated into another one of our weird Catholic family arguments, with him explaining that as a layperson, I couldn't possibly understand all the subtle and complicated Church doctrine that would completely back him on his position. This is why I don't talk to Tim much.

Mr. Desmond hunched forward in his seat and looked away, gazing into the distant past as he resumed speaking. "You aren't supposed to have favorites. But Ignacio—oh, he hates that name, I suppose I should call him Evan like his friends do. Evan is so good-natured. He was the happiest little baby you ever did see."

I laughed to picture some fat little almond-eyed baby with black hair and eyes, waving a rattle and gurgling at a much younger Mr. Desmond. I had a little moment of dissonance, imagining myself holding a baby like that, and Evan beside me. That made me momentarily angry—the sheer impossibility of it, the unfairness of wanting it now when I could never, ever have it. I balled my hands up into fists and dug them into the seat cushion on either side of me.

"He's going to wake up." Evan's father clasped my left hand in his own, and we sat that way in silence for a long time.

I went to get us coffee and came back to find Mr. Desmond speaking with a familiar nurse, someone from the station outside Evan's room. She turned and included me in her speech.

"He's regained consciousness. He can't say much—we just took out the breathing tube. But we gave him a pen and paper, and he keeps writing two names, over and over. Sabrina's one of them. The other is Christian."

Evan's dad turned to me. "It looks like we'll be going in together, won't we, Miss O'Hara?"

Twenty-Two

Evan took the news about Christian hard. He cried. Real tears streamed down his cheeks, and I hardly knew where to look. I hadn't seen a man cry since I was ten and our dog died, and my dad went all to pieces in front of me. I would have dashed forward to hold Evan, but by then they'd called his mother to the hospital. She was the one who hugged him to her chest. I guess they'd both still had that prodigal brother fantasy in their heads.

They moved him to a private room the next day, out of Shock-Trauma. When they took out the breathing tube, his voice was hoarse and faint from its irritation. I couldn't say much to him, because his dad and mom came in together and stayed in his room for as long as they could. A sister—his only sister, I learned later—had arrived from Houston, along with two more of his brothers. The only reason the remaining two weren't there is that they were both serving in Iraq. Quite an eye-opener for me. Even after my surgery, I'd never seen all my family members in my hospital room together at one time— and none of them had the excuse of fighting in a foreign war. They just couldn't all stand to be in one room at the same time.

Tyrese and Chuck stopped in as well. They knew his parents from way back, so it was like one big, happy, extremely loud reunion in Evan's room. I drifted toward the back of the room and then slipped out.

We'd had less than forty-eight hours together. Sure, he'd written my name down first when he woke up, but it only meant he had a kind heart and wanted to know I was safe. Now he knew, and now I in turn knew he'd be fine. Despite the horrible waywardness of Christian, it looked as if Evan had a much stronger family than my own, full of affection for one another and able to put aside differences in a crisis. Even Christian, in the last moments of his life, had chosen loyalty to his brother over loyalty to the Mendozas—however stupidly belated that choice might have been.

I needed to return to the office and start getting my life in order. I'd done a lot of thinking while sitting in that waiting room, and I knew I wasn't going back to accounting. I would hand in my resignation, finish out the year, and sell my condo. Maybe I'd go back to Arizona and move in with my mom, maybe I'd head to my sister's in North Carolina. Maybe I'd stay right here and go to work for one of the accounting firm's clients, a woman who ran a small art gallery in Baltimore. She'd talked to me about the possibility in the past, and I'd always blown it off. I might call her today when I got home. No, I would definitely call her.

I strode down the long hospital corridor with my head up and my shoulders back, telling myself I didn't feel let down. I'd made it to the elevator and pressed the button when someone called my name.

"Ms. O'Hara!"

I paused at the elevator doors and turned to see Tyrese breezing down the hallway, his trench coat flapping away.

"Do you ever take that thing off?" I asked.

He flashed one of his rare smiles and walked up to my side. "Not when I have a great big gun in a holster underneath it. That tends to make bystanders nervous."

I smiled and reached out to push the button again. Tyrese laid his hand over the panel to stop me.

"He wants you to come back. He saw you leave, but his throat is too sore to yell. He says, and I'm quoting, 'Everybody else get the hell out, I want to talk to her.'"

I turned away and leaned against the wall beside the elevator doors. My eyes filled up, and I felt horribly female and weak.

"Come on." Tyrese took my arm and guided me back down the corridor. Evan's siblings had drifted back to the waiting room near the nurse's station, and I glimpsed a collection of smirks and stifled laughs as we went by.

We passed Evan's parents outside the room. Mr. Desmond beamed at me and winked. His wife glared at me and did not.

"I'm thinking of hiring this woman," Tyrese said to Evan as he ushered me back into the room.

Chuck was still in there, standing at the foot of the bed and snickering. Evan pushed himself up to a sitting position, a look of horror on his face.

"I've been considering how well she stayed ahead of the game," Tyrese continued.

I have to hand it to him—he was so gruff and convincing, even I thought he might be serious.

"Leaving the laptop out in the car that night. Inspired genius," he concluded.

Which was interesting, because in the immediate aftermath, what he'd actually said to me was, "Woman, are you a lunatic?"

Evan seemed seconds away from shouting, sore throat or not. Tyrese waved a beckoning hand at Chuck and exited with one more parting jibe.

"Ms. O'Hara, let me know if you're interested in a career change, okay? We could make it happen. Come on, Chuck."

The two of them made their way to the door.

"Evan, you've got a lot of stitches, buddy," Chuck

267

called over his shoulder. "Don't do anything I wouldn't do, okay? And hey, look forward to working with you in the future, Sabrina!"

Evan made a move as if he would speak, but I dashed over to the bed and covered his mouth with my hand.

"I'm not going to become a Federal agent. Good Lord, I'd probably shoot myself in the foot the first day of training."

He shook his head.

"Okay, no, I probably wouldn't," I admitted. "But something catastrophic would happen. I'm an artist, not a fighter."

"You're both," he whispered.

He patted the bed beside him, so I sat down. Right away, he raised a hand and stroked his fingers over my face, so light and delicate, like a silk scarf wafting against me. I couldn't help it; I closed my eyes and tilted my head up, like a cat begging to have its neck scratched. He did better—he leaned forward and pressed his lips to my throat, leaving a trail of soft kisses down to my collarbone.

"I keep thinking I've lost you." His voice was faint and ragged. "First when you ran away, then when I got shot, and now when you walked out of the room."

"I would have come back at a less busy time." I said it to be kind. I probably would never have had the nerve to come back without being asked. "Your mom especially doesn't look too thrilled to have me here."

"Of course she doesn't. She doesn't know you like I do. She'll like you fine when she gets to know you."

"Will she?" My question came out nice and level, belying the butterflies fluttering all around in my stomach.

"Yeah," he nodded. "And there'll be plenty of

time for that."

"Oh?"

"Sabrina, don't be coy." Evan struggled into a more upright position. "Say you were worried sick about me. Say you hardly left the hospital—I know you were here every day, Chuck told me."

I flushed and bit my lip.

"Oh, babe, it's okay." He caught a strand of my hair and pushed it back behind my ear. "I was glad. I woke up thinking of you, but I couldn't say your name. I couldn't say anything, and at first I was too out of it to even write anything. But you're who I thought of first, I swear it. Even before Christian."

I couldn't find my voice. It was like I wanted to compensate for his talking too much by saying nothing. Instead I sighed and laid my head against his shoulder. He tangled his hands up in my hair, and I warmed to him easily, like I'd known his touch all my life. I kicked off my clogs and stretched myself out on the bed beside him.

"I was afraid you'd die," I admitted. "I didn't want to care so much. But I did."

He pressed his lips to my forehead. "I want to go on seeing you when I get out of here. And more. I want to be with you all the time. I want to wake up next to you and go to sleep next to you. I'm thinking I might even want to have a family and get old with you."

I jerked myself out of his embrace and sat up abruptly.

"Evan, a family is out of the question for me."

"There's adoption." His eyes had a glittery, feverish look, reminding me that only a day before, even his survival had been open to question.

"Evan, that's way too much to think about, and way too soon."

"Okay, yeah," he agreed cheerfully. "It is too soon to decide that. But what I'm saying is, we could do it. Or you could do that without me. Without Scott. Without any man. You sounded so sad about the baby thing that night when we—when we talked."

I couldn't help but smile at his sudden attack of modesty.

"I only want to raise the possibility that if you ever do something like that, you might want to do it with me. I'd make a great dad. I could teach him to ride a horse and fish and play basketball."

I arched an eyebrow. "And if it's a girl?"

"Well, I could teach her to ride a horse, too. And fish and play basketball."

I'd have gotten pissed off if he'd said something about how I could teach her to bake or wear make-up or be all soft and lady-like. It meant a lot that he'd already figured that much out about me. One of his arms was pretty much immobilized on a board with a couple of IV's trailing out of it. I patted the other arm absently.

"Evan, that's sweet."

"We could set the date right now," he rasped, grinning a little drunkenly.

I don't get speechless too often, but right then, I sure was. My mouth opened and closed a few times, making little popping noises.

"Set the date for what?" I finally managed to sputter.

"Our wedding."

"Wouldn't you want to test the waters first?"

"I already have." He leered at me.

"Evan!" I swatted at his good arm. "I meant like, living together. Or something."

"Nah. I'm an all or nothing guy, babe."

As he spoke, he closed his eyes and shook his head, a little over-emphatically. A creeping suspicion dawned on me, and I got up from the bed to take a look at the chart hanging from the footboard. It looked like Latin. At any rate, I sure couldn't make any sense out of it.

"What exactly are the doctors giving you?" I asked.

"I don't know what they're giving me." Evan opened his eyes and beamed at me. "But I know what I'm saying."

"I'm sure you think you do."

"Okay, don't believe me. I'll ask you again when I get out of here."

"Yeah, you do that. But I'll wait to sign up for the bridal registry at Macy's, if it's all the same to you."

He shrugged and didn't answer. I found myself a little upset he'd given up on the topic, and that got me flustered and irritable.

"Besides," I groused. "That growing old thing is probably not a safe bet with the likes of me. I've barely been cancer-free for a full year. It could still come back. I could still die from it. That's a lot of uncertainty for any man to accept, even a man like you."

He grabbed my hand and pulled me close. "I'm not worried."

He should be worried, he really should. I drew back and studied his face, remembering his brother's bleak stare. I shook off that memory with difficulty and focused on the face presently in front of me, full of tenderness and an almost child-like delight. For the first time, I noticed he resembled someone in his family other than Christian. His father. He had his father's cockeyed optimism, and it was pretty darned adorable.

I leaned into him and brushed my lips against his, afraid I might suffocate him or something. We stayed that way, mouths closed and lips together, like two virgins at the high school prom.

"Man, even a kiss like that is hard work after

you've had a collapsed lung." Evan coughed. We both started to laugh, and I sat back down on the edge of the bed, laying my head on the pillow beside him.

"I understand the cancer could come back." He brushed a hand against my cheek. "And you understand I could get shot again. But no one gets a guarantee of long life and a happy ending. I think we just have to enjoy whatever time we get while we're here. And I'd like it if you would spend that time with me. I could make you very happy."

And you know what? He was right again.

A note about the author...

Lynn Reynolds is a writer, wife, and mom—not necessarily in that order. A city girl currently trapped in Green Acres, Lynn works as a newspaper reporter in real life. She writes romance novels because she genuinely believes in Happily Ever After.

Visit Lynn at www.lynnreynolds.com

Thank you for purchasing
this Wild Rose Press publication.
For other wonderful stories of romance,
please visit our on-line bookstore at
www.thewildrosepress.com.

For questions or more information,
contact us at info@thewildrosepress.com.

The Wild Rose Press
www.TheWildRosePress.com

Other titles to enjoy from
The Last Rose of Summer line:

A TRAIL OF LOVE by Bess McBride—A Smokey Bear uniform, "baby mooses" and oh-so-handsome Dace—if this was any indication, Kerrie's summer hiding place suddenly looked a lot like Paradise.

BALANCED HEART by Betty Hanawa—Martha was not going to cave to Phil's smile this time or accept the invitation in those sea eyes. She'd been stupid enough to fall in love with this idiot when she was seventeen, but that didn't mean that at thirty-seven she still needed to be stupid.

FORTY SOMETHING by Mary Eason—To anyone who has ever thought life ended with divorce, this book will bring a smile and give hope.

LET NOTHING YOU DISMAY by Linda Swift—Kala Vandergriff has a good job at the Welcome Center, so getting her car fixed shouldn't be so much trouble, and neither should having a few people stay over during the big snow storm....

RIVER OF DREAMS by Vanessa Harvey—When Beth Black dreams of escaping an unhappy past and finding success in her new job at a boatyard owned by the wealthy Radcliffe family, she finds dreams don't always translate to reality in this tender romance set along England's idyllic River Thames.

SOLDIER FOR LOVE by Brenda Gale—An award-winning novel set on a lush Caribbean island. As CO of the American peacekeeping force, Julie has her hands full dealing with voodoo signs and a handsome subordinate who suspects treachery by someone determined to keep the strife stirred up.

Breinigsville, PA USA
20 January 2010
231100BV00004B/9/P